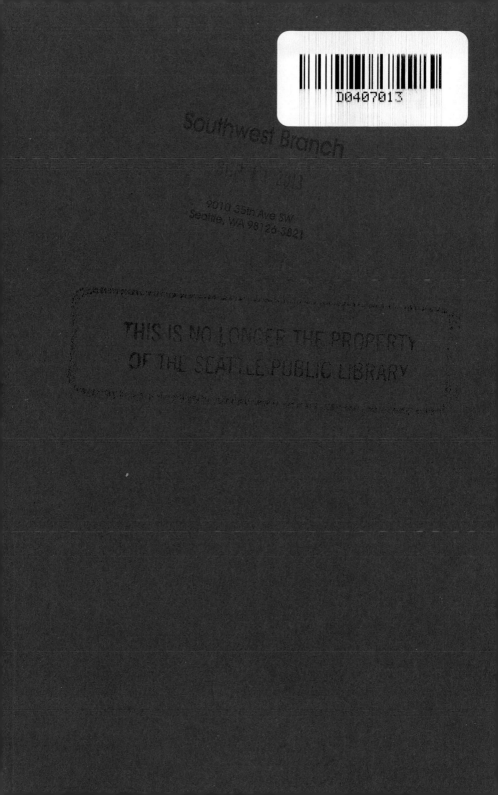

GOBLINS

PHILIP REEVE
GOBLINS

| SCHOLASTIC PRESS | NEW YORK

All rights reserved. Published by Scholastic Press, an imprint of Scholastic Inc.,
Publishers since 1920, by arrangement with Scholastic Children's Books, an imprint
of Scholastic Ltd, Euston House, 24 Eversholt Street, London, NW1 1DB, UK.
SCHOLASTIC, SCHOLASTIC PRESS, and associated logos are trademarks and/or
registered trademarks of Scholastic Inc.

Library of Congress Cataloging-in-Publication Data available

ISBN 978-0-545-22220-4

10 9 8 7 6 5 4 3 2 1   13 14 15 16 17

Printed in the U.S.A.   23
First American edition, September 2013

The text type was set in Constantia.
Book design by Yaffa Jaskoll

For **SAM REEVE**,
for his VERY OWN.

CONTENTS

THE DARK TOWER

In the lands of the west, where men are few and some of the old magic lingers still, there stands the ancient fortress of Clovenstone. A wide wall rings it, tumbled now and overgrown with weeds. The trees and waters of the wild have crept inside and made their home again among its steep, deserted streets and crumbling buildings. At its heart a crag rises, Meneth Eskern, most westerly of the Bonehill Mountains, and on the summit stands a black Keep, tall as the sky, with sheer walls and horns of stone. Around this dark tower, like a stone crown on the crag's brow, there runs a lofty inner wall, guarded by seven lesser towers. All are in ruins now, the men who raised them long since gone. Crows caw about their sagging roofs, and gargoyles lurk in their ivy like lice in beggars' beards.

The highest of these seven towers is called the Blackspike. Although it is dwarfed by the great mass of the Keep behind it, it is still taller than any tower in the lands of men. From its snow-flecked battlements to the ground at the crag's foot is a very long drop indeed . . .

And that was bad news for Skarper, because he had just been catapulted off the top of it.

"Aaaaaaah!" he screamed, rising up, up, up, pausing a moment, flailing for handholds on the empty air, and then beginning his long fall. "Aaaaaaaaa . . ." But after the first thousand feet or so he realized that he was just going ". . . aaaaaaaaaaaa . . ." from force of habit, so he stopped, and from then on the only sounds were the whooshing of the cold air past his ears and the occasional cottony rustle as a cloud shot by.

Of course it's not so much the falling that bothers me, thought Skarper, as the ivied stones and mean little windows of the Blackspike rushed past him. *It's the hitting the ground that's the trouble. . . .*

Below him — now that he had got used to the feeling that the wind was pushing its thumbs into his eyes —

he could see plump white clouds dotting the middle air like sheep. Below *them* the bleak buttresses of Meneth Eskern spread out like the fingers of a splayed stone hand, with ruined buildings clustering between them. Weeds and little trees had rooted themselves in the rotting roofs and between the flagstones of the silent streets, and as the land sloped downward toward the Outer Wall, five miles away, the trees grew thicker and thicker, forming a dense wood, from whose canopy old bastions and outbuildings poked up like lonely islands.

This was Skarper's world, and as he looked down upon it he was interested to notice several details that *Stenoryon's Mappe of All Clovenstone* had got wrong. But not *that* interested, because the details were rushing toward him at great speed, and long before he could tell anyone of his discoveries he was going to be splattered all over them like a careless delivery of raspberry jam.

Indeed it was maps, and books, and things of that sort that were to blame for Skarper being in this sticky situation in the first place. He felt quite bitter when he thought about it, and glared fiercely at a passing crow.

▼   ▼   ▼

Skarper was a goblin, as the crow guessed at once from his amber eyes, clawed paws, long flapping ears, and the tail that snapped behind him like a whip as he fell. There were goblins in all the seven towers of Clovenstone. They were born of the stone of the mountains, and they had a fierce greed for gold and silver and other shining things, which they spent most of their time searching for in the ancient armories and storerooms, or stealing from one another, and from the goblins of the other towers.

There had been a time when all goblins had been servants of the same great sorcerer, the Lych Lord, who had raised Clovenstone and ruled the whole world from his Stone Throne, high in the Keep. But years without number had passed since the Lych Lord's army was defeated at the battle of Dor Koth by the armies of the kings of men, and for as long as any living goblin could recall, each of the seven towers had been home to a separate goblin gang. Sometimes the gangs from two or three different towers would form an alliance and go roaring out of Clovenstone to raid the fisherfolk and miners of the little man-kingdoms on the Nibbled Coast, but they were untrusting, untrustworthy creatures and their alliances didn't last. It was never long before they were fighting one another over the loot, safe in their home towers again with the entrances blocked up by barricades of rubble and old furniture.

Blackspike Tower, where Skarper lived (or *had* lived, until he was catapulted off its roof that morning) was ruled by a large and dangerous goblin named King Knobbler, and the goblins who lived in it were called the Blackspike Boys. There were no crueler raiders, greedier hoarders or more ruthless robbers anywhere in Clovenstone. Fighting and loot was what they lived for; fighting and loot and eating. Fighting and loot and eating and then more fighting.

Except for Skarper. Skarper was different.

Old Breslaw had seen it as soon as Skarper hatched. Breslaw was different too. He had lost an eye, an ear, a leg, and most of his tail in a raid on the Nibbled Coast forty years before. He was only half the goblin he used to be, and since he could no longer go out raiding with the rest of the tribe, King Knobbler had made him hatchling master.

Once a year, on the night when the horns of the new moon seemed to rest on the summit of the Keep, Breslaw would descend into the Blackspike's deep cellars, unlock a heavy cobweb-covered door, and steer his squeaking wheelbarrow down steep and lonely tunnels that plunged beneath the roots of Clovenstone into the dark under the mountains where lay the lava lake.

There, in the cauldrons of the earth, the restless silvery-hot magma roiled and churned. The lake spat out little gobs of lava, which hardened shiny black upon the walls and floors of its great cave. Once a year it spat out something else as well: eggstones.

Patiently, using a long-handled shovel, and wrapped in wet skins to save himself from being shrivelled by the heat, old Breslaw would hobble back and forth along the hot shores collecting the eggstones. Sometimes, through the fumes that hung above the lake, he could see the hatchling masters from other towers patrolling their own stretches of shoreline, but he did not interfere with them, or try to stop them gathering up their own eggstones: *Each to his Beach*; that was one of the few scraps of the old law which all Clovenstone's goblins still obeyed.

Nor did he try to peer up the great chimney-holes that opened above the lake and were supposed to reach right up inside the Keep. When Breslaw was a younger goblin, the idea of getting inside the Keep had kept him awake at night, but he'd long since come to accept that there was no way in. Mad Manaccan's Lads from Slatetop Tower had tried it once, creeping out over the lake on scaffolding made from old floorboards. The scaffolding had fallen apart and dropped into the lava before the goblins climbing it got anywhere near those black openings.

So Breslaw just kept his eye on the basalt beach and scooped up the dully glowing eggstones as they landed, and when they were all safely in his barrow he trundled them back up the steep miles to his chamber high in Blackspike Tower, which was called the hatchery. There he kept them warm beside his fire until they began to jiggle, and to crack . . .

The goblins who had hatched from the same batch of eggstones as Skarper did not look alike. Earth-born creatures do not resemble one another in the way that members of a human family or a human race do. The sizes and shapes of Skarper and his batch-brothers had been decided by some strange whim of the earth itself.

Some had scales and some had fur; some had squashed-in snouts like pigs, others long pointed noses and trailing ears. Most had fangs, and claws, and beady black eyes in which a little gleam of vicious glee appeared when they kicked aside the fragments of their eggstones and saw the minimallets and little training cudgels that Breslaw had left leaning against the hatchery walls. With scratchy cries they snatched the tiny weapons up and began belting one another over the head. Breslaw watched them, and nodded in satisfaction. More good, brutish Blackspike Boys, who would be a credit to the tribe of King Knobbler.

Then he spotted Skarper. He was smaller than the other hatchlings, with long ears, a mat of reddish hair, a ginger tuft at the end of his tail and an odd light in his yellow eyes. Breslaw saw the way he hung back unnoticed in the corners of the cavern, as if he thought it might not be such a good idea to let other goblins swing huge lumps of timber at his newly hatched skull.

Breslaw rummaged through the heap of eggstone shards and picked up the still-warm fragments of the stone that Skarper had emerged from. Sure enough, thick veins of slowsilver ran this way and that across its surface. Slowsilver: the strangest and most magical of all metals. It shone like real silver, but you could knead it like putty, and when exposed to certain types of flame it would burn with a strange fire. In olden times great sorcerers like the Lych Lord had used it in their spells. These days it did not seem much use for anything, but it was rare and valuable and shiny, and goblins loved rare, valuable, shiny things. Breslaw stuffed Skarper's egg-shards away inside his clothes before the hatchlings saw them. Later, he would prize out the slowsilver and add it to the little ball of the stuff he kept in a secret place in one of his hiding holes in the walls of the hatchery.

It was years since he'd found an eggstone with that much slowsilver in it. From such a stone, long years before, Breslaw had hatched, and now he saw in young Skarper another like himself; a goblin wiser and more cunning than the rest. "I must keep an eye on this youngling," he told himself.

Sure enough, Skarper learned to talk much more quickly than his batch-brothers, whom Breslaw had named Yabber, Gutgust, Bootle, Wrench and Libnog. He was the only one who paid attention when Breslaw tried to teach them the goblin-lore. And while the others fought over food at mealtimes in the big, busy chamber called the scoffery, Skarper always found some way to spirit hunks of meat and cavemold cheese out from under their squabbling snouts and carry it away through Blackspike's maze of passages and wobbly wooden ladders to some dark little disused room where he could eat alone, undisturbed and unobserved — except by Breslaw, whose beady eye was on him always.

Breslaw watched the clever way young Skarper sneaked little shining trinkets from the other goblins and hid them away in his own secret places, where he could fetch them out and gloat over them when he thought no one was watching.

"He reminds me of me, when I was new," the cunning old hatchling master chuckled.

One day, when a storm was racketing its way through the Bonehills and the rest of the tribe were all outside on the battlements, netting crows or hurling boulders and rude words at Mad Manaccan's Lads, Breslaw found young Skarper lounging in the scoffery. He was sitting in King Knobbler's own chair and nibbling leftovers from King Knobbler's own dinner.

"What are you doing here?" the hatchling master demanded. "You should be out with the others! Boulders don't throw themselves, you know!"

Skarper shrugged and popped a plump cave spider into his mouth. "It's raining up, down, and sideways out there," he said. "Hailing too. It's warmer and drier in here, and while those idiots are busy, I can get close to the fire and eat."

Breslaw drew himself to his full height (he stood about five foot six, which was tall for a goblin) and his eyes glittered. No hatchling had spoken to a hatchling master like that since . . . well, he thought, not since *he* had spoken like it to *his* hatchling master, old Wheezingbottom, more years ago than he cared to recall.

So instead of screeching at the impudent young sprout and giving him a clout with his teaching mallet, he said, "Come with me, young Skarper," and led him down the Blackspike's winding, wormy stairways to a half-forgotten chamber near the tower's foot. Thick skeins of cobweb stretched and tore as Breslaw heaved the door open. "Behold," he said. "The Bumwipe Heaps!"

THE BUMWIPE HEAPS

There were chambers beyond numbering among the labyrinths of Clovenstone. Huge, crumbling, abandoned buildings crowded right up to the foot of the Keep, and the goblin explorers who ventured out from Blackspike Tower didn't usually have to go very far before they discovered a stronghold or a store-hole that they'd never seen before. Some of those rooms were full of treasure, which would be looted and fought over and carried up the stairways to King Knobbler, who kept the best bits for himself and made gifts of the rest to his favorite lads. Others held moldering curtains and tapestries (which could be turned into goblin clothes), or heavy old items of furniture (which could be used to make weapons), or weapons (which could also be used to make weapons), or pots and pans and cauldrons, which the Blackspike Boys turned into armor. Still other rooms were home to colonies of fat black rats, which were always tasty, or the bones of men and goblins and other things from long ago, which could be gnawed, or used to make nice ornaments (or weapons). But sometimes the goblins would come upon a locked chamber or a promising-looking ironbound chest that, when opened, turned out to contain nothing but bundles of thin white crinkly stuff, covered in little wriggly black marks. This they deemed useless. They had found a lot of it in Blackspike itself, and it had all been thrown into a deep storeroom. "Bumwipe," the goblins called the stuff, and sometimes they helped themselves to a handful on their way to the pooin' holes, but mostly it lay undisturbed, for goblins seldom bothered about wiping their bottoms.

It was to this storeroom that Breslaw now led young Skarper. There lay the bumwipe, in a great heap, with whiteworms burrowing through it and the blind white bats of Clovenstone snoozing among the stalactites above and scattering their luminous droppings over it so that the heap glowed with a sickly green light. It was ten times as tall as Skarper, and as smelly as King Knobbler himself. The lower levels had gone to compost, but on the top were mounds of books, papers, charts, letters, documents, and drawings.

"What's all this then?" asked Skarper, who had never heard of any of those things.

Breslaw knew at once that he had been right to bring the lad there, because "What's all this then?" was more interest than any other goblin had shown in these old things during all his time as hatchling master.

He picked up a thick, leather-bound book and scraped bat poo from its cover with a thoughtful claw. Opening it, he held it out to Skarper.

"See them black wriggly things all over it? Them are what the softlings call *lettuce*," he said. "When you get lots of lettuce strung together it's called a *worm*. That's what all these are: *worms*. Because they look a bit like worms, I suppose, although they're black instead of white and you can't eat 'em. And when there are lots and lots of *worms* on lots of different sheets of bumwipe they stitches 'em all together and puts these leather flaps on back and front and calls it a *burk*. That's what these things be called: *burks*."

He gave Skarper the burk to hold and pulled a big furled-up sheet of bumwipe out of the side of the heap. Unrolling it revealed a lot of spindly squiggles, with worms written between them. "This thingy here be called a *map*," he said. "All these lines be pictures of things, see. It's like a picture of the whole hugeness of Clovenstone. When softlings lived here back in oldy-times they'd use such *maps* to find their way about. Look," he said, pointing to a place near the map's center. "Here's the old Blackspike."

Skarper peered closely at the lines and saw that Breslaw was right. He recognized the spiky outline of Blackspike Tower, and next to it its neighbor towers, Redcap and Slatetop and Sternbrow, Natterdon, Grimspike and Growler, with the Inner Wall stretching between them to form a ragged ring around the Great Keep itself. Any goblin could have recognized the distinctive pointy outlines of those towers if they had taken the trouble to look, but apart from Breslaw and Skarper none ever had, and none but Skarper would have thought to do what Skarper did next, which was to look at the squiggly black worms written on the map and think, *The worms beside Slatetop and Sternbrow both start with that big squirly* mark. S. *And there it is again, in the middle of that worm next to the Blackspike. So maybe the squirly S mark means "Sssss." And maybe all them other marks mean different sounds . . .*

("I wish I'd never lit eyes on that flamin' map!" wailed Skarper, two thousand feet above the ground and falling fast.)

But he *had* lit eyes on it, and that was how it had all begun. From then on, while the other goblins went bird's-nesting among Blackspike's turrets or practiced fighting on its narrow ledges and crumbly battlements, Skarper always found a way to slip off unnoticed and creep down to the bumwipe heap. There, by the glow of the luminous bat droppings which he smeared on his nose to light his studies, he pored over the mysteries of lettuce, worms, and burks. Before many moons passed he had taught himself to read, using the names on the old map as a key to help him work out the sound that each of the lettuce stood for. He had learned that the "lettuce" were really called *letters*, the "worms" were *words*, and the proper name for "burks" was *books*. There was even a book there called *Dictionary*, which held lists of words, with other words beside them explaining what they meant. From this Skarper learned the meaning of words which no goblin before him had ever known, words such as *kindness* and *gazebo*.

There were other books too; books that held whole stories, although sometimes their endings had been nibbled off by whiteworms, and even when they hadn't, Skarper had no way of knowing which were true and which were false. For instance, had someone called Prince Brewyon of Tyr Trewas really been taken up into the sky by a cloud maiden who had fallen in love with him? Skarper didn't think there were such things as cloud maidens, and he wasn't at all sure about these "prince" things either, although there seemed to be quite a few of them in the books. Prince Brewyon cropped up in a lot of different stories, fighting giants and trolls and rescuing things called princesses.

Bat droppings showered down on Skarper; cave spiders crawled over his feet; from the chamber above came the bickerings of the older goblins squabbling over the loot from their latest raid, and from somewhere outside a long, fading shriek and a distant crunch announced that one of the bird's-nesting younglings had fallen off the battlements. Skarper noticed none of it. The stories in the old books carried him far away from the Blackspike and away beyond the walls of Clovenstone to worlds of mystery and wonder.

The only place the old books did not tell him about was Clovenstone itself. It was barely mentioned in any of them, except for a reference here and there to "ye Darke Tower of ye Lych Lord that is called Clovenstone," or "Clovenstone, the Tower of Sorrows." All that he could find out about Clovenstone came from that map, which he now knew was called *Stenoryon's Mappe of All Clovenstone*. It had been drawn a long time ago, because it showed the buildings and roadways all whole, with not a wood or a marsh to be seen within the Outer Wall, and Natterdon Tower still standing where there was now only a stump. (Goblins didn't like to talk about Natterdon Tower.) But it was enough to make Skarper understand the size of this place he lived in, and to make him wonder how and why it had fallen into ruin.

TOO CLEVER BY HALF

Enjoying the strange new snippets of knowledge which he found in the old books, Skarper longed to share them with someone else. If only there had been somebody else like him in Blackspike Tower; somebody he could talk to . . .

At first he'd talked to Breslaw, but slowly he had started to realize that the old hatchling master was watching him, and so he began watching Breslaw in return. He soon found out about the egg shards Breslaw stole, and once he even glimpsed the ball of slowsilver, big as an eyeball, that Breslaw kept hidden in the hatchery wall. *Some of that came out of my eggstone,* he thought. *That should have been mine, by rights.* He was so angry that he sometimes thought of stealing the slowsilver ball and taking it to his own hiding hole. At least, he did until he remembered that Breslaw was batch-brother to King Knobbler himself (he was always boasting that he might have ended up as king, had it not been for his missing bits). Hatchlings who stole from Breslaw got reported to Knobbler, and Knobbler always saw to it that they came to sticky ends. *You wouldn't want to end up catapulted off the roof, for instance,* Skarper told himself.

No, you did not steal from a wily old goblin like Breslaw. But neither did you trust him, and you *certainly* didn't tell him things that might help to make him cleverer than he already was.

Instead, Skarper did his best to share his newfound knowledge with his own batch-brothers.

"Men down-below don't hatch from stones like us goblins," he said one evening in the scoffery. "That's why we call them softlings. They grow in the tummies of things called 'ladies.'"

His batch-brothers looked at him, so bewildered that several of them actually stopped eating for a moment or two.

"What?" said Yabber.

"Anchovies!" said Gutgust. (*Anchovies* was the only word Gutgust ever used. No one knew why, or what he thought it meant. He was big enough and tough enough that no one had ever asked.)

"No wonder softlings is weak as cave bats then!" said Libnog.

"What are 'ladies'?" asked Wrench.

"Ladies is the ones with long hair," explained Yabber. He was the biggest of the batch and had been out already on a big raid into the man-towns along the Nibbled Coast; he always liked to show off his knowledge of foreign parts. "They squeal higher-pitched than the ordinary men. I hate it when they do that. It hurts my ears like . . . like . . . ."

"Fingernails on a blackboard?" suggested Skarper.

The others looked blankly at him again.

"What's 'fingernails'?" asked Bootle.

"What's a 'blackboard'?" asked Libnog.

"What's 'on'?" asked Wrench.

"Anchovies!" shouted Gutgust.

"He's talkin' rubbish anyway," said Yabber airily. "I've seen these 'ladies' and they ain't no bigger than ordinary softlings. Smaller, maybe. There'd be no room inside them for a whole man."

"Men aren't born full-grown," said Skarper wearily. "They starts out little and they grow, just like us goblins do when we hatch from our eggstones."

"And I has grown mighty indeed!" agreed Yabber, seizing his chance to steer the conversation toward a subject which didn't make his brain hurt so much. He proved it by flexing his huge muscles and then punching Wrench and nicking his dinner. Wrench picked himself up and tried to brain Yabber with a handy club, but Yabber ducked and the club hit Bootle instead. Bootle bit Yabber; Libnog stabbed Wrench with a fork; Gutgust smashed a table over Bootle's head. Sighing, Skarper picked up his bowl of spider stew and left the fight behind, sneaking off to the bumwipe heaps to catch up on his reading. He wished he could join in their innocent fun, but he seemed to have less and less in common with his batch-brothers. He knew so much *more* than they did. . . .

Yet in the end, he thought, as he plummeted toward the rocks, all that knowledge and learning had been his downfall. It was difficult, when you knew so much, not to try to explain things to people, and set them right when they made mistakes. And that was not always a good idea. . . .

Tumbling over and over in the bitter gusts that roared up the face of the mountain, Skarper recalled the previous night, and the great mustering of the tribe that King Knobbler had called in the scoffery.

All the goblins of the tower had gathered there, from the mightiest warriors to the lowliest snot-nosed hatchlings. The king, magnificent in all his armor, had stood on his special kinging chair in the firelight. King Knobbler was a giant of a goblin, almost as big as a man, which was how he had managed to make himself king in the first place. His craggy face was seamed with scars from countless raids and battles, and he wore a black patch to hide a missing nose. His fangs gleamed as he shouted, "Great news, boys! In two nights, us lot are going to join with Mad Manaccan's Lads and the Chili Hats from Redcap and launch a great raid on the towers around the eastside!"

The eastside towers — Sternbrow, Grimspike and Growler — were home to cheeky goblins who'd lately taken to ransacking old armories in the very shadow of

Blackspike. It was high time they were taught a lesson, and their towers were probably full of treasure too. A raid that roared through all of them should come home laden with loot. The Blackspike Boys cheered, and the noise boomed and echoed under the stone ribs of the feast-hall's roof.

Old Breslaw, who was standing at the king's side, nodded wisely. The idea for the raid was his, of course — Knobbler and his captains were all big and strong and good at hitting things, but they didn't really have ideas; it was Breslaw who did the thinking in the Blackspike. Still, he didn't mind Knobbler taking the credit, as long as he ended up with a share of the loot. He raised a tattered umbrella to try to shield himself from the royal spittle, which gusted like rain into the faces of those goblins in the front row as Knobbler went bellowing on.

"Us are going to sweep down on them eastside mobs and kill 'em all, and take their gold and silver an' that. And you lot is going to be right at the fronts of things; the hammer of the Blackspike! We'll show Mad Manaccan's lot and them Redcap Pepperheads why King Knobbler's Blackspike Boys is the best . . . the best . . . the best *land pirates* in all Clovenstone!"

That was when Skarper, with his head stuffed full of facts and words, raised his claw.

King Knobbler saw the movement. It put him off his speech. He forgot what he'd been going to shout next. His angry golden eyes were drawn to Skarper. He grunted and leaned forward, peering at this weedy little runt whom he'd never noticed before, but who had done what nobody else had ever dared do: interrupt him. The firelight shone sharp on the spines of his armor and the tips of his tea-colored fangs.

"What?" he said.

"There's no such things as land pirates, your majesty," said Skarper uneasily. He already sensed that he had made a mistake, but he could see no way back.

The glow in the goblin king's eyes deepened, as if a fire somewhere behind them was being stoked up. (Down deep beneath the Bonehills' roots the lava lake glowed much like that.) "We robs people," he said. "We smashes in doors and burns houses and kills people and comes home laden with loot. What is we if we ain't land pirates?"

"Well, it's just that pirates generally work at sea," Skarper explained. His voice got smaller and smaller as he spoke, but it was still easy to hear in the appalled silence that filled the Kingcave. "We're bandits, your royal immensity. Or brigands."

"Brigands?" said Knobbler.

"Yes, your magnificentness. '*Brigand*: noun: somebody who lives by plunder, usually as part of a gang of marauding thieves.'"

The *Dictionary* definition of *brigand* rocked the king back on his heels like a blow from a well-aimed war hammer. He didn't know quite what it meant, but it sounded like softling-talk to him. Knobbler had no time for softlings. "What did softlings ever do that was any good?" he often asked his goblins, and roared the answer along with them: "Nothing!" (Although actually there was one softling invention that secretly impressed him. He admired the softlings' underpants; so snug and comfortable and toasty warm. He had stolen himself some very cozy pink flannel ones, extra large, with frilly bits, which he wore at all times to protect his bottom from the Blackspike's icy drafts and the hard seat of his kinging chair. Of course, he made sure they stayed safely hidden beneath his armor and his goat-hide trousers: It would never do to let his goblins see he wore pink flannel knickers.)

And it would never do to let himself be contradicted by a little half-grown runt like Skarper, either. The Blackspike goblins only let Knobbler lead them because they knew he'd dish out dreadful punishments to anyone who questioned him. He scowled at Skarper for a moment, trying to think of something suitably bad to do to him.

Luckily he didn't have to think very hard. The goblins of Blackspike Tower had an age-old way of dealing with impertinent, rebellious or unwanted hatchlings.

"To the bratapult!" roared Knobbler.

UNHAPPY LANDINGS

The bratapult had stood upon the topmost pinnacle of Blackspike Tower for as long as any goblin could recall. It had been designed to throw stones and pots of blazing oil at besieging armies, but nobody bothered besieging Clovenstone anymore, and when goblins from other towers attacked Blackspike, King Knobbler's boys usually just dropped rocks on them from upstairs windows. The bratapult was now mostly used for fun, and there was nothing that the goblins thought funnier than flinging a cheeky hatchling high into the air and watching him plummet to the ground far, far below.

It was made from wood, stone, iron, bone, old mineshaft props, the hides of pit ponies, and anything else the goblins could get their paws on and drag up the steep stone stairways to the tower's summit. Snow covered it, icicles trailed from its long throwing arm, and all night Skarper shivered in the cold, trussed up and left in its vast cup.

King Knobbler had been all for launching him as soon as they got him there, but it was dark by then, and the other goblins complained that they would not be able to watch him fall, which was always the best bit of firing a hatchling from the bratapult. "We could set him on fire first," someone suggested, but there was a north wind howling around the tower, driving thin, slushy snow, and Skarper proved impossible to light. So they left him there and went back to the scoffery, planning to come back and launch him in the morning.

But what if it's foggy tomorrow? he wondered as he lay there, roped, regretful and slightly singed. He looked up at the huge bulk of the Great Keep towering into the night, hidden behind the murk most of the time, except when a lessening of the storm cleared the sky for a moment and showed him those empty black windows and bare battlements. The Keep of Clovenstone, doorless, impenetrable, and full of mysteries. It didn't even look like the towers and walls that had been built around it: It was older, and it did not seem to have been made from individual stones but from one sheer black mass of rock. Goblins had tried to get inside and loot it sometimes, but there was no way in: When the Lych Lord died, every door and window into the Keep had sealed itself shut with a scab of thick, dark stuff called lychglass which no mortal instrument could break or even make a mark on. All the treasures and wonders of the Keep had been locked away forever, all alone.

Of course, goblin legends said that there were still things living in the Keep — servants of the Lych Lord, waiting for the day he would return — but Skarper had never believed that. At least, not until now . . . He squinted upward, imagining the terrible cold eyes that might be gazing back at him, and for a moment, just a moment, he thought he saw a light up there, an impossible light in one of those empty windows.

Then the snow swirled back, and with it Skarper's worries about fog. *They won't be able to see me fall if it's foggy tomorrow; they'll have to wait for it to clear. . . .* Sometimes it took weeks for fog to clear from the heights of Blackspike. He could starve to death waiting in the cup of the bratapult for the weather to improve. He wondered whether starving would be better than being splattered on the stones at the tower's foot, but he couldn't decide. He drifted into an uneasy sleep, still worrying.

He was in luck, or out of it. The next morning dawned clear and bright, and as soon as the sun had heaved itself up over the eastward towers a crowd of goblins came tumbling out of Blackspike to watch the fun. Dungnutt, Knobbler's second-in-command, came and cut Skarper's bonds, because it would be funnier if they could see him flapping his arms and legs about on the way down. Yabber, Wrench, Libnog, and Bootle took bets on how long it would take their batch-brother to reach the ground, and whether he'd bounce off anything interesting on the way down. "Anchovies!" shouted Gutgust. Breslaw the hatchling master sadly shook his head.

King Knobbler drew his sword. It was a massive broadsword, and although it wasn't as richly decorated as some swords, a sort of sullen magic seemed to live in it: It was said that its blade could slice through stone. Knobbler had heard somewhere that kings and heroes in the lands of men gave names to their swords, so he had named his. It was called "Mr. Chop-U-Up." He raised it so that the sunrise bloodied its blade.

"This," he yelled, "is for being too clever by half!"

Mr. Chop-U-Up swept down, hewing through the rope that held the bratapult's cup in place. The throwing arm sprang upright, crashing against the frame. The icicles flew off it with a thousand little pretty tinkling noises, and Skarper flew with them, like many a cheeky young goblin before him, hurtling up and out into the howling emptiness above the tower.

"Aaaaaaaaa . . ." he said.

The goblins cheered, and rushed to the edge of the roof to watch him fall.

Down and down and down he went, his escort of icicles filling the air around him. Sometimes he fell with his face to the wide sky, sometimes facedown. Facedown was worst, because as the ground drew closer he could see, between the clouds, the smashed-up skeletons of all the bratapult's previous victims, spread about between the buttresses down there like white shingle at the foot of a sea cliff. Tears came from his eyes as he fell, and whirled upward in his slipstream like lost raindrops. They were tears of bitterness, because he was regretting every moment that he had spent with books and words. Wrench and Yabber and the others had been right; what use had it ever been to him to learn about far-off lands and long-forgotten kings? Few goblins had even ventured as far as Clovenstone's Outer Wall in Skarper's lifetime; what help was it to know about the lands beyond? Most of what he had read had probably been made up anyway. He didn't believe there had ever been any such person as Prince Brewyon, or any such places as Coriander or Tyr Trewas. As for cloud maidens, who would believe that old tripe?

There was a soft tearing noise, a louder *whoof*, and he landed heavily on something that yielded beneath his weight like a blanket bog. *I'm dead!* he thought, and then realized that, if he was thinking it, he couldn't be. He opened his eyes, which he had shut tight as he landed, not wanting to watch bits of himself being strewn about the landscape.

He was lying in thick, cottony white fluff at the bottom of a deep, Skarper-shaped shaft. The walls of the shaft were all made of the same pale fluff, and at the top of it there was blue sky in the shape of his own spread-eagled silhouette. He realized that he had plunged into the top of a low-flying cloud, and had sunk about half-way through it.

At about the same moment that he worked this out, a face appeared at the top of the shaft, looking down. It was a cloud-white face with a lot of smoky hair, and when it saw Skarper it frowned and flushed an angry bruise-gray. "What do you think you're doing on our cloud?" it demanded.

Skarper groped through all the memories of all the books he'd read, searching for a witty or a courteous answer.

More heads were appearing at the top of the hole he'd made. "What is it, sister?" asked one of them.

"Is it a prince?" asked another, hopefully.

"Of course not! It's much too small."

"Perhaps it's a very small prince?"

"Anyway, what would a prince be doing up here?"

"It's just a horrid goblin!"

"Seize him!" said the first cloud maiden. She darkened like a thunderhead and little zigzag sparks of lightning started to dance in her cloudy hair.

"If you don't mind," called Skarper hopefully, "that would suit me very well. Just set me down anywhere and I'll trouble you no more."

The cloud maidens peered down at him suspiciously.

"He's very polite, for a goblin," said the one who'd hoped he was a prince.

But the rest blushed black, spitting and sparking with lightning. "Take him to the ground? The very idea! We must cast this creature back into the sky, sisters, before his weight drags us to the earth!"

INTO THE WOODS

"Seize him!" shouted the cloud maidens.

But Skarper wasn't waiting to be seized. He had spent enough time escaping from other goblins to know when to make himself scarce. He started to writhe and wriggle against the cloud that pressed around him, and found that it had the texture of light, dry snow. He could kick holes in it, and dig out handfuls. Turning over onto his hands and knees, he started digging like a dog, shoveling up great handfuls of the dense vapor and flinging it over his shoulder, where it drifted uncertainly up the shaft. By the shrieks and hisses coming from above he could tell the cloud maidens didn't much like him doing further damage to their home and, when he glanced up, he saw that several of them had started to climb toward him down the shaft he'd made, kicking footholds in its vapory walls like climbers coming down a snow-face. They glared angrily at him with eyes as hard and bright as hailstones; in their smoky hands were blades of ice.

Skarper whimpered and dug faster. He'd rather be smashed on the flagstones after all, he thought, than sliced to bits by angry cloud maidens. He dug and dug, clawing up big handfuls of cloud and throwing it frantically over his shoulder, fighting his way down into the deepening hole. The farther he went, the darker grew the cloud, and soon the handfuls that he was scooping up became wetter and heavier, packed with hailstones or sodden with unfallen rain, like cold gray sponges. At last, through a growing crack in the bottom of the cloud, he glimpsed daylight.

A cloudy hand reached down and grabbed him by the tuft on the tip of his tail. Considering that it was made of cloud, the hand was surprisingly strong, but it was not as strong as gravity, which seized Skarper from below at exactly the same moment, because the thin cloud floor had given way beneath him. He dangled there a moment, screaming, "Let me go! Let me go!", suspended by his tail while the cloud maiden's wrist stretched out longer and longer, thinner and thinner. Finally it tore, and Skarper was tumbling again, only to land with a soft squelch in thick mud about six feet below.

Freed of his weight, the cloud bobbed upward, caught by the breeze that curled around the base of Blackspike Tower. Bits of it had unraveled like fraying banners, and Skarper could see the cloud maidens scrambling about all over it like sailors on a ship, trying to plait it back together. He wondered why he had never noticed such interesting clouds before. Presumably they were rare, and their crews stayed out of sight of ground-lings. It was a pity they'd been so unfriendly, he thought, flicking wisps of the cloud maiden's fingers from his tail like clinging smoke. He would have liked to ask them about their life in the sky.

He stood up shakily and looked around. He was standing in a bleak little bog about a mile from the base of the Inner Wall, formed where a stream of fresh water overflowed from its channel and spread across a weed-grown area which had once been a square between two massive ruined buildings. On either side of this marsh were stretches of ancient paving, the huge flagstones cracked and tilted by misshapen trees which had grown up from beneath them.

I'm outside the Blackspike! he realized suddenly. *Beyond the Inner Wall!* Never having set foot outside his home tower before, he felt frightened by the huge space around him, so much wider and brighter than the halls and passageways that he was used to. All his life he had been trying to find peace and quiet and places away from other goblins, and now that he had finally reached one he found he *missed* the sounds of their constant squabbling and bickering, their snores and farts and burps. For a moment he felt tempted to run straight back to the Inner Wall, climb inside Blackspike Tower again, say he was sorry, and beg King Knobbler to forgive him. But goblins were not good at forgiveness. He would have to find somewhere else to make his lair, he decided. He looked south, at all the old bastions and towerlets which rose among the trees between the Blackspike and the Outer Wall. Surely one of those could hide him? He'd hole up there and think what to do. Maybe there'd be treasure to find; just a few small trinkets, left behind in those old buildings. He'd sort out a nice new hoard for himself. There might even be goblins down there;

some little outcast tribe that wouldn't mind an extra member . . .

So he turned his back on his home, squelched his way out of the bog, and set off southward down a broad, paved road, stopping now and then to munch a handful of the dead thistles that stood man-high between the flagstones and enjoy their peppery flavor.

At first the margin of the road was marked by mounds of tumbled masonry, with the chimneys of fallen-down buildings sticking up like bony fingers, and meres between them where water had flooded the old cellars. But as it sloped downhill, away from Blackspike Tower, the trees came to meet it: Skarper could see them crowding in ahead until they appeared to close over the road like a twiggy tunnel. He began to feel uneasy. He didn't know much about trees and growing things. The saplings that sprouted from the crevices of Blackspike made good eating, but these great trees were so *big* and *old*, and their creaks and rustlings had the sound of secret whispers. Skarper couldn't help noticing the ease with which their roots had managed to split and crumble huge slabs of stone.

He walked slower and slower, and he was about to

turn back when there was a crackle and a flash, and a clump of alders that had been minding its own business nearby burst suddenly into flames. Skarper yowled and looked around again, then up. The cloud which had broken his fall had recovered itself, and it was hovering over him, black as wet slate, with lashes of lightning flicking from its belly. It looked like a fierce, shaggy monster with electric legs.

Skarper set off at a loping run while lightning bolts lanced down all around him, sizzling when they hit the meres and starting small fires when they touched the dry bits in between. Above the steady boom of thunder and the fizz and prickle of the lightning he caught another sound: the high, scornful laughter of angry cloud maidens.

Zigzagging between forks of their white fire, jumping a line of fallen pillars that had collapsed across the old road, he sprinted toward the edge of the woods. The trees looked more welcoming than forbidding now. Big and bare and wintry, they clustered close together, branches bearded with lichen, forming a cage of green shadows. Once he was under there, surely the cloud maidens would not be able to see him . . .

Krazzzzzap! A lightning bolt crisped past his ear, making his hair stand on end.

Pfritzzzz! Another touched down in a puddle just ahead of him and turned it to scalding steam.

Krakkk! A wobbling globe of witch-fire drifted by and blasted a nearby boulder into bits.

Skarper zigzagged his way between the explosions and threw himself into the shelter of the woods. There he lay, bruised and panting, on a bed of thick, wet moss under a fallen tree, while his heartbeat thundered in his ears like all the war drums of all the goblin holds of Clovenstone.

The cloud maidens steered their thunder-grumbling cloud around above him, trying to peer down through the dense branches. "Oh, goblin!" they called. "Come out, little goblin!" They sent a few more lightning bolts down just for fun, and then let the wind take their cloud and blow it away toward the east, to join a herd of others above the Bonehill Mountains.

Skarper waited until the last faint sounds of their voices had faded, then slithered out of his hiding place, checked the corners of the sky for lurking clouds, and set off again through the trees, looking for a new home.

THE BRIDGE

After that, several whole hours went by without anybody trying to kill him. No tree monsters or angry dryads appeared to drive him from the wood, and he saw that goblins had sometimes been this way on raids, because he recognized their crude graffiti on the ruined buildings that stood on either side of the roadway. That made him feel a little more at home, and he decided that things were looking up (although he kept looking up too, checking those tiny flakes of sky that showed between the bare branches, just in case that cloud was still around).

Skarper cast his mind back again to *Stenoryon's Mappe of All Clovenstone* (how he wished he could have brought it with him!). The vast Outer Wall which ringed

Clovenstone was roughly circular, with four gates in it: north, south, east and west. This road that he was walking down must be the way from the Keep to Southerly Gate. In the days of the Lych Lord whole armies had marched down it, off to carry terror and war to the lands of men. The buildings on either side would have been their barracks and armories, their kitchens and saddleries, and the stables for their steeds. Now there were only ruins, subsiding into the undergrowth like sinking galleons. Everything was furred thick with dense green moss and filled with dim green light and the song of unseen birds and the chuckle of running water. Streams that had once run obediently along neat channels of dressed stone had now escaped to find their own ways through the wood, sometimes flowing knee-deep across depressions in the old roadway.

Leaving the road, Skarper pushed his way through the undergrowth to start exploring the old buildings. He soon decided that he did not much like them. Even before they rotted into ruin they must have been mean, cramped, low-ceilinged places. Now they were floored with heaps of slates or moldered thatch that had slumped down through their roofs as the rafters rotted. Goblins from Blackspike and the other towers had long since taken any treasure they had held, but in many of the rooms lay bones, and in high corners the black bees of Clovenstone had built huge paper nests from which low and dangerous buzzings emerged whenever Skarper blundered too close. He was pretty sure that worse things than bees had made their homes among the ruins too. His ears kept prickling: a sure sign that he was being watched. Scuttling sounds and half-glimpsed movements filled the shadows. The trees creaked and whispered, peering down at him through the holes where roofs had been.

Warily, he found his way back to the old road. He could do better for himself, he decided, if he kept going south; Stenoryon's map had shown great bastions just inside Southerly Gate. So he kept walking until the road turned into shallow stairs, descending into a valley where the trees grew even more thickly, winding their leafless, moss-shaggy branches together in great green nets that overhung a river full of big stones.

Skarper guessed at once that this must be the River Oeth, which flowed down out of the Oeth Moors and curved through the outer regions of Clovenstone before flowing on to meet the sea. It was swift and white and startlingly loud, but he was glad to see it, because he knew that once he was on the far side of it he would be only a short way from Southerly Gate. The road spanned the river on a bridge; not one of the primitive clapper bridges that goblins made to cross the streams behind the Inner Wall, but a proper, man-built bridge, with piers and buttresses and things. It must have been elegant back in better days but was now looking overgrown and crumbledown and rather sorry for itself.

It was just the sort of place where trolls might lurk, according to the books that Skarper had read. He had never seen a troll and wasn't completely sure that they existed, but after his meeting with the cloud maidens he wasn't going to take any chances, so before he crossed the bridge he went carefully down the riverbank and peered beneath it.

Nothing stirred in the green shadows, but the place still made him uneasy. The ferns and mosses grew so thick beneath the bridge that he could not see all the way through. He climbed back to the road and was about to go down and take a look from the other side when a voice from the far side of the river called: "Aha!"

Skarper looked up. There, striding toward him across the bridge, was a softling; a human; a real, live, actual human being: quite a young one by the look of him, with a dark cloak, travel-stained boots and breeches, and a leather tunic with iron studs. Skarper stared at him. He had heard of softlings venturing into Clovenstone — outlaws and fortune hunters, drawn by stories of the Lych Lord's treasure chambers — and he had seen the skulls of some of them, decorating King Knobbler's kinging chair. But it had not occurred to him that he might actually meet one, and he could only stand and watch as the softling swung a long sword down from his shoulder. Hanging from its notched and obviously not very sharp blade were various bags and satchels and blanket bundles, which the softling hastily unhooked and shed on the flagstones of the bridge as he hurried across it toward Skarper.

Skarper ducked, and felt the blade slice through the air where his head had just been.

"Stand and fight, foul troll!" the softling shouted.

"I'm not a *troll*!" Skarper said indignantly, scuttling sideways.

The softling swung at him again. "I saw you with my

own eyes!" he cried. "You were creeping out from under this bridge to waylay me!"

"I'm not waylaying anybody!" shouted Skarper.

"You lie!" said the softling, panting with the effort of swinging that big sword to and fro as Skarper ducked beneath it. "Stand still, can't you? Make your peace with your fell trollish gods and prepare to die!"

"Trolls are taller!" shouted Skarper. "*Much* taller! I've seen woodcuts . . ."

Dodging past the swordsman, he turned and started to flee over the bridge, but as he set his foot on it there came a wet, echoey roar from below, and out from among the moss and the ferns beneath the arch there oozed a great gray-green shape. Thick-fingered hands seized the parapet as the figure heaved itself up to block the bridge; dull, dark eyes gleamed hungrily behind a fall of pondweed hair; a gout of vapor and a musty smell enveloped Skarper as its broad mouth opened to let out another roar.

He pointed at it, and turned to look back at his attacker. "Now *that's* a troll," he said.

HENWYN

Skarper had expected the troll to reach straight past him for the softling, who was so obviously larger and more tender and better to eat. Instead, to his surprise, it closed one of its big hands about his leg and lifted him upside down in front of its face, blinking at him with those black, wet-pebble eyes. Trolls, he realized, as it opened its spike-toothed maw to gulp him down, are *really* stupid. . . .

The softling must have been stupider still. He came charging in under the dangling Skarper and swung his blunt and rusty blade straight at the troll's chest. Had no one told him that troll hide was as tough as stone? The sword rebounded; it clattered to the flagstones as the softling yelled in pain and stuck his jarred hands in his armpits. The troll knocked off his hat and lifted him by his curly golden hair. As it did so, Skarper managed to lash out with one foot and catch it in the eye with his heel. The troll grunted and stepped backward. Over-balanced by the weight of its struggling prey, it stumbled against the bridge's parapet, and the rough old ivied stones gave way. Down they went, man, troll, and gob-lin, into the cold dark swirl of water under the bridge.

The troll let go of Skarper, but that didn't help much; water is no place for goblins. He sank, choking and flail-ing, until a firm hand grabbed him and heaved him up into the air and then ashore. The softling let him go and turned back to the river, drawing a knife from his belt as the water heaved in the bridge's shadow and the troll burst up roaring, looking for its prey.

"Over here, spawn of evil!" shouted the softling, waving his little dagger.

"Hush! Shhh! Psst! Don't attract its attention! Running's our only hope!" hissed Skarper, grabbing the flapping end of the softling's sodden cloak and trying desperately to pull him backward.

It was too late; the shouting or the flash of the blade had caught the troll's attention. Its big head turned; it roared its fury at the pair on the bank.

Fortunately the parapet of the bridge had not quite finished falling to pieces. One huge stone still teetered, leaning far out over the river but held in place by a tether of ivy stems. At the troll's roar the last stem broke; the stone toppled, fell, and landed with an ugly thud on the troll's flat skull. The troll collapsed into the water and did not come up again; a few bubbles rose, and the river whirled them away. The white rapids downstream flushed a rusty red.

"Victory!" cried the softling triumphantly, and started to wade toward the pool where the troll had sunk, holding his knife aloft. "I shall cut off its head!"

"Not with that, you won't," shouted Skarper, still holding on to the raggedy end of the softling's cloak and pulling hard to hold him back. "Don't you know the king of Coriander dresses his bodyguards in trollskin armor because it deflects the blows of any man-forged blade?"

The softling looked back, a glimpse of doubt in his large blue eyes. "You have been to Coriander?"

"I read it in a book," said Skarper. "And I read in another one that trolls' bones are hard as upland stones," he added, and fell backward on the bank as the softling turned and waded back to shore.

"You think it might only be stunned?" he asked as he scrambled out of the water.

"Let's not wait around and find out," said Skarper.

"No; perhaps that would not be wise," the softling said, showing some sense for the first time since Skarper had met him, and together they scrabbled their way up the bank to the road and hurried along it until the river was well behind them. The softling had retrieved his baggage and his sword, and Skarper eyed him warily as they both paused to catch their breath and wring water out of their soggy clothes.

"Henwyn," said the softling.

"Eh?"

"My name. Henwyn of Adherak."

He held out his hand, though Skarper did not know what he was supposed to do with it. He looked the softling up and down. *He's not much more than a hatchling,* he thought. *Maybe that's why he's so stupid . . .*

"You must be a man of great learning," Henwyn said earnestly. "To have read books and things. I hope that you can forgive me for trying to . . . Well, I mistook you for a troll, you know. It was quite understandable, seeing you creep out from under the bridge like that, and what with you being a rather strange-looking fellow, if you don't mind me saying so. Where I come from, in Adherak, people are taller than you and, well, different altogether, so when I saw you I naturally assumed . . ."

He paused, and suddenly bowed low and dropped his sword on the road with a clang that made Skarper leap back nervously.

"Allow me to apologize and to lay my sword at your service. I should be glad of company in this fell place. Everyone knows that Clovenstone is full of ravening, rampaging goblins of the most wicked and unsightly sort."

"Really?" asked Skarper. He glanced sideways at his companion. Surely this idiot must have noticed his goblin ears, his goblin paws, and the goblin tail that stuck out from under his thick leather goblin jerkin? "So what do these goblins look like, then?" he asked.

"Oh, they are great big hulking brutes," Henwyn explained. "Taller and broader than men, dressed all in iron armor, with red, glowing fangs and terrible pointy eyes."

"You're sure of that?"

"I may have got the eyes and the fangs the wrong way around, but otherwise, yes, quite sure. That's what all the songs and stories say. They are supposed to infest those tall towers around the Great Keep, but who knows how far they might creep in search of loot and victims? Even on this road I feel that I may be close to a goblin . . ."

"So what's brought *you* here?" asked Skarper, thinking, *You have no idea how close . . .*

"Oh, I am a hero," said Henwyn airily, and then, as if he sensed that Skarper did not quite believe him, "at least, I mean to be. Like in the old tales. I am of humble birth, but I've always had a feeling that I am destined to do great deeds. My mother came from the line of King Kennack, you see; a daughter of heroes. So I decided to try my hand at heroing. Slaying monsters, rescuing princesses. Though there's not much call for that sort of thing in Adherak these days. That's why I came to Clovenstone. I haven't actually done any great deeds yet, not unless you count that troll, and that wasn't really a deed, more of an accident. I wish I could have got its head . . ."

He paused, looking thoughtfully back toward the river, and Skarper said, "So you decided to just come and wander about in the ruins till you found something heroic to do?"

"Oh no," replied Henwyn. He sat down on the mossy curb and took his boots off, tipping the water out of each before pulling them back on. "No, no; I am on my way to Westerly Gate."

Skarper's eyes narrowed as he recalled Stenoryon's map. "Why's that?" he asked.

"It is the home of the giant Fraddon," said Henwyn.

That meant nothing to Skarper. "I don't know what a giant fraddon is," he said. "I don't even know what a normal-sized fraddon is."

"No, he's a giant *called* Fraddon," explained Henwyn. "A very wicked, villainous giant. There is a song about him, 'The Ballad of Princess Eluned,' all about how he carried off Princess Eluned of Lusuenn and keeps her prisoner in the old fortress that guards the Westerly Gate of this evil place. It's quite catchy. Shall I sing it to you?" And without waiting for an answer he began singing in a thin, tuneless voice:

> *"O, 'twas on a summer's morning,*
> *A Tuesday, I've heard tell,*
> *The princess of Lusuenn sailed*
> *Upon the gray sea's swell . . ."*

"Some other time, maybe," said Skarper hastily, for although he didn't know that particular song, there had been books in the bumwipe heaps full of others like it, and some of them went on for pages and pages.

Henwyn stopped singing. "Well, anyway," he said, "if I can rescue Princess Eluned and slay the giant, the king of Lusuenn is certain to reward me with half the kingdom and her hand in marriage."

"Her *hand*?" said Skarper (for the ways of men were strange to him).

"Oh, and the rest of her, of course. At least, that's the way it generally works. Lusuenn is only a small kingdom, but it would be a start, and the song says that Princess Eluned is a great beauty . . ."

He stopped talking and looked around in surprise, for Skarper had started to make a strange creaking, croaking, snoring sound, which turned out to be laughter.

"You?" cawed Skarper. "You, defeat a *giant*? With that overgrown butter knife? Oh, hee, hee, hee!"

"Well, I don't see what's so amusing about it," said Henwyn huffily. "I am a hero, and that is the sort of thing that heroes do."

Skarper shook his head. This wasn't funny anymore. It was sad. He had read about giants in the bumwipe heaps, and once, from one of the roofs of Blackspike Tower, he and Breslaw had watched one moving about among the ruins up northerly way. "All sorts of old things are coming here out of the Bonehills and the tangleywoods," Breslaw had said. "There ain't no place for them in man-country anymore, so they comes to make their homes at Clovenstone. That's why wise goblins stay safe within the Inner Wall." The giant had been a long way off, and fog had been brewing in the bogs that lay north of the Inner Wall, so it had been hard to say just how tall the giant was, but he'd stood high enough to lift the roofs off buildings as if they were the lids of treasure boxes. *It would need a whole army of softlings to defeat him,* Skarper thought.

"I came in through Southerly Gate because it seemed easier than skirting around outside the walls, through all the mires and crags and things," said Henwyn. "I hoped to find a road through these woods to Westerly Gate. Have you passed one, friend?"

Skarper shrugged. All sorts of paths had branched off the road he'd come down, but there was no telling where any of them went. "You'll have to follow your nose," he said rudely, and pointed vaguely westward, where scraps of golden sunlight showed between the trees.

Henwyn did not seem offended. "Very well. It looks a difficult and dangerous path through these haunted trees, but that is where my fate must take me. Will you join me on that road, Master, er . . . ?"

"Skarper," said Skarper. "And no: I'm heading south . . ." He had no idea where his fate was taking him, only that it wasn't going to involve giants. Or would-be heroes. He raised a paw in farewell and scurried on along the road. He looked over his shoulder twice as he went. The first time he could see Henwyn standing staring after him. The second time, the road was empty. He paused, and thought he heard the young man's voice raised in song, dwindling westward between the trees.

What an idiot, he thought.

THE CHEESEWRIGHT
OF ADHERAK

Let's pause a moment and take a good look at Henwyn as, stout of heart and damp of socks, he squelches off in search of his adventure. Tall, slim, curly-haired, he certainly *looks* like a hero, or would if his tunic weren't quite so old-fashioned, his wet cloak quite so ragged. "I am of humble birth," is what he's told everyone he's met on the way from Adherak, "but my mother was of the royal line of King Kennack . . ." Only that's not quite true: His mother was not descended from one of the great king's sons or daughters, but from his dairy maid. Henwyn son of Henmor comes from a long line of dairy maids and cheesewrights, and he did not grow up in a castle or a manor house but in his father's cheesery in Adherak.

Not that it wasn't a good cheesery. It was a very good one; the best in Adherak, and his father's famous cheeses were carted off to stock the larders of the high king in Coriander and the pantries of all the little kings of the Nibbled Coast. Among the low, thatched roofs of Adherak the house of Henmor stood tall and proud, built from creamy-colored stone, triangular and two stories tall, with round windows and doors that made it look like an enormous slice of cheese. A brass weather vane in the shape of a cow twirled on its rooftop, and the wind that spun the weathervane wafted delicious smells across the neighborhood, reminding all of Adherak that Henmor made the finest cheese in the Westlands.

There were probably young men — good, sensible young men — who would have given anything for a chance to be the great cheesewright's apprentice and a hope of inheriting the cheesery from him. It was just bad luck that his own son wasn't one of them. Henwyn didn't even *like* cheese, and he certainly did not want to be a cheesewright all his life.

He felt that fate had something far more interesting in store for him.

For as long as he could remember, Adherak had felt

too small and ordinary a place for him. He liked to stand at the edge of the town and look north to where, beyond the safe, soft hills, you could just make out the brindled moors and high blue mountains massing. Sometimes, on clear days, he even glimpsed the dark spike of Clovenstone, like a tentpole holding up the sky. *That's where I should be,* he thought. *Not here in the soft-lands, among merchants and traders; up there in the north, where there is still magic, like in stories. I wasn't born to be a cheesewright! I was born to be a . . . a hero!*

He wanted magic and adventures so badly that it was almost unbearable. But there was no magic anymore in Adherak, and no adventures to be had, so he got them the only way he could: secondhand, from stories. Henwyn had never been much of a reader, which was lucky, because there were no books in the cheesery. But Adherak was a market town, plonked down plump and prosperous in a green valley where the road from Coriander crossed a winding river. Up that road, from Coriander and the Nibbled Coast, came fish and sealskins, spice and silk, all the produce of the Sundering Sea and the lands that lay beyond. Down the river to Adherak's docks came barges filled with grain and timber and all the good things of the softlands. And up and down both road and river there came stories: tellers of tales, singers of songs; whole traveling shows arrived in Adherak every few days, and Henwyn, running through the town on errands for his father, always found some excuse to stop and listen.

"The boy has his head in the clouds," said Henmor the first time his son spent a whole afternoon watching a play about Prince Brewyon and the cloud maidens when he should have been collecting a shipment of cheesecloth from the floating market.

"He's only young," said Henwyn's mother. "He'll grow out of it."

"He's away with the fairies!" Henmor raged, the day Henwyn was sent to buy chives to flavor a special wheel of cheese for the wedding of the Lord of Adherak; he came back without the chives, and without the money he'd been given either. He had been hanging around the secondhand weapons stall where the old washed-up warriors went to pawn their gear and tell tall tales, and one of them had sold him a rusty old sword, which he said had once belonged to King Kennack.

"All this nonsense he fills his head with!" Henmor

railed. "Heroes and monsters! Quests and battles! What sort of dreams are those for a young man? When I was his age, I just dreamed of cheese! The world would get on very nicely without battles and quests, but where would be it be without cheese, eh? Heroes and monsters were all very well in the olden times, but nowadays a young fellow needs a sensible trade."

"He's still just a boy," said Henwyn's mother, though even she was getting tired of making excuses for her son. "Wait till he turns thirteen; he'll gather his wits and settle down to cheesemaking, like his father and his grandfather before him."

But Henwyn turned thirteen, turned fourteen, turned fifteen, and still he was more interested in stories than in cheese. He did his best to pay attention to the things his father told him: the best ways to make milk coagulate, how to separate curds from whey, the ripening times of different cheeses. Sometimes, as he concentrated on wrapping the cheeses and pressing them in the great round molds, he would tell himself, *Yes, this is the life for me* . . . But then, across some empty, sunlit meadow of his mind a rider would go galloping, off to save a princess or defeat a tyrant, and his work would go all to pieces. Often the cheeses went all to pieces too: He would leave them too long in the brine bath or drop them down the cellar steps, or forget to add rennet at the right moment so that the cheese never thickened properly.

Whenever he could, he would leave his sisters to do his work — there were three of them, Herda, Gerda and Lynt, and they were all better cheesewrights than Henwyn. If only *they* could have been Henmor's heirs, and carried on the family business! But cheeseries were passed on to sons, not daughters, and Henwyn was Henmor's only son. It made him feel ashamed of himself when he left Herda, Gerda and Lynt to do the wrapping and salting and pressing for him while he went off to hear whatever new storyteller the trade winds had blown into town — but not ashamed enough to stop him from doing it. By night, in his attic room, where the smells of the ripening curds drifted up between the floorboards like invisible, cheesy smoke, he would fetch out King Kennack's sword and mime great battles, practicing the moves he knew good swordsmen had to know, such as Thrusting and Parrying and Not Getting It Stuck in the Ceiling.

One day — a blue day in his fifteenth summer, the west wind blowing fat white clouds in over the hills where the cows that made the cheesery's milk were grazing — Henmor took his son aside.

"I have business down in Nantivey," he said. "A cheesewright there has devised a new sort of vat, and I want to take a look at it. While I'm gone, you'll be in charge here. The cheesery is yours for a week. It will be good practice for you, for the day when I retire and it is yours forever."

"Yes, Father," said Henwyn.

He looked so serious and earnest as he said it that Henmor thought, *He's a good boy after all; I should have given him responsibility sooner.* Perhaps his son was settling, just as his mother had always said he would; maturing like a good, hard cheese. He set off for Nantivey with a secret smile, because the cheesewright there didn't just have a new sort of vat, he had a daughter too, and Henmor thought she'd make a good wife for young Henwyn, and stop him daydreaming of princesses. He couldn't know that Henwyn had been daydreaming all through their little talk, and that when he'd said, "You'll be in charge here," Henwyn had been imagining that it

was a castle he was being left in charge of, not a cheesery, and that he must defend it from ravening hordes of
goblins for a week, not just make cheese.

For the first day, and the second, all went well. Henwyn
tried hard to concentrate, and whenever he found himself daydreaming he would tell himself, "Cheese!" and
drive the warriors and dragons and princesses from
his thoughts. But on the third day there was not much
to be done; only the cleaning of the cheesery, which
his mother, Herda, Gerda and Lynt were busy doing. To
get himself out of the way of their mops he walked down
to the floating market, wondering if the latest barges
had brought in any players or bards. They hadn't; there
was only an old man singing "The Ballad of the Blind
Giantslayer," a tale so familiar that even Henwyn was a
little tired of it. He listened to a few verses, but it lit no
pictures in his mind, and he turned to walk home, wondering if perhaps he was settling down, and would be a
good, sober cheesewright from now on.

He didn't see the three travelers who followed him
out of the marketplace. He didn't hear the quick, muttered conversation that they held.

"That's him!"

"Who?"

"Henwyn; the one I told you of. They say he's a day-dreamer: away with the fairies; believes in goblins and trolls and any old folly the harpers sing of."

"But so do we."

"That's not the point."

"Then what is the point?"

"The point is . . ." said the one who had spoken first, and shook his head angrily, because all these questions had completely broken his train of thought. "The point *is* that we need money to hire ourselves some transport if we're to get to You Know Where, and young Henwyn, son of Henmor, there is going to give it to us." And he hurried ahead of his two companions, calling out, "Young man! I say! Cheesewright! Henwyn, son of Henmor!"

Henwyn turned, at first surprised and then intrigued to be accosted in this way, by these three strangers who looked — well, like something from a story. Their leader, the one who had just spoken, wore a deep hood, from the shadows of which a long white beard emerged like a waterfall from a mountain cave. One of the others was a dark-skinned man from Musk or Barragan, wearing silk robes embroidered with symbols of stars and suns and moons. The third was tall and lanky, with curly gray hair and ears that stuck out like two pink handles and held up the horn frames of a pair of spectacles, a new invention, seldom seen in Adherak.

"Yes," said Henwyn, "I am Henwyn, son of Henmor." He assumed that the unlikely trio wanted to buy some cheese.

"Your father is away in Nantivey," said the white-bearded one, throwing back the hood of his robes to reveal a disappointingly ordinary face. "He has left you to run the cheesery in his absence."

"How can you possibly know that . . . ?"

The stranger smiled a secret smile. "I am Fentongoose. These are my colleagues, Carnglaze and Prawl. We are sorcerers of the Sable Conclave, and sorcerers know everything."

"There are no such things as sorcerers anymore!"

"You see? We *knew* you were going to say that!"

Henwyn gaped. He knew that there had once been real and powerful magic in the world, and he believed firmly that there were wild places where it lingered still, but even he had never imagined that he might meet three sorcerers just walking around the marketplace, accosting passing cheesewrights. Yet these strangers knew his name, and his business . . .

"The Sable Conclave . . . ?" he said.

"It is a secret society," said Fentongoose impressively.

"Well, I've never heard of it."

"You see? Secret."

"Sable means black, doesn't it? I hope you're not *evil* sorcerers."

"Good and evil; these are terms for children," said Carnglaze. "In the worlds of magic which our studies have opened to us, they have no meaning."

"What matters is this," said Fentongoose. "Word of your skill as a cheesewright has reached our brotherhood, and we have traveled far to offer you our aid. The great cheese magnates of Coriander would pay us in mountains of gold, but we should rather use our powers to help a young man of great skill. And you are the most skillful cheesewright in this patch of the world, and the most handsome, and the truest of heart. That is why we offer you this."

Henwyn looked down and saw a little brown glass bottle, teardrop-shaped, lying on the sorcerer's out-stretched palm.

"For ten gold pieces," said Fentongoose, "it shall be yours. It is an elixir of great power, which I brewed myself. Three drops in the next cheese you make will give it such a flavor as no mortal man has ever tasted. It will make you famous the length of the Westlands; the name of Henbane . . ."

"Henwyn."

". . . Henwyn will go down the coming years in song and legend."

"Gosh," said Henwyn, taking the bottle, staring at it. He could see his own face reflected in the glass, distorted like a reflection in the back of a spoon. Inside the bottle some thick liquid swirled. The wind blew Henwyn's golden curls around his head, and seemed to blow his thoughts around inside it too. It looked very magical, and magic led to trouble; all the old stories were agreed on that. But to hold real magic in his hand, in real life, was thrilling. It was as if he had stepped into a story of his own. He glanced around quickly, to make sure no one had noticed him accept the sorcerers' gift. Surely his father would be pleased, when he came home from Nantivey to find that Henwyn had created the world's best cheese while he was gone?

"Ten gold pieces?" he said uncertainly.

"We cannot possibly ask less than ten gold pieces," said Fentongoose solemnly. "All right; eight."

Henwyn hesitated for just a moment longer, then untied the purse from his belt. It held eight gold pieces, a few steel and copper coins, and a spare button. He tipped them all into Prawl's cupped hands, and looked down at the bottle again. Was it just the sun shining through the glass, or did the stuff inside glow with a golden light? "At what stage of the process do I add the three drops . . . ?" he asked, looking up again at the members of the Sable Conclave.

But the sorcerers, if sorcerers they were, had gone, and although Henwyn went looking for them all through the floating market, he saw no sign of them again. He walked home thoughtful, one hand in his coat pocket, clutching the bottle of magic.

Back at the cheesery, all was quiet. His mother and sisters had finished the cleaning and gone out to shop or see friends. Sunshine poured in through the windows and shone on the newly washed floors. It seemed hard to believe in magic in a light like that; hard to believe in *dangerous* magic, at least. Henwyn took out the bottle and held it up, and the sun shone through it, splashing his fingers with gold.

In the big cheese vats the cheese milk that he and his sisters had prepared the day before was waiting, slowly setting into curds. Henwyn lifted the wooden lid off one of the vats and unstoppered the bottle. *Drip, drip, drip*: three drops, that's what the sorcerer had said. He watched them fade into the pale curds. He waited to see if the mixture in the vat would change color. Would it take on a strange and lovely aroma? Would there be unearthly music? There was always something of that sort in stories.

But this was not a story, and nothing happened at all.

Henwyn shrugged. He put the lid back on the vat and turned away, pocketing the little bottle. He was starting to regret those eight gold coins, not to mention the loose change and the button. Perhaps the so-called Sable Conclave had just been a gang of tricksters, or people playing a prank. The fact that they had known about Henwyn's father going to Nantivey and leaving him to mind the cheesery was no proof of magic powers; Henwyn realized now that the self-styled sorcerers might have learned those things from half the other merchants in the market. This was just Adherak, after all. Magic didn't happen here.

Burrrrk, went the cheese vat behind him. A sort of deep, wet belch. An odor reached his nostrils: cheesy, and yet not quite cheese. Henwyn had known socks that smelled like that.

He looked around. In the silence of the cheesery the lid of the vat he'd doctored rattled softly, like a pot coming to the boil. A wisp of pale green vapor curled out from under it. Something was happening to the cheese after all . . .

He was halfway back across the room, reaching out to lift the lid, when the lid lifted itself. It shot up and shattered against the ceiling. From beneath it something white and glistening came boiling out of the cheese vat, stretching forth thick, cheesy, quivering ropes like tentacles in all directions. One found Henwyn's ankle and wrapped around it.

It was only then that he understood the cheese was alive.

A tug from the tentacle tipped him off his feet. The cheese was still rising from the vat; far more cheese than a vat should hold, as if the mixture he had added had made it grow as well as move. It formed itself into a lumpish shape, like a bad snowman. The tentacles kept whipping out of it, sticky hawsers of cheese, and whenever they touched something that was not nailed down — a chair; a spoon; his sister Gerda's best apron, hanging on the door — they started to retract, reeling the captured objects in until they vanished with soft sucking sounds into the body of the cheese-thing. It was reeling Henwyn in too, pulling him across the tiled floor by his ankle, but only slowly, as if his weight was more than it could easily drag. He saw a curd knife pass him, one of the big slotted paddles that was used for cutting the curds. He snatched at it and tugged, and the leash of cheese that held it parted, the end that had been wrapped around the paddle hanging limp, the rest withdrawing quickly into the cheese-thing. Gripping the curd knife in both hands, he used it to strike at the thick strand that held his ankle. After a few blows, that parted too, and he was up and out of the room, slamming the door behind him, leaning against it to catch his breath.

Through the door's planks came the sound of falling furniture and clattering pans. That monstrous cheese would dismantle the whole cheesery if he didn't stop it.

What would his parents say? What would the neighbors think? At all costs he must not let it escape.

He dragged a bench across the door and went up the stairs, two at a time, to his room. His secondhand sword lay under the bed and he took it out and strapped it on. His hands were shaking, but he told himself not to be such a coward. Wasn't this what he had always waited for? A chance to prove himself in combat? And it wasn't as if it were a dragon or a troll crashing about downstairs; it was only cheese gone bad . . .

He reached the foot of the stairs just in time to see the door he'd barricaded give way; the cheese oozed through the splintered planks, bulked out with all the objects it had eaten, reaching out its pale, whiplike tentacles to seize more. Soon the whole cheesery was festooned with the sticky strands. Henwyn swung his sword at them, chopping and lopping, but although the strands parted, the cheese stuck to the blade like some awful fondue, dulling the cutting edge and making the weapon heavier and heavier. And all the time more strands were lashing at him, sticking to his face, his arms, his hair, until at last with a great wrench he broke himself free of them and ran, crashing out into the street, where passersby stopped to stare at him, surprised by this cheese-stained swordsman, and by the crashes and clangs, the weird belching sounds, and vile socklike wafts that were emerging from inside Henmor's usually quiet cheesery.

"It's nothing," said Henwyn, as casually as he could, trying to put his sword back in its scabbard and discovering that it was so thick with cheese that it would not fit. He felt sure that if the city authorities found out he had created this cheese monster he would be banished, and the cheesery closed down.

"We're having a bit of trouble with, um, mice," he said, unconvincingly.

The people in the street stood and stared, but it was not Henwyn they were staring at. Behind him, the cheesery bulged. The roof heaved.

"Well, rats," said Henwyn hopefully.

One whole wall of the building collapsed with a roar, and out through the hole the cheese-creature came sprawling, soft and glistening and shapeless, except that as it reared up part of it seemed to briefly form a face, with little holes for eyes and a wide, dark, stringy mouth.

There were screams, shrieks, curses. The towns-people turned to run, tripping over the cats which had come scurrying to lap up the flood of cheese milk spilling from the wreckage. Tiles and timbers smashed on the cobbles as the cheese-creature wrenched itself out of the ruins. Henwyn thanked his lucky stars that Herda, Gerda, Lynt, and his mother weren't at home. Where the cheesery had stood there was now only the cheese-thing, its hundred tentacles as thick as the ropes of a ship, lashing out to pull down chimney pots. He felt both scared and embarrassed as he stood there in its cheesy shadow, wondering what to do. If only he could think of some really brave and decisive way to deal with this thing, he might make up for having made it in the first place. He wiped the cheese from his sword as best he could and wondered how to use it. Did the cheese-thing have a heart? A brain? He looked for a head that he might lop off, but it had nothing that looked even vaguely headlike. The only good thing was that its move-ments were growing slower, as if it were weighed down by all the vats and benches and lumps of masonry it had engulfed. It seemed unwilling to drag its lumpy bulk far from the ruins of the cheesery, and the cats, which were the only living things left nearby, easily avoided its slug-gishly groping tentacles.

He glanced down the street, toward the heart of town, the looming gray bulk of Adherak Castle on its walled mound. Three figures watched him from the corner of an alleyway. "Fentongoose!" he shouted. "Carnglaze! Prawl! Help me! Use your magic! Undo what your potion has done!"

He ran toward them, but the three sorcerers looked as horrified as Henwyn by the thing that their elixir had created. "Water," Fentongoose said, in a weak voice. "Colored water. That's all it was . . . How can this be . . . ?"

Henwyn snatched at his beard, meaning to force an explanation and an antidote out of him, but the sorcerer was too swift for him; he ducked aside. The white beard slithered through Henwyn's fingers, and the three sorcerers turned and fled.

"Oh," wailed Henwyn, turning back toward the ruins of the cheesery. "Oh, what have I done? I should have known better, after all the tales I've heard! I have summoned up a monster from the underworld, and it has turned on me the way they always do! I shall be destroyed by my own unholy fondue . . ."

But even as he spoke, he saw that the cheese-creature was starting to change. It was shuddering, subsiding, shrinking. With unpleasant sucking and bubbling sounds it gathered itself into a taut, quivering blob upon the ruins of the cheesery, like a vast, restless pearl. Then something picked Henwyn up and flung him; as he hit a wall and crashed down on the cobbles he heard a high-pitched boom and a ghastly belch. Warm, sticky cheese began to rain down all around him, and he realized that the creature had exploded.

Henwyn scrambled up, still clutching his sword, his face blackened by the blast, the rags of his clothes all scorched and smoldering. All that remained of the monster was a thick coverlet of rubbery yellowish sludge draped over the ruins of his home, making it look like a piece of toasted cheese that had been left too long in the oven.

That was the reason that Henwyn was banished from Adherak. He had tried to explain about the Sable Conclave, but the sorcerers had vanished, not to be found anywhere, so no one believed him. Few people had actually seen the monster for themselves, and the idea that real magic had been at work in their own town seemed so disturbing and unlikely that most Adherakis preferred to explain it all away as just a freak cheese-making accident. "Too much rennet," they reasoned. "Or a new form of mold. Whatever it was, it was all the fault of that careless young cheesewright."

Still, the elders had been very good about it. There had been talk at first of sending Henwyn to face the high king in Coriander, but it was decided that it would be embarrassing if word got about that Adherak had been menaced by, well, cheese. So they sent the foolish young man away, and warned him never to let his shadow darken the gateway of their town again, unless he wanted to end up like the brigands and cutpurses whose heads and trunks and chopped-off limbs were displayed on the spikes above it like the pieces of a Build Your Own Brigands and Cutpurses Kit.

They let him keep his worthless old sword, though, and a little money that his mother slipped into his hand as he was leaving (his father wanted nothing more to do with him). He spent the money on a pair of boots and that tunic with the studs, the closest thing to armor he could afford. He had decided to seek adventure in the wilderlands.

As he left Adherak behind him his eyes turned to the north. A few days' walk would take him to wild hills where people were few and legends walked. "Clovenstone!" he whispered to himself, and the word woke all the old, wild feelings in him. It reminded him of that strange certainty he'd always felt that he was meant for something more than dairy produce. At Clovenstone there would be adventures. At Clovenstone there would be evils to fight: proper ones, not made of cheese. At Clovenstone, in the lost kingdom of the Lych Lord, he would find his destiny, or death.

Destiny, hopefully, he thought to himself, as he parted from Skarper and squelched on his way through the overgrown ruins toward Westerly Gate. *Unless my destiny is death . . . but hopefully it's just destiny . . .*

He was sure that if he could just do something really brave his father and the Lord of Adherak would change their minds about him. Adherak had never produced a hero before.

AT SOUTHERLY GATE

Skarper hurried on his way south, and the road rose up in long, low stairs again, climbing away from the river. As it rose, the trees around it thinned, and soon he could see ahead of him the high battlements of the outer wall, and the guard towers clustering around Southerly Gate. The towers were topless and battered-looking, and parts of the wall on either side had been smashed down, for here the armies of the lands of man had fought their way right into Clovenstone on a long-ago day so terrible that it was still remembered in goblin lore: Bad Wednesday, the day the Lych Lord was defeated. As he neared the gate he began to pass heaps of bones lying scattered on the road or gleaming white among the roadside weeds. There were loads of old skeletons lying around all over

Clovenstone, and Skarper would hardly have spared them a glance usually, but many of these were still encased in rusting armor, and around them lay corroded swords and the crumbling heads of axes, spears, and pikes. In all the years since the Lych Lord fell no goblin had ventured this far from the Inner Wall to rob the dead who lay here.

The gateway was huge; big enough for giants to pass through three abreast. Splinters of the shattered gate still hung from rusted hinges. Weeds grew up thickly in the shadow of the arch, and a path had been trampled through them; trampled quite recently, judging by the smell of crushed leaves and stems. Skarper sniffed suspiciously, detected man-scent, and guessed that this was where that numbskull Henwyn had crept into Clovenstone earlier that day. For a moment he wondered how the young hero was faring, away in the woods between here and Westerly Gate, and whether anything had eaten him yet. The oddest feeling came to him; a pang of regret that he had not talked a little longer with Henwyn, or walked a little farther with him. He hoped that the softling had *not* been eaten. He shook himself, feeling unsettled, for he had never actually cared about anyone but himself before, and he could not find a name for this strange new emotion. Perhaps one of the words he'd learned in *Dictionary* would describe it. "Kindness"? "Compassion"? "Gazebo"?

None of them sounded quite right, so he shook the feelings out of his head with a determined flap of his ears and crept along the trampled path to stand on the very threshold of Clovenstone, under the curve of the great arch. He looked south across the plain of Dor Koth to where cloud shadows walked upon the hills of Oeth Moor, and for a moment he was gripped by an odd excitement as he realized that he was *free*; there was nothing to stop him stepping out through the gate if he wanted and setting off in search of an adventure, just as Henwyn had. Then he flicked his ears again and told himself not to be so foolish. South of those hills lay man-country, and anyway, the last thing he wanted was more adventures.

He turned away from the hills and stepped back into Clovenstone, and instantly a net came down on him, weighted with stones all around its edges so that it knocked him to the ground and pinned him there. Booted footsteps clapped and clattered, coming down a long stone stairway from the battlements above the gate. Excited voices called, "I got him!"

"It's a goblin, I'm sure it is!"

"Let's have a look at him!"

Skarper thrashed and struggled on the old flagstones, getting himself hopelessly tangled in the net. Through the ropes he saw three softlings peering down at him. First Henwyn, now this lot: He had never realized that Clovenstone was quite so busy.

"Yes," said one of the softlings, nodding until his long white beard bobbed, "it is quite definitely a goblin!"

"I had not expected to meet any so soon, so far from the Inner Wall," said a second, a tall, pale fellow whose ears stuck out like handles. He had little round panes of glass perched on his nose in a horn frame, and these made his large, nervous eyes look even larger and more nervous.

"We must beware!" the third said. He was shorter than the others, and his skin was peaty brown. He wore a dark brown robe embroidered with suns and stars and moons, and he carried a sword. "Where there is one, there may be more. Make sure he can't escape,

Fentongoose! Maybe he's been sent out from one of the old towers to see who we are, and how many. If we let him go we could have a whole gang of them down on us by nightfall."

"Then we shall not let him go," said White-beard. "Not yet. Not until we have explained ourselves." He stooped over Skarper, peering in at him through the knots of the net. "If our quest is to succeed then I must win the friendship of the goblin tribes. What is your name?"

There was a pause, while Skarper worked out that the man was talking to him. "Skarper," he admitted.

"And what is your tribe?"

"King Knobbler's Blackspike Boys, but . . ."

"Very good," said the white-bearded man, smiling and rubbing his hands together. "I am Fentongoose, and these are my companions, Carnglaze and Prawl. We are the Sable Conclave. Alone among men we have kept alive the memory of the Lych Lord and his powers. Now magic is stirring again in the world. We have seen the portents, and we have come here, to the source and center of it. To Clovenstone!" He pointed toward the Great Keep. The clouds had cleared now, and it soared above the summit of Meneth Eskern with the afternoon sun shining on its impossible walls.

"Magnificent, isn't it?" asked Fentongoose, and without waiting for an answer he went on, "King Kennack's armies never found their way inside, for all the entrances were sealed up with lychglass before they got there. But a way will be opened for those of us who have been loyal to the memory of the Lych Lord all these years. Behold: I bear his token, to prove that I am heir to Clovenstone."

Out from the collar of his tunic he pulled a little stone amulet, which hung around his scrawny neck on a cord. It was an old and tarnished thing, carved in the likeness of a grim, handsome face with wings sprouting from its temples.

"Look, goblin!" said the sorcerer. "Gaze upon the face of the Lych Lord!"

"He didn't really have those wings on his head," explained Prawl, tugging his spectacles off and buffing them on a corner of his cloak. "They're symbolic."

"Of course they are," agreed Carnglaze. "He'd never have been able to get his hat on if they'd been actual wings."

"They symbolize his great learning, and the way his will could fly forth from Clovenstone to work upon men and creatures far away," said Prawl.

"Indeed," said Fentongoose. He popped the trinket back inside his clothes. "Anyway, the point is that the Sable Conclave are your new masters. That's what I wish to explain to your King Knobbler when you introduce us."

"Introduce you?"

"Yes. You will lead us back to Blackspike Tower. There you will announce our arrival to King Knobbler, and ask him to grant us safe passage into the Keep. In return we shall make him our chief general when we become the new lords of Clovenstone."

"But . . ." said Skarper, and then put a paw over his mouth to stop himself blurting out what he been about to blurt: that he was an outcast who had been thrown out of Blackspike — *catapulted* out of it, in fact — and that if he went back there with these softlings, Knobbler would tear him to pieces as soon as he'd finished tearing *them* to pieces.

"But what?" asked Fentongoose sternly.

"Nothing!" said Skarper. "I'm a particular favorite of King Knobbler's, and I'll be happy to show you the way to Blackspike and introduce you and all." He knew that if he told them the truth about himself he'd be no use to them, and if he was no use to them they'd have no reason not to kill him. He would just have to go along with them. Somewhere between here and Blackspike, he would find a way to escape from them.

THE PRINCESS

All this time, Henwyn of Adherak had been making his way westward, or as nearly westward as he could. He pushed between the trees, hacking through thick undergrowth with his sword, finding his way along old streets and alleyways that weeds had swallowed. And the farther he went, the more he wished that he still had Skarper's company, because the ruins were strange and forbidding, full of odd rustlings and mysterious sudden movements.

To keep his spirits up, he started to sing an old song from home. It was called "The Ballad of the Cheesewrights of Adherak," and it went like this:

A Cheesewright, a Cheesewright, a
Cheesewright am I,

A master of rennet, an artist of whey,
Preserving the Secrets of Cheesewrights of Old;
The Lore of the Cheesecloth,
The Mysteries of Mold,
So raise up your curd-cutters, hold them high
please,
And give three lusty cheers for the Wrights of the
Cheese!

"Hurrah! Hurrah! Hurrah!" he cried, and stopped, because when those merry cheers came back to him, echoing off the dead houses, they did not sound merry at all but empty and eerie and a little ghoulish, and at the same moment he thought he heard other voices, little creaky ones above his head and all about him, sing, *"A Cheesewright, a Cheesewright, a Cheesewright is he . . ."* before dissolving into scratchy whisperings and thin giggles. It was as if the trees themselves had taken up his song.

"Hello?" called Henwyn, readying his sword and turning around, his eyes on the trees and the green shadows between them. "Who's there? Show yourself!" Shapes scattered along the big, mossy boughs. Henwyn waved his sword. "I'm not afraid!" he yelled, then added, "Eeek!"

One of the shapes had dropped to the ground in front of him. It stood in a beam of sunlight and he saw it clearly. It was half as tall as him, and it seemed to be made of twigs. It looked a little like the head of a witch's broom, except that it was gathered in at the middle by a kind of belt made of more twigs, from the midst of which two black eyes gleamed. Instead of a broomstick it balanced on two spindly twig legs, and two twiggish arms with little spidery hands emerged from its sides. In one it clutched a willow branch that had been whittled into a sharp green spear.

A goblin? wondered Henwyn. It did not look like goblins did in stories.

Now, all around him, more of the twiggy creatures were plumping to the ground like windfall fruit. Others swarmed along the overhanging boughs and down the trunks of the trees. One balanced on the stone pineapple that topped a nearby fountain and called out in a voice that sounded like the wind rattling dry leaves, "Men not come! Men bad! Bring fires and axes! Trees hold this place now!"

"Well, I'm, ah, just passing through," Henwyn tried to explain. "I don't have an axe. I'm on my way to Westerly Gate, perhaps you could . . ."

But the twiglings (as he had decided to call them) were not listening. They pressed in all around, rustling their twig-tops, blinking up at him with eyes like little drops of oil, and a couple of spear points jabbed experimentally at his legs and bottom.

"Ow!" he cried. "I'm warning you; I shall smite you with my sword! The next one who pokes me will get smited. I mean smitten. Or is it 'smote'? *Hewn*: I shall hew you!" He swung the sword, and the twiglings drew back with disapproving whispers, but after a moment they pressed in again, and Henwyn found that they were not really solid enough to smite or hew; the blade just brushed through their twigs, and when he lopped off an arm another emerged in its place, picked up the lopped arm and its fallen spear and jabbed him in the knee.

"Ow!" he shouted again. He was starting to get frightened now. The things were all around him; there were a great many of them, and now that he had started using his sword he did not think it would be possible to reason with them. A flung spear missed his face by inches; another snagged in the folds of his cloak. He turned to run, hoping that his greater size and weight would let him shove his way out through the ring of twiglings.

"Man not come here!" the twiglings clicked and chattered. But once man *had* come there they didn't mean to let him go, it seemed. Through a crack in the flagstones at Henwyn's feet a shoot emerged and grew with astonishing speed, reaching up until it was taller than him, swaying like a snake charmer's snake. He stepped sideways to go past it, but another grew there. He chopped it in half, but after another few seconds he had no more space to swing his sword in, for the thin, strong trunks were sprouting all around him, and stretching out little side branches which entwined with one another, forming a cage of living wood.

The twiglings formed a circle around the cage, creaking and rustling. A few fetched sharp-edged stones and roof tiles from the ruins and began whittling their little willow spears to even keener points. Somewhere in the woods a deep drum began to beat.

Henwyn gulped. A nasty idea came to him, slipping in through the crannies of the sapling-cage. What if he wasn't meant to be a hero at all? In most stories, when the hero reached the lair of the giant or the dragon he was to slay, he would pass the bones and rusted gear of other, less fortunate warriors who had tried and failed before him. What if Henwyn was just going to be one of those? In a few months from now some proper hero, a prince or a king or some such, might pass this way to rescue Eluned from the giant and barely notice Henwyn's skeleton whitening amid a grove of young trees . . .

The drumbeats grew louder. They shook the ground, and shuddered more slates from the sagging roofs. They startled crows and woodcocks and a bleary-eyed owl into the sky. The twiglings heard them, and drew back from Henwyn's cage with little fearful twitterings, while their bead-bright eyes went up and up to look at something in the trees behind him.

Oh, he thought, *what now?*

A vast leg stepped over his prison, and set down a foot as big as a small boat among the weeds in front of it. Another foot came down to join it, twiglings scattering out of its way. Old bones creaked as the huge figure stooped to thrust its face against the saplings. A great gray face, shaggy with lichen, bearded and crowned with twiggy hair and a shapeless felt hat the size of a cottage roof. A gust of musty breath enveloped Henwyn, and a bloodshot brown eye as big as a dinner plate considered him through the gaps between the branches.

It's F . . . F . . . Fraddon! he thought, stammering even in his thoughts with the terror of it.

He hadn't imagined that a giant would be so . . . well, so *big*.

"Man come!" the twiglings were all complaining, hissing like woods in a high wind. "This isn't man place! This is tree place! Man chop and burn trees!"

"Now, now," said the giant, in a voice so deep and rumbly that it seemed like something you felt in your chest and your stomach rather than heard with your ears. "This is no woodsman. That's a sword, not an axe. You leave him be now, hear?" And he took hold of the tops of the saplings that had grown up around Henwyn and uprooted them with one huge heave, flinging them into some nearby ruins like a gardener throwing prunings on a trash heap.

The twiglings hissed and twittered and scattered away, like a twiggy tide withdrawing quickly into the shadows of the surrounding trees.

Henwyn and the giant stood looking at each other.

"Who are you, boy?" the giant said.

"I'm Henwyn of Adherak," said Henwyn.

"I'm Fraddon," said the giant, and pulled off his hat. "What brings you to Clovenstone, Henwyn of Adherak?"

"I came to fight you, and rescue the Princess Eluned."

They both looked at the sword in Henwyn's hands. Henwyn was afraid Fraddon might laugh at him, or simply reach out one of those huge hard hands and kill him where he stood. Instead, the giant just nodded mildly, and fiddled with the necklace of old millstones that was strung around his neck on a rope. He was a well-turned-out giant, Henwyn noticed; his huge shirt seemed to have been stitched together out of the sails of ships, and his hide breeches were patched at each knee with gaily striped awnings. His fingernails and toenails were trimmed and clean, and once you got used to his thunderous voice and the tusks that poked up out of the corners of his mouth he seemed quite mild-mannered; not at all what Henwyn had expected. He began to feel a bit embarrassed, and wondered what to do next.

"Tea?" asked the giant.

Henwyn lowered his sword. This really wasn't how giant-killing was meant to be, he felt.

"There's cake," the giant said.

"Ooh," said Henwyn, and his stomach gurgled, reminding him that he hadn't eaten anything since he'd arrived at Clovenstone's southern border that morning.

Fraddon seemed to take that as an answer. He put his enormous hat back on, then scooped Henwyn up in one hand, set him in the crook of one huge arm, and strode on through the forest, bending the big trees gently aside, stepping across the ivied ruins, until, out of the treetops ahead, the battlements of Westerly Gate arose. Henwyn saw that a stranded ship was perched on the high tower above the gate, and that some sheets were drying on a washing line strung between its masts.

Princess Eluned was in the little garden she had made on a south-facing slope sheltered behind Clovenstone's western wall. She had taken off her shoes and tucked the skirts of her dress into her belt and she was knee-deep in the fishpond, scooping out duckweed with a rake. The afternoon sun dazzled her, shining in under the brim of the broad straw hat she wore, but she did not mind; it was good to see the sun, and to be reminded that the spring would soon be here. She liked this end of wintertime in the garden: the first shoots just showing, the crocuses shouldering their way up through the grass, and the sense of the earth's green life waiting, getting ready to burst forth in leaves and buds and blossom.

The old song that Henwyn had heard about her was quite true. One day, when she was sailing south on the king of Lusuenn's royal yacht to be married to King Colvennor of Choon, the giant Fraddon had come wading out into the sea, snatched up her pretty little ship, and carried it away, with her still aboard, back to his lair on the edge of Clovenstone.

But songs sometimes leave out the important details of things, and the harpist who composed "The Ballad of Princess Eluned" had not bothered to mention that the young princess was a headstrong, intelligent sort of girl who had no wish whatsoever to be married to King Colvennor. Colvennor was loud, lazy and stupid; there were no books in his castle, and he believed a queen should do nothing but sit about all day looking soulful amid a gaggle of silly ladies-in-waiting.

Unfortunately, Eluned had no choice.

She was not the king of Lusuenn's daughter, just his niece, and the only reason she had been given house-room in his palace all through her girlhood was so that he could marry her off to Colvennor of Choon in exchange for a couple of islands that he fancied. Her own father and mother had both been killed when she was quite small, on a terrible night that she still remembered faintly, in her worst dreams.

They had been king and queen of Porthstrewy, a tiny kingdom on the rockiest and northernmost stretch of the Nibbled Coast, not many miles from the Northerly Gate of Clovenstone and still haunted by mermaids, sea serpents, and other watery hangovers from the Lych Lord's time. It was a good place despite that. The sea serpents and mermaids hardly ever made a nuisance of themselves. The bright-painted houses were stacked up the sides of a steep valley, overlooking thick harbor walls, which cradled a space of calm water where the fishing boats moored.

The castle of Eluned's father stood on the headland above the town. From her nursery window she had looked out and seen the cliffs and islands of the Nibbled Coast reaching away and away into the blue distance, and it really *did* look nibbled; like a great stony cookie that the sea had been taking bites out of since the world was new. She still remembered the sound of the waves; how they sloshed and boomed in the sea caves under the castle and snored on the inaccessible shingle beaches at the foot of the cliffs. She remembered how, when the tide was high, the foam came feathering out of blowholes in the cliff tops with a great *Ker-chooof!* and the spray drifted across the harbor, filled with rainbows. That was how the town had got its name: *Porthstrewy*, which meant *sneeze harbor* in the olden tongue.

Then, when she was nearly eight, a dreadful thing had happened. Goblin raiders had come racketing down from Clovenstone, burning the farms and manors inland, marching on the town itself. The people of Porthstrewy had crowded inside the castle while Eluned's father led his best men out to meet the goblins. A desperate battle raged across the cliff tops, but the goblin band was not as large as had been feared, and soon they were all lying dead in the gorse. All except one. One little cringing goblin, who sniveled and whimpered and begged for the warriors to spare him. He was covered in blood from half a dozen wounds, and Eluned's father, who was a kindly man, found that he didn't have the heart to kill him. (Sometimes, in her worst dreams, Eluned could still hear the goblin's plaintive, wheedling voice: *Spare me! Spare me!*) Her father had brought him inside the castle. He had said, "We'll patch him up and send him home to Clovenstone to tell his friends of the welcome they had from the men of Porthstrewy."

But the goblin's friends were not at Clovenstone. That was why the raiding party had seemed so small. Most of them were waiting, hidden, among the rocks on the cliff top. As soon as the sniveling one was inside and left alone, he stopped sniveling and opened the castle gates, and let the rest of his band come charging inside.

In the fight that followed, both Eluned's father and her mother died, and she found herself shipped south, to the court of her uncle in Lusuenn, where most people were far too civilized and educated to even believe in goblins, let alone sea serpents and mermaids. When she told them how her parents had been killed they shook their heads and said, "Poor child! She is a little touched. It was brigands, not goblins, who attacked Porthstrewy." The girls of the court made fun of her north country accent and called her "Princess Sneeze of Sneeze Harbor." And when she turned sixteen her uncle announced that he was marrying her to the king of Choon.

So she had been in a foul mood on the day when her uncle made her go aboard his ship, and when she dried her eyes and looked out through the windows of the stern cabin to see that huge gray figure climbing down the cliffs of Choon Head and sloshing toward her through the waves she did not think, "Oh no, a giant!" so much as, "Oh good, *this* will upset the wedding plans . . ."

How the sailors and the servants and the maids of honor howled when Fraddon plucked the ship out of the water in his huge hands! Some wailed for help, some jumped overboard, and some let off crossbows and catapults, whose shots, if they hit the giant at all, were no more than gnats' stings to him.

The king shrieked and tried to hide under the cabin table, but it kept sliding away from him as the giant tilted the ship this way and that to admire its pretty paintwork. "We'll be eaten alive!" he whimpered, bum in the air, spurs jingling, as he quivered with terror. But Eluned, peering out of the cabin at the huge face peering in at her, could see at once that there was no harm in this giant.

She had read about giants, and she knew that they are creatures of the woods and the high hills and that while they drink great quantities of water they do not really eat very much at all, and certainly not human beings.

So she opened the window and called out to him. "I am a princess," she told him, "and the holds of this boat are full of treasure. Just set down all the mariners and passengers safe ashore, dear giant, and it is yours. But not me. You must take me with you. All the best giants have a royal prisoner."

And that was what he had done. Eluned's uncle and his people were set down in a frightened huddle on the tip of Choon Head, and Eluned had Fraddon scoop up the silly ones who'd thrown themselves into the sea and set them safely ashore too. Then he tucked the ship under his arm and went striding back to Clovenstone, and there she had stayed with him ever since. He was a very peaceable giant, who spent much of his time just daydreaming, standing like a tree in the woods or like an old stone up on Oeth Moor. Eluned helped him to make some clothes to replace the rags and uncured skins he was wearing when they met, and in return he cleared a garden for her, and brought fruit trees uprooted from the orchards of the south to plant in it, and whole cupboards full of books from the libraries of lazy kings who had never bothered reading them. Her ship, set squarely on the topmost tower of Westerly Gate, was a perfect place to read and think, and although she was a little scared at first to know that there were goblins close, and even heard them sometimes, caterwauling inside the Inner Wall, she quickly learned that they did not stray far outside it, and that they were far too scared of Fraddon to come anywhere near Westerly Gate.

She missed people a little at first, but she soon learned to do without them; if she wanted conversation she could always seek out some of the other strange creatures who made their homes in Clovenstone. It was far more interesting than being queen of Choon.

For a while there had been the annoyance of heroes coming to try and rescue her. Quite a few had ridden up the shattered road to Westerly Gate, tooting their war horns and waving swords about. Most had wisely turned and fled as soon as they saw Fraddon; a few had insisted on fighting, and he had been forced to sit on them. Eluned had strung their shields and weapons from the trees outside the gate as a warning to the others. But the shields were rotted now; the weapons rusty; nobody had tried to rescue her for ages.

That was the other thing about the song Henwyn had heard. It was a great deal *older* than he had thought. That bright day when Fraddon plucked Princess Eluned's ship out of the waves and brought her to live at Clovenstone had been nearly thirty years ago.

She could see the shock of it in the young man's face as soon as Fraddon set him down on the grass beside her pond. The poor lad had expected to find a beautiful young princess, not a lady of forty-something, with laughter lines around her eyes and her hair more gray than not. He would not want to win *her* hand in marriage! But, to his credit, he did his best to hide it, and he bowed and said, "Princess Eluned, I am Henwyn of Adherak, and I came here to rescue you."

Eluned laughed and said, "But I don't want to be rescued!" And then, because he looked so very disappointed, she added kindly, "But thank you anyway. And you may call me Ned."

THE TROUBLE WITH GOBLINS

As soon as the Sable Conclave left Southerly Gate and began their journey to the Inner Wall, Skarper started looking for a way to escape. He was sure there would be some gap among the ruins that he could slip away down, and plenty of nice dark holes where he could hide. Unfortunately they had not gone ten yards before Carnglaze called a halt, pulled a length of rope from his pack, and used it to make a halter for him.

"Oi!" Skarper protested, struggling as the sorcerer drew the rope tight around his neck.

"Come, Brother Carnglaze," grumbled Fentongoose, "that hardly seems friendly!"

"You may trust him, Fentongoose, but I do not," replied Carnglaze. "I have read much about goblinkind, and all of it was bad. This one has a shifty look. We do not want him to abandon us somewhere in this maze of ruins, do we? We can let him go once we reach the Inner Wall."

"Very well," agreed Fentongoose reluctantly, and they went on their way with Skarper trotting ahead of them like a dog on a leash.

"This way," said Carnglaze, "if your goblin friends attack, you'll be the first to feel the bite of their blades."

He seemed to think that Skarper might not already have thought of that.

They went past ruins full of lovely shadows, but there was no way now that Skarper could slip away. He began hopefully scanning the sky, for even another attack by cloud maidens would have been a welcome diversion; but the air above the ruined roofs was clear, and all the clouds were far away, clustered about the snowy summits of the Bonehills. Soon the trees closed over the road and it began its long descent toward the Oeth.

The three self-styled sorcerers looked about them warily. It was one thing to dream of reclaiming the Lych Lord's kingdom; one thing to read about it in secret books and scraps of age-old documents; it was quite another to actually be here.

Down secret centuries in the lands of men the Sable Conclave had kept the stories of Clovenstone alive. *A time will come when magic returns to the world,* each generation of the Conclave's elders told the next. *We shall return to Clovenstone; one of our number shall sit upon the Stone Throne, and the power that was the Lych Lord's shall be ours.*

But they couldn't live *only* for that far-off day. While they were waiting they had to have jobs, and families, and homes to live in. So, although they claimed to be dark sorcerers and the servants of the Lych Lord, the dark sorcery thing was really more like a hobby for most of them. They would creep off to their secret meetings to practice magic (which never worked) and pore over old books of spells (which they only pretended to understand) while their wives sighed wearily, told them not to stay out too late, and reminded them about the shelves they'd promised to put up in the pantry. Over the years the darkness had been bred out of them. Few people in the lands of man believed in magic anymore. Lately a philosopher named Quesney Prong had proved that there was no such thing, in a series of popular lectures called *Why Magick Doth Not Exist*. Many former members of the Conclave had been convinced by this intelligent Prong, and had drifted away to take up other hobbies, such as basket-weaving, or reenacting the Battle of Dor Koth with little model soldiers. Now only three were left.

In their pleasant little homes in Coriander, Fentongoose, Carnglaze, and Prawl had felt very daring and dangerous when they greeted one another in the Lych Lord's name and lit black candles before the image of his winged head. Here, among the gaunt ruins of his kingdom, they were starting to feel distinctly nervous.

"It is a solemn thought indeed that after so many lifetimes of waiting it should fall to *us* to come here," Fentongoose said, as they went deeper and deeper into the woods. Although he was trying to sound brave he could not stop his voice from trembling a little.

"When the Lych Lord's power is ours and we have great goblin armies and things at our disposal," Prawl grumbled, "the first person I shall wreak my terrible revenge on is the cobbler who sold me these boots. They pinch like anything."

Carnglaze said nothing. In his youth he had been a soldier for a few months in the service of the king of Zandegar, and he felt that made him responsible for the safety of the expedition. Certainly he could not rely on Fentongoose and Prawl to look after themselves; they were clever men, and very learned, but in his opinion they should not be allowed out alone. So he kept one hand on the hilt of his old army-issue sword, and when they reached the bridge over the Oeth he stopped, and jerked on Skarper's rope so that Skarper stopped too.

"What's wrong?" asked Fentongoose.

Carnglaze nodded toward the bridge and its tumbled parapet. "That damage is recent. See how no moss or ivy has overgrown it?" He gave Skarper's halter another yank. "What happened here, goblin?"

"I dunno, do I?" Skarper protested. "Nothin'. Bridges fall down, don't they? 'Specially in Clovenstone."

"That sounds quite reasonable," admitted Fentongoose. "Everything else here is in ruins, Carnglaze. Why should this bridge be any different?"

"Very well," said Carnglaze grumpily. "But you go first, goblin."

This was exactly what Skarper had been hoping for, for as they descended into the valley a plan had come to him. It wasn't a very good plan, but it was the best he had, and it involved leading the softlings onto this bridge and escaping when the troll emerged to eat them. Of course, there were many things that might go wrong, of which the most likely was that the falling stones of earlier might have killed the troll, or at least hurt it so badly that it had slunk back down into its hole beneath the water to lick its wounds. Still, it was better than no plan at all. Skarper went cautiously out onto the bridge and stopped in the middle.

"What's wrong?" called Fentongoose again, stepping quickly behind Carnglaze and Prawl in case danger threatened.

"I'm just being careful," retorted Skarper. "Bridges is *trollish* sort of places. Sort of place you might find a *TROLL*," he added hopefully, and the word echoed from one bank of the Oeth to the other and then back again, but nothing stirred in the dark pool beneath the bridge; nothing rose from the water to attack his captors. He sighed, and hung his head, and plodded on. The others followed him, and he led them up the stairs on the northern bank. Obviously the poor old troll was dead, he thought, and for a moment he felt almost as sorry for it as he did for himself.

They walked on, the road climbing steeply. The ruins and the woods were quiet; there were none of the furtive rustlings and scuttlings that Skarper had noticed on his way south. Perhaps the things that lived among the trees had been frightened away by the coming of these big, loud human beings, he thought. But he knew that the goblins in the old towers would not be scared of them. The Inner Wall reared above the old buildings ahead like a petrified wave. Hundreds of twisty thorn trees grew from the crevices of the stonework, and the afternoon sun spread their shadows across the wall's face like nets. Skarper knew that from the nearest of the towers — Blackspike and Slatetop — goblin eyes might already have glimpsed the travelers making their way through the ruins. Behind them, huge and terrible, the Keep thrust its pronged head into the heights of the sky.

Up and up they climbed, scrunching over the mounds of roof slates that had avalanched across the road. At last a great gateway came in sight, a high black archway opening like a mouth in the base of the wall. A portcullis of rusted iron spikes grinned at them from its shadows.

"You won't get in that way," Skarper said, keeping his voice to a whisper for fear that sharp goblin ears might hear. "Them iron gates is rusted shut, and there's all sorts of rubble blockin' up the passage through the wall behind."

"How do you goblins come and go then?" Fentongoose wondered.

"There are secret little ways," said Skarper. "I don't know them, though. I never been outside the wall before today, and I came over the top, not under."

Prawl looked up and whistled. "You climbed all that way?"

"Not *climbed*, not exactly . . ."

Carnglaze looked left and right along the foot of the wall. "If the gate is really blocked then we must scout about and find one of these goblin ways . . ."

But Fentongoose had grown impatient. "Why should we sneak into our domain like thieves?" he demanded, stamping his foot. "We are the Sable Conclave! Goblins are feckless, feeble-minded creatures. They have been leaderless since the Lych Lord fell. They will be glad to know that we have come to rule and guide them. I shall announce our arrival."

"No! Don't do that!" Skarper started to say. But the sorcerer had already scampered back a few paces and scrambled up onto the plinth of a toppled statue, from where he felt sure he could be seen by anyone looking from the towers and battlements above.

"Goblins of Clovenstone!" he shouted, his thin, reedy voice echoing back at him off the wall. "The time of waiting is at an end! The old powers of the world are stirring again, and the sorcerers of the Sable Conclave command them! Look, one of your own kind, bold Skarper, has come with us to prove that we are your friends . . ."

No reply came down to him from the watchful window-slits of Blackspike or the silent battlements of the Inner Wall. He rummaged under his collar and pulled out the amulet which he had shown to Skarper earlier. "Behold! The Lych Lord's token! We are his heirs, and the inheritors of the magic that was once his! Why, only the other day we used our powers to brew a potion which summoned up a dreadful creature of the underworld, in the form of some cheese . . ."

He faltered; somehow that hadn't sounded as

impressive as he'd meant it to. He wished he hadn't mentioned the cheese.

"Imagine what wonders we will be able to work once the Keep is open to us and I sit upon the Stone Throne!" he continued. "So open your gates to us in friendship! We are the new lords of Clovenstone!"

The echoes faded, and only the wind stirred, blowing dead leaves along the wall's foot. Then, from high in the Blackspike, a dreadful, shrill, metallic honking sound began, and from Slatetop Tower there came an answering tinny bray.

"What's that?" gasped Prawl, clapping his hands over his ears.

"Goblin horns," said Carnglaze.

"They are welcoming us!" Fentongoose said eagerly.

Skarper shook his head, but it didn't really show, because every other part of him was shaking too. "That's war horns!" he said, and would have run, except that Carnglaze still held his halter, and Carnglaze seemed to have been frozen solid by the trumpet blasts. "War horns is the only sort of horns goblins have!"

He knew too well what would be happening, hundreds of feet above. High in Blackspike Tower the goblin lookouts would be running to warn King Knobbler about the softlings. High in neighboring Slatetop Tower, Mad Manaccan's lookouts would be telling him the same news. The sounds of the horns would alert the goblins of other towers too, but Skarper was not too worried about them, because by the time they arrived the massacre would be over. Blackspike and Slatetop would be buzzing like beehives by now, as Knobbler and the others snatched up whatever weapons came to hand and hurled themselves down the stairways, trampling smaller goblins underfoot in their eagerness to reach the intruders.

"We must run away!" quavered Prawl, which Skarper thought was the first sensible thing he'd said since they'd met.

"No, no," said Fentongoose. "A simple misunderstanding; I'm sure it can be ironed out . . ."

From above them now there came another sound: a deep, reverberating twang that Skarper recognized. Some overeager goblin had filled the bratapult with roof rubble and released it. He glanced up and saw a speck in the sky above him; a speck which swelled swiftly into a huge, falling stone. "Look out!" he screeched, and shoved Carnglaze sideways. The sorcerer, thinking that Skarper was attacking him, cursed loudly and raised his sword, then stopped in surprise as the great slab of masonry smashed down onto the flagstones where he had been standing. Dust rose in clouds; shards and splinters scattered, and before the travelers could gather their wits, a flagstone at the wall's foot was shoved aside and the goblins were upon them.

RACE THROUGH THE RUINS

At first Skarper was not sure whether it was Knobbler's gang or Mad Manaccan's that was attacking them. Soon he realized it was both. The goblins from the rival towers had met one another as they scrambled down through the little passageways which ran through and beneath the Inner Wall, and instead of fighting one another as they usually did, they had joined together in their hatred for the softlings. Manaccan was first out of the passage, waving his great three-headed flail and screeching madly, but Knobbler was close behind, standing taller than any man on a shield that four straining goblins carried high above their heads, and swinging Mr. Chop-U-Up. Behind the two kings there came pouring a swarm of Slatetop and Blackspike boys, as if the whole Inner Wall were just a bucket full of goblins and Fentongoose's speech had poked a hole in it.

"But *look*!" he shouted, waving the little winged head on its cord. "We are the Sable Conclave! The old powers of the earth flow strong in us!"

Some of the goblins seemed impressed, but Knobbler charged forward swinging Mr. Chop-U-Up, and Mad Manaccan, never one to be out-berserked, foamed at the mouth as he came snarling at the travelers. Fentongoose turned with a squeal of terror and ran away.

Prawl had already fled. Carnglaze let go of Skarper's leash and ran after them. Skarper hesitated for just a moment, wondering if he should try to explain himself to Knobbler — *Look! I brought you these nice softlings!* — before he turned and followed the scampering sorcerers. Knobbler and the other goblins did not look as if they were in any mood for explanations.

The three sorcerers already had a head start on him, but he saw Prawl's robes disappearing around a corner, and ran after him. There were the sorcerers, stumbling down the steep streets and vaulting fallen pillars, putting on a good turn of speed for such learned men. Prawl had cast his backpack off so that he could run faster.

Skarper almost swerved aside to see if there was any-thing valuable in it, but the screech of hunting goblins echoed through the ruined colonnades behind him, driving him on. *No point in trying to hide,* he thought, glancing wistfully at the deep tree tangles clogging side alleys. *No point doubling back and trying to blend in with the hunt. There must be so much man-smell on me now they'd sniff me out easy . . .*

He ran on, and soon he could hear the River Oeth chuckling through its gorge ahead. Footsore and pant-ing, he caught up with the sorcerers as they blundered down the long stairs into the green shadows of the gorge, where twilight was already gathering between the trees. They were moving more and more slowly after their long sprint from the Inner Wall, and the goblins were swiftly gaining on them. Long before they reached the bridge the smaller ones were keeping pace with them, running along the roofs of roadside ruins and shying slates and slabs of stonework at them. Luckily goblins did not use bows, and had nothing deadlier than slates and stones to throw. Luckily their aim was lousy. But it would take more luck than that, thought Skarper, if he and the stu-pid sorcerers were to escape.

The bridge was in sight now. Skarper could hear the river swirling under it, and the *pop, plop, pop* of the bubbles that rose and burst in the pool beneath it.

Bubbles? he thought.

The troll came up out of its lair with a roar and a white gush of water. Its battered head was bandaged with pondweed; it was hungry and headachy and in no mood for nonsense as it vaulted onto the bridge.

The sorcerers, who had just been about to cross, shrieked and stumbled back toward the foot of the steps. Carnglaze threw a stone, which rebounded off the troll's scaly forehead without leaving a mark. None of them seemed to notice Skarper, or think it strange that he was still with them. They all stood there helplessly, troll on one side, goblins on the other, like the filling in an ugly sandwich.

"I command you in the name of the Sable Conclave . . ." Fentongoose said to the troll, but it didn't seem interested. His voice died away as it turned its black eyes on him and bared its grimy fangs.

Skarper looked up, wondering if he might leave the softlings to their fate and escape unnoticed up one of the overhanging trees or ivied walls, but goblins had already crept up onto the wall tops and the old roofs all around.

"'Ere, ben't that Skarper?" he heard one shout.

"Can't be. He got bratapulted," sneered another.

"It is!" yelled a third.

"But what's he doing with them softlings?"

"He's bein' a traitor, that's what," snarled Knobbler, stomping down the stairs with the main body of the goblin force hopping and scuttling behind him. His yellow eyes lit on Skarper and brightened like blown embers as he recognized the scared speck he had sent hurtling out of the bratapult that morning. He was not sure what angered him more: that Skarper had taken up with these softling trespassers, or just that he had somehow avoided being splattered in the first place. "I'm going to have his skin for a nice *scarf*," he bellowed.

He raised Mr. Chop-U-Up and started to move forward, but Mad Manaccan shoved him aside, eager for first blood and first share of the loot. Whirling his flail above his head, he flung himself through the air toward Skarper and the sorcerers.

But before he reached them there came a great crashing and tearing from the trees beside the stairs. A shape big enough to be a tree itself strode out of the green shadows; huge hands swung an uprooted oak stump like a bat, and there was a meaty crunch as it hit the hurtling goblin king and sent him flying back over the heads of the other goblins to crash down among the boulders near the top of the stairs: a clatter of armor, the dropped flail jangling, a long slither of metal on stone, and then stillness.

The goblins reeled backward. Some shrieked, "Giant! Giant!" But even as they cowered before that massive figure, even as Knobbler prepared to swing Mr. Chop-U-Up at its mighty knees, another terror came upon them from out of the trees. Knobbler heard whisking sounds, and yowls of pain from the lads behind him, and suddenly a rain of little sharp sticks was falling all around.

The goblins were masters of all weapons that hacked and hewed and stabbed, but they had never got the knack of archery. Their paws and claws were much too clumsy to fiddle about with bows. They thought archery was *cheating*, and one of the few bits of history all goblins knew was how the softlings had defeated the goblin army on Bad Wednesday by firing cheaty storms of arrows at them. They cowered under this terrifying new attack, squealing, "Arrers! Arrers!"

Knobbler caught one of the missiles as it ricocheted off his breastplate. "These en't arrows," he shouted, trying to calm the goblins' panic. "They're just pointy sticks."

"Pointy sticks! Pointy sticks!" the goblins wailed, not calmed at all.

Knobbler looked up, and saw twig-things swarming through the trees, hurling the sticks down at his boys. *Curse 'em*, he thought. He'd heard tell of these woodlings, who'd infested Clovenstone along with the foul trees that bred them. He'd never heard of them attacking goblins openly before. Still, they were flimsy things, just sticks themselves really, and he didn't see what harm they hoped to do. One or two of the boys, looking up to see who was pelting them, had been hit in the eye and were reeling about howling and cursing, but the willow spears weren't heavy or hard-thrown enough to pierce through goblin hide, let alone armor. "Ignore 'em, lads!" he shouted. "Get the softlings . . ."

But when he turned toward the bridge again, there were more softlings than before. A young warrior with a long, rusty sword was running at him, yelling some-thing that sounded like, "Adherak!"

Knobbler had just time to wonder where he'd sprung from and think what a nice plume his curly golden hair would make before the sword came crashing against his helmet. There was a flash of sparks, the blade rebounded, Henwyn said, "Yowch!" and Knobbler tottered backward and was caught up in a scrambling, panicking mass of goblins, convinced that they were under attack by a whole army of softlings now.

The giant Fraddon brandished his oak-tree club and bellowed at the fleeing goblins to speed them on their way, then turned. Two strides took him to the river's edge, and a swipe of his club batted the unlucky troll backward into the river. "Back to your pond, old toad," he growled.

Skarper and the sorcerers looked on in wonder. At first they had been as frightened of these newcomers as they were of the goblins and the troll. Was there no end to the monstrous shapes that Clovenstone was send-ing to attack them? But when the troll went tumbling, they finally understood that their luck had changed. The giant looked again toward the goblins on the stairs, but they were scattering northward, dropping shields and cleavers clanging on the flagstones as they fled. Then he turned and noticed Skarper standing near the softlings by the bridge. He bellowed again and swung his club up ready to flatten him, but the young warrior who had appeared out of the trees with him called, "Fraddon, no! That's no goblin; that is Master Skarper!"

The giant lowered his club and bent his huge gray head to stare at Skarper. "*Looks* like a goblin," he rumbled. "*Smells* like a goblin . . ."

"He *is* a goblin." Carnglaze's hand came down on Skarper's shoulder and gripped it firmly. "But this goblin saved my life," he said. "I don't know what his reasons were, but it would not be right to kill him now."

The giant pulled off his hat and scratched his thatch of hair. "Softlings vouching for a goblin? I've never heard the like of that before."

"A giant and a man fighting side by side?" said Fentongoose. "That's new to me."

The young man bowed. "I am Henwyn of Adherak," he said. In the dim light and all the excitement he had not recognized the three trembling sorcerers. The sorcerers recognized him, though, and exchanged uneasy glances while he explained, "This is Fraddon: He's a giant. I came to Clovenstone to slay him, but he turned out not to need slaying, and when we heard those goblin horns honking and realized someone was in trouble we came as fast as our legs could — that is, as fast as *Fraddon's* legs could carry us. I thought I might as well slay something, since I'd gone to all the trouble of coming here . . ." He looked regretfully at his dented sword. He felt rather proud of the way he'd gone straight for that big goblin. He'd had no idea its armor would be so thick.

"Goblins," rumbled Fraddon ominously, and looked northward, as if he were regretting not having flattened King Knobbler and a few of his boys while he had the chance.

"He is quite *safe*, I take it?" Fentongoose asked Henwyn, looking up nervously at the giant.

"And what about all these twiggy things?" quavered Prawl.

The trees that overhung the river were thick with twiglings. Hundreds of black eyes peered down at them through the twilight.

"There's no real harm in the twiglings," said Henwyn.

"They don't like people much, and they sort of captured me earlier, but they hate goblins even more, and Fraddon persuaded them to come with us. While Fraddon's here they'll do us no harm — oh, but do not make a light!" he added, for he had seen Fentongoose pulling out flint and kindling, ready to light a torch.

The twiglings rustled ominously. "No fire. Fire bads, bads."

"Put it away, Fentongoose," said Carnglaze.

"Fentongoose?" cried Henwyn, and he suddenly understood why these three travelers seemed so oddly familiar. "You! The Sable Conclave!"

"We can explain everything!" the sorcerers said hastily.

"We didn't mean for the cheese spell to work as it did . . ."

"Indeed, we didn't know that it would work at all!"

"Then why did you make me pay eight gold pieces for it?"

"Er . . ."

"We needed that money!"

"We had to have supplies and transport for our journey to Clovenstone."

"Boat fare up the Sethyn as far as Sticklebridge, a guide to lead us across the Oeth Moor . . ."

"Such things aren't cheap . . ."

"So we mixed up that elixir . . ."

"We'd heard from your neighbors in Adherak that you were a bit of a fool . . ."

"That is, they'd said that you were broad-minded and open to new ideas . . ."

"So we thought you might buy it from us . . ."

"It was supposed to give life and body to your cheese."

"Well, it did that all right!" shouted Henwyn, knowing that he would be well within his rights as a hero to chop off the heads of these treacherous magicians, and wishing they didn't look quite so much like harmless, dithery old men.

"If you can work magic on cheese," said Skarper, "why can't you work it on goblins? Why couldn't you have turned Knobbler into a bat or a hat or something?"

"To be quite honest," said Fentongoose awkwardly, "we cannot work magic. Not yet, in spite of all our studies. Except for that one time, with the cheese, and we are none of us sure quite how that happened."

"We'll pay you back, Henwyn," promised Prawl. "Won't we, Fentongoose?"

"Well, I suppose . . . Yes, yes; as soon as we're inside the Keep, we'll pay you back tenfold. We are the Lych Lord's rightful heirs, you see; look, I bear his token."

He fished inside his robes for the amulet, frowned, fished deeper. A look of horror came upon his face. "It's gone! The Lych Lord's token! The amulet! It's gone! The string must have snapped when we were running from those beastly goblins . . ." He started bustling toward the steps. "Come on, we must go back and look for it."

"We shall do no such thing, Fentongoose!" said Prawl, grabbing him firmly by the collar of his robes.

"But without the token, how shall we prove our right to the Stone Throne?"

Carnglaze shook his head. "You don't really think we're going to get inside the Keep now, do you? Not after what just happened? It is over, Fentongoose. We shall stop the night at Southerly Gate, but when the morning comes I, for one, shall be starting for home."

The giant Fraddon, who had been listening to all of this, said in a sudden rumble, "Best not go to Southerly Gate tonight. The goblins could come back and sniff you out. I killed a king of theirs, and that's apt to make them revengeful. Come to Westerly instead. Ned will tend your wounds, and give you food."

"Ned?" asked Carnglaze.

"Food?" said Skarper hopefully.

"Excellent plan!" said Prawl. "We can discuss all this at greater length over supper."

"Eight gold coins and some coppers and a button," grumbled Henwyn. "Not to mention the price of a new cheesery."

"I knew that string was wearing thin," said Fentongoose, still in mourning for his lost treasure. "I knew I should have put an extra knot in it. Oh, what a fool I am!"

They set off in single file along a riverside path that the giant had made for himself, winding between trees and ruins. Darkness was settling over Clovenstone and, as it deepened, so the voice of the river seemed to grow louder and the white water of the rapids and the little waterfalls showed whiter still, and everything else was gray, except for the stars, which winked at them some-times through the treetops. And all around them they could hear the soft pitter-pat of small things falling, so that Skarper wondered if it was starting to rain. Then, as the moon rose and slipped its pale light down through the branches, he saw that the falling things were tiny, spiky balls that dropped from the boughs of trees where they'd been growing. When one of these balls rolled into a patch of moonlight it would twitch and split open, and two black-bead eyes would squint out from inside for a moment; then twiggy hands would reach out and make the gap wider and a tiny twigling would emerge and go scampering up the trunk of the nearest tree. *So the wood makes twiglings just like the earth makes goblins,* Skarper thought, and he wondered why, and what it meant.

"We'll ask Ned," said Henwyn, when Skarper pointed out the new-hatched twiglings to him. "She'll know."

"Who's Ned?" asked Skarper.

"Ned is a princess."

"Is he the one you came to rescue?"

"*She.* And yes, sort of. You'll see for yourself in a minute. Look; we're nearly there!"

The river curved in front of them in the dark, narrower here, and laughing softly to itself. A broad slab of moorland granite had been laid across it as a bridge, and beyond the bridge there was a little path leading up through moonlit bushes, and beyond the bushes were some bare bean-rows, and beyond the bean-rows the towers of Westerly Gate rose dark against the sunset. A ship was perched upon the tallest one, and warm yellow light spilled welcomingly from all its portholes.

SIX STARS IN THE HONEYBAG

"**W**hen everything was young and new," said Princess Ned, "long before the first men were born, the world had its own ideas about who should live in it. From the trees of the forests came the twiglings; from the cold hills came the giants; on the floors of the rivers stones stretched their limbs and became trolls; in the vaults of the sky, puffs of water vapor and ice crystal stirred and woke and called themselves cloud maidens. Under the mountains the lava lake hawked up the first eggstones, and the forefathers of all goblins smashed their way out of them and started squabbling.

"For long, long ages things went on like that, and the old creatures of the world were a wonder and a terror to the first men when they began to settle the Westlands, to farm and mine. But some men learned to feel the magic running in the earth and in the air, and they learned how to harness it just as they harnessed fire and wind and water. Sorcerers, they were called, and it was thanks to them that the softlands were tamed, the deep-woods felled, and the old things of the world's beginning driven into secret places. Many of them sought refuge in the Bonehills, where the magic had always been strongest. But the sorcerers followed them there, and to show how easily they could control the old powers, they split open the summit of Meneth Eskern and a tower rose from it, and they called it Clovenstone, and made it their stronghold. From here they ruled over all the lands of men, and the kings of men sent tribute to fill their treasure houses, and even the old things bowed down to them, and under their rule there was peace throughout the Westlands.

"But although they set out meaning to do good, it did not stay that way. Their magic gave them great power, and we all know what even a little bit of power does to people."

Skarper said, "Like King Knobbler. It makes tyrants and bullies of 'em."

"Quite so," agreed Princess Ned, glancing at him a little nervously (for she still felt uneasy about letting a goblin into her ship). "My uncle was just such a man, and King Colvennor was another. And there are plenty of queens who are just as bad, not to mention dukes and landlords and teachers. When you give someone power over other people they soon grow mean, cruel, and self-righteous, unless they are the very best of people. The sorcerers of old were not the very best of people, and they had more power than we can easily imagine. They turned the goblins into their soldiers and began to conquer all the lands around, and when all the kings of men were their slaves they turned on one another, until only one was left."

"The Lych Lord!" said Henwyn.

"His real name is no longer known," said Ned, "but that is what men called him, when he sent his armies out to strip their granaries and mines, and when his black fleet set out on winds of magic from the havens of the Nibbled Coast to take tax and tribute from lands beyond the sea.

"Then, slowly, the powers of the earth began to wane. The magic faded. Instead of breeding goblins by the millions the lava lake began to cough out only thousands, and then hundreds. The spells of the Lych Lord lost their potency. His empire crumbled. The kings of men threw off his yoke; they gathered under the banner of King Kennack. On the plain of Dor Koth they routed his armies, and even the walls of Clovenstone could not protect him. So perished the last of the sorcerers of the world, and good riddance too, most people say. But here at Clovenstone the old powers linger, or at least a faint echo of them does. And that is why the old things of the world still find their way here, and make their homes among the ruins."

It was late, and owls were hooting in the woods around Westerly Gate. The fight with the goblins and the frightening trek through the trees were just unpleasant memories now. Fraddon stood guard outside in the night like a watchful tree. Everyone else was sitting with Ned in the stern cabin of her old ship, eating apple cake and drinking tea. It was a snug and happy feeling to be packed into that crowded cabin, seated on packs and blankets because there weren't enough chairs, listening while the princess told her story.

Of course, when it was over, they had many questions.

"Where do you get hold of tea?" Henwyn wondered. "And flour and sugar and things?"

"Oh, one of those heroes who tried to rescue me when I first came here turned out to be quite nice," she explained. "He had never really wanted to marry me in the first place, being in love with someone else already, so when I explained that I was happy here with Fraddon he rode down to Netherak and made arrangements for me with a merchant there. There was a great deal of treasure in this old ship's holds, and in exchange for some of it the merchant sends me a cartload of life's little luxuries twice a year. He leaves it by a stone out on the moor, poor man, being afraid to pass the walls of Clovenstone."

"Sensible fellow," muttered Prawl, who was regretting his own eagerness to come to Clovenstone.

"How did your giant carry this ship so far from the sea, and lift it up onto this tower?" asked Fentongoose. "He doesn't look big enough."

"Oh, Fraddon was larger then," the princess told him. "Giants grow down, not up: They start large and shrink, like mountains do. I have gone walking in the Bonehills with Fraddon and talked with newborn ones; rock-faces, just shouldering their way out of the earth. And I have met Fraddon's great-great-grandfather, who has been worn down by years of wind and weather till he can sit quite comfortably upon my open hand."

"What is this 'tea' stuff, anyway?" asked Skarper, sniffing suspiciously at the steaming mug he held between his paws.

"What I want to know," said Carnglaze, before Ned could start telling them about the tea trade, "is this: Is Clovenstone really awakening again, as this old fool Fentongoose keeps telling us?"

"Old fool?" cried Fentongoose. "I may not be as ruthless or as wise as the men who founded our conclave all those years ago, but I still know the promise that they made to we who come after them."

"Promise?" asked Ned.

"It is more of a prophecy, really."

"Oh, one of those."

Fentongoose closed his eyes, put his hands against his temples to make the sign of the winged head and said ominously,

"When the Lych Lord's light within the Honeybag doth burn

Then magic shall return

And the Lych Lord's heir shall come to Clovenstone

To take his place upon the Throne of Stone."

"But what does that mean?" asked Ned, frowning. "It doesn't even scan."

"It's not meant to be poetry," Prawl said primly. "It's a prophecy."

"Prophecies are rubbish," said Ned. "There are only two sorts of prophecy. The ones which fortune-tellers make because they know that people want to hear them, like 'You will meet a handsome stranger,' or, 'You will come into some money,' and the dotty ones that are always about the far-off future, about the world ending on a certain day or some such, when the prophet knows he'll be safely dead and buried by that time so that nobody can complain to him when it doesn't. Or, of course, they're wrapped up in such a lot of silly riddles that you can make them mean anything you like. What does it mean, 'When the Lych Lord's light within the Honeybag doth burn'?"

"It is a secret," Fentongoose said primly. "It is not meant to be understood by any but adepts of the Sable Conclave."

Ned was not satisfied. "How can you have a light in a honeybag?" she asked. "Who keeps honey in a bag anyway? You'd think it would get awfully sticky . . ."

Henwyn looked up hopefully. Ned was not the sort of princess he'd been expecting, but she seemed very kind and clever and he was keen to impress her in some way. "The country folk around Adherak use that name for one of the constellations; the five stars we usually call the Spoon. And a light *does* burn in it! I mean . . . I noticed it from my window in the cheesery, a few weeks ago. There are *six* stars in the Spoon now."

Ned's frown grew deeper. She put down her mug, and rose, and opened a small door in the bulkhead behind her and stepped out into the cold night air on the open balcony at the old ship's stern. The others trooped out to join her, even Skarper, although he didn't have much idea what they were looking at; he'd never paid very much attention to stars. Fraddon stood among the beech trees at the far side of the garden, fast asleep and snoring. Beyond him in the moonlight the tumbled, tree-drowned ruins stretched away and up toward the Inner Wall, where the great towers stood black around the darkness of the Keep.

"Look," said Henwyn, pointing to a constellation that was just rising from behind the Bonehill Mountains.

"It doesn't look anything like a spoon *or* a honeybag," complained Skarper.

"Constellations never look like the things they're named after," said Henwyn. "Have you ever looked at the Great Huntsman? If you join up the stars in that you get a shape more like a squashed pastry . . ."

"Henwyn is right," said Ned. "I am not usually awake at this hour, or perhaps I would have noticed it for myself. There *is* a sixth star . . ."

Skarper shaded his eyes from the moonlight with one ear and looked where she was pointing. There, in the heart of the Honeybag, one star shone brighter than the rest, and paler too. It didn't even twinkle like the others. It looked to him like the ghost of a tadpole, hanging in the sky.

"It is bigger than when I first saw it," said Henwyn.

"It is the Lych Lord's star," said Fentongoose. "It is the star that looked down upon the Lych Lord and his fellow sorcerers when they first raised Clovenstone from the earth."

"It is a comet," said Ned. "Comets do return. Is it

possible that this one was somehow connected with the Lych Lord and his power? And perhaps . . . Perhaps Clovenstone *does* feel strange these days. As if something more than just the spring is coming . . ."

"Why would it be *bigger*, though?" asked Henwyn.

"Because it is coming closer," said Ned. She sounded half worried, half excited. "I suppose, as it draws closer still, that all *sorts* of strange things may start to stir, and waken . . ."

All over Clovenstone, strange things *were* stirring; strange things were wakening. In the heights of the Keep itself things moved; a rustle of dry, papery skin, a tiptoeing tread of clawed feet. They came to the windows and peered out through the thick, rippled, reddish panes of lychglass, and the light of the comet gleamed in their slowsilver eyes. At another window, farther down, a tiny crack had opened in the lychglass and a little batlike something struggled and battered there and finally squeezed its way out and went fluttering up into the moonlight, screeching in a thin, high voice, flying and flying around the Keep's black walls until at last, exhausted, it dropped upon a passing cloud.

The cloud maidens came creeping to where it lay and looked down wonderingly at it. One of them — her name was Rill, and she was the kindest of them; the same one who had pleaded for Skarper earlier that day — picked it up gently in her cloudy hands, spreading the webs of its wings between her fingers.

"Sisters, look!" she said. "It is a little dragon!"

In Blackspike Tower King Knobbler rubbed ointment on the scrapes and bruises of that day's battle and made his plans for tomorrow night's raid, when he would lead his own lads and all of kingless Slatetop's against the unsuspecting goblins around on the eastside. Mad Manaccan was no more, flattened by Fraddon's club, so Knobbler was king of two towers now, not one.

And why stop at two? thought old Breslaw, as he climbed stiffly up the stairway to Blackspike's roof and stood beside the bratapult, looking along the moonshiny curve of the Inner Wall at Slatetop, Grimspike, and Growler. A bright, silvery star shaped like a tadpole hung above Slatetop, and there was something in the air that made him feel unusually chipper. *Knobbler's an idiot,* he thought. *He's got no ambition. Why stop at two towers?*

He could be king of all of them. King Knobbler of all Clovenstone, with old Breslaw the power behind the throne. Think of all the treasure I could get my paws on if I had the run of all the towers! Why, I might even be able to find a way inside. . . .

And he turned his greedy eye toward the Keep, and wondered.

In the northern parts of Clovenstone the Lych Lord's servants had dug great cellars once, and underground chambers full of furnaces and smithies, but since his fall the streams and rivers of the Bonehills had flowed into them and flooded them, and now a great swamp called Natterdon Mire sprawled between Northerly Gate and the Inner Wall. It had undermined the foundations of Natterdon Tower, causing it to slump down into the ooze. Since then the goblins of the other towers had learned to leave that part of Clovenstone alone, and they had blocked up all the passages and walkways that used to link their towers to Natterdon.

What had become of the Natterdon Tower goblins nobody knew; all that was certain was this: Deep in the marsh's poisoned pools, little globes of gray jelly appeared, and clumped together like frogspawn, and hatched out things that seemed half goblin, half frog. Boglins, they were called, and the Natterdon Mire was their domain.

They had taken the rubble of the ruins there and heaped it into a shapeless, ramshackle hall, moss-thatched and drafty, which they named Bospoldew in honor of their king, an ancient, bloated, toadlike thing called Poldew of the Mire. There he squatted, lit by moonbeams poking through the rotting thatch, and fiddled with scraps of mist that blew in through the glassless windows.

In the Lych Lord's day the boglins had known the knack of weaving mist; they'd plaited it into traps and snares to catch unwary travelers in the great marshes to the north, and no enemy had dared to approach Clovenstone from that direction, for fear that they'd end up as boglin snacks. For years beyond number the secrets of mist-weaving had been lost, but lately Poldew had begun to feel a tingling in his webbed fingers, and now, as his boglins crowded close to watch him with their lamplike eyes, he looped the strands of mist around his finger ends, and twisted, and pulled, and knotted, until a pale cat's cradle stretched like a web between his hands.

"Look!" he bubbled delightedly, holding the little snare aloft. "The mist obeys us! The mire is waking up again!" He let go of it, and it drifted upward like a smoke ring to hang beneath the mossy rafters. He made another, and scowled thoughtfully for a while, wondering how best to use this gift. "Find me some softlings," he said at last. "Fetch 'em here. Soon 'drakes will be stirring down in the deeply pools and we'll need hot softling blood to fetch 'em to the surface and fresh flesh to tame 'em with. With 'drakes' help we can spread the mire and drown all Clovenstone in lovely marsh, but not without 'drakes, and 'drakes won't rise for naught but blood. Find me some blood to wake them with, my dears."

"B-b-but there *ain't* no softlings in Clovenstone," said one of his war chiefs.

Poldew shot out his long, pink, muscly tongue, snatched up the chief and swallowed him whole. A wide, contented grin spread across his face as he crunched and munched. "Find me softlings," he ordered, spitting out the bones.

STENORYON'S MAP

Skarper slept late next day, as goblins will when there are no other goblins to kick them awake or steal their bedding, and they don't have to worry about fighting for their breakfast. When at last he opened his eyes, it took him a long moment to remember where he was. There were no piles of straw as soft and clean as this in Blackspike . . . These wooden walls were not the stones of Blackspike . . .

He was in a little narrow cabin on the bottom deck of the old ship, and daylight showed through the gaps between the planks. He scrambled out from under the old blankets that Princess Ned had given him and set off to see what was happening. Outside his cabin door there was a porthole, and through the glass he saw low gray clouds rushing over Clovenstone on a southwest wind, with spokes of sunlight spiking down between them, trailing over the ruined rooftops.

Skarper looked around the cabin. There were shelves on the walls, and on the shelves sat little knickknacks; things that Princess Ned had brought with her to Clovenstone or found upon her walks among the ruins since. Some of them looked valuable, or at least shiny, and with a goblin's instinct he started to fill his pockets with them, quickly assembling the beginnings of quite a decent hoard. Then, feeling hot and angry at himself, he stopped, and slowly started to return the things to where they belonged. Princess Ned wasn't some goblin to be robbed and sneaked from: She'd been — *kind*, Skarper supposed was the word. *Hospitable*, even. He could tell that she didn't think well of goblins generally — she had looked quite afraid of him when he was first introduced — but she hadn't said, "Eugh, a nasty goblin, he's not coming inside *my* ship-balanced-on-a-building." No, she'd mastered her dislike and smiled and welcomed him. It seemed to him suddenly that it would be pretty mean, low-down, gobliny sort of behavior to steal her knickknacks.

So he left the cabin and climbed a companionway to the upper deck and peeked into the larger cabin where they had all sat and talked the night before. They were there again, and when the princess looked up and saw Skarper standing uncertainly in the doorway her eyes went wide and her face pale and for a moment she looked scared, but then she smiled and said, "Master Skarper . . ."

"Skarper!" said Henwyn happily. "Won't you join us?"

Skarper was a bit unnerved by that — he wasn't used to people being pleased to see him — but he trotted in anyway. There had been some eating going on, and all kinds of breakfast things were still laid out on a long table under the window: fresh baked bread, goat's cheese, honey, and a pot of Princess Ned's tea.

While Skarper was piling his plate, Carnglaze said, "Tell me, Princess, in all your time here, have you ever found a way to get inside the Great Keep?"

"Not that there's any point now," said Fentongoose wistfully, and his hand went to the place at the base of his throat where the Lych Lord's token used to hang.

Ned looked at them thoughtfully. Then she shook her head. "I have never looked," she said. "Let old evil lie, that is what I say. Besides, I have a great dislike of . . ." (She stopped herself; looked warily at Skarper.) "But Fraddon has looked in over the Inner Wall sometimes," she went on, "and he says the Keep is sealed tight."

"You have never heard of the secret way?" asked Prawl.

"No," said Ned, looking blank.

"I never heard of any way in," said Skarper, through a mouthful of toast. "Old Breslaw is the only one in Blackspike with any brains, and he never mentioned no secret way."

"But it must exist, all the same," said Fentongoose. "Stenoryon spoke of it."

"Stenoryon?" Skarper's ears pricked up.

"Who was this Stenoryon?" asked Henwyn, always eager for a story.

"Stenoryon," said Fentongoose, "was a loyal servant of the Lych Lord, who fled to live in secret among the lands of men after his master's fall. It was he who founded the Sable Conclave, so that there would be sorcerers ready to take up the Lych Lord's mantle once the magic woke again. It was he who made that prophecy I told you last night."

"He is also said to have made a map," added Carnglaze. "*Stenoryon's Mappe of All Clovenstone*, on which the secret way into the Keep was shown, for any who knew how to see."

"Ah," said Fentongoose sadly. "That map! It would have been the greatest treasure of our order. But it was lost. Stenoryon's grandson took it with him when he returned here, hoping to enter the Great Keep himself. That was many years ago."

"A foolish thing to do," said Carnglaze. "He should have waited till the star rose."

"The goblins killed him, no doubt," said Prawl. "The stupid creatures plainly have no loyalty left to the Lych Lord or his memory."

"No use for maps either," said Princess Ned. "I expect this wonderful map of yours was flung into some stinking pit to rot."

It was! It was! thought Skarper. He was quivering with dark excitement at the thought he had actually touched and studied this fabled map. No doubt Stenoryon's grandson was one of the treasure hunters the Blackspike Boys had caught trying to sneak through the Inner Wall; his skull was probably one of those that decorated

Knobbler's kinging chair. The map he carried had meant nothing to goblins, who had flung it into the bumwipe heaps, where Breslaw found it. But Skarper could not recall seeing any secret passages marked on it.

"What do you mean, 'for any who knew how to see'?" he asked Fentongoose.

"That must remain a secret of the Sable Conclave," replied the sorcerer shiftily.

"Only those of us who have studied long in secret and forbidden books could hope to understand how to see the secret pathway hidden in the map," agreed Prawl.

"It's probably just slowsilver ink," said Princess Ned. "Slowsilver used to be mined here in olden times. Ink made from it is invisible, unless you burn some more slowsilver in a magical fire and look at the writing by the light of it. Nobody uses it anymore, but in Stenoryon's day . . ."

The three sorcerers tutted and humphed and looked crossly at her. What was the use of guarding mystical secrets down the generations if it turned out that perfectly ordinary people like princesses had known them all along?

"All very interesting," said Carnglaze. "But not much use without the map. It seems to me that this quest of ours is finished, Fentongoose. I say we start packing our stuff and making ready to return home to Coriander."

"Not today, you won't," said Ned. "You will rest, Master Carnglaze. You are quite safe here. Fraddon is certain that the goblins will not trouble us. If they were going to come, they would have come last night, he said. He has gone up into the Bonehills to speak to others of his kind about this comet, and what it means. He would not have gone if he thought that we were in the least danger."

Skarper had stopped listening. He took an apple and went out onto the balcony to eat it, and watched cloud shadows sliding up the face of the Keep. *Treasure!* he kept thinking. *The Lych Lord's dearest treasure, just waiting to be looted! If only I could get my paws on that map . . .* He scowled at his old home tower. He could visualize where the bumwipe chamber lay inside it, and where in the bumwipe heaps the old map was hidden; he'd rolled it tight and buried it good and deep, where no passing goblin would grab it to wipe his bottom on. *I know just where to put my paws on it,* he thought bitterly, *if only Blackspike wasn't stuffed full of goblins who want to kill me.*

And then, like a revelation, it came to him. Blackspike *wouldn't* be stuffed full of goblins who wanted to kill him! Not *tonight* it wouldn't! He remembered the announcement that King Knobbler had made two nights ago, just before Skarper interrupted him. Tonight was the night of his big raid on the eastside towers! Apart from old Breslaw and a few dozy guards, the Blackspike Boys would all be off killing *different* goblins in Sternbrow, Grimspike and Growler.

Skarper clamped a paw over his mouth to stop a yelp of excitement slipping out. Did he really dare to slink back into Blackspike and steal that map? Of course he did! He was a goblin! Slinking and stealing was what goblins were best at!

But how could he get there? There were miles of woods and rivers and ruins between him and the tower. There might be more trolls, or cloud maidens. There'd certainly be those woody twigling things; they'd seemed safe enough when the giant was around, but there was no knowing what they'd do to a goblin they caught alone among their precious trees.

So don't go alone, he told himself slyly. *Get one of these softlings to come with you, just as far as the wall . . .*

Not the sorcerers; they'd want the treasure for themselves. Not Princess Ned; she had no love for goblins. That just left . . .

"Henwyn!" he said, ten minutes later.

The breakfast party had split up. Fentongoose was talking with the princess, while the other members of the Sable Conclave had volunteered to do some digging in the vegetable patch. Henwyn was being helpful too, wheeling a barrow of dung and straw from the cowshed to shovel onto Ned's rose bushes. He looked happy enough to set the heavy barrow down and talk. Skarper jumped up on the heap of dung, which kept his toes nice and warm while also bringing his face more or less level with Henwyn's. "I hope you're not angry with me for not telling you yesterday that I'm a goblin," he began.

"Well . . ." admitted Henwyn doubtfully. "I do think you might have mentioned it. I didn't realize you goblins come in all shapes and sizes. That's a detail the songs never bothered mentioning. It was very embarrassing when those sorcerers saw that I don't even know what a goblin *looks* like." He sighed. "I wish I was a real hero."

"You *are* a real hero," said Skarper encouragingly. "You rescued us all from Knobbler's lot."

Henwyn just shook his head. "That was Fraddon's doing," he said.

"You walloped Knobbler with your sword," Skarper pointed out.

"I stunned him, but I didn't slay him," Henwyn said. "So it doesn't count. And apart from that I've done no heroic acts at all. I was beaten by a troll. I was beaten by the twiglings. I was even beaten by cheese."

He looked so dejected that Skarper felt quite sorry for him. He glanced around quickly to check that no one else was nearby and said, "What would you say if I told you that I know how to find Stenoryon's map?"

Henwyn didn't say anything, but the sun seemed to be coming up behind his eyes. "The *Mappe of All Clovenstone*?" he gasped. "The map that shows the secret way into the Keep?"

Skarper nodded, and tapped his nose with one claw. "I've seen it," he said.

"We must tell the others!" said Henwyn eagerly, and would have turned and run to tell them there and then if Skarper hadn't grabbed him by his tunic sleeve and held him back. "Hsssst!" he said angrily. "What did you think I was tapping my nose with one claw for? That means 'Shhh!' It means 'Secret!' It means, 'Let's keep this 'tween ourselves.'"

"Oh, sorry. I thought you had an itch."

"You don't want to tell the sorcerers," Skarper reasoned, "because they're rubbish, and what's more, they're evil."

"Well, they keep *saying* they serve the powers of darkness," said Henwyn, "but they all seem quite nice really. I don't think Princess Ned would have invited them to stay the night and let them weed the vegetable patch and everything if she thought that they were really evil sorcerers."

"Well, this is your chance to show them all you're a real hero. Come with me, and we can find that map and get inside that old Keep and get our paws on all the Lych Lord's stuff."

"His greatest treasure . . ." whispered Henwyn, and in his imagination he was suddenly far from this garden, being welcomed back into Adherak at the head of a column of wagons laden with gold and jewels. "I could build a new cheesery for Father," he murmured, "and stone houses for Herda and Gerda and Lynt. And I'll hire the best harpist in the Westlands to write 'The Ballad of Henwyn,' and make sure he gets all the details right . . ."

Then his face fell. "No. I would feel wrong, sneaking off without telling Princess Ned. She's been so kind."

"You can share some of the stuff with her when you get back, if it makes you feel better," Skarper promised. "There's bound to be books and maps and spells and things in there that a lady of her learnedness would want. Give something to Fentongoose's bunch too, if you must; something harmless. But if you tell them before you go, they'll want to come too, and then they'll be the ones the harpists end up writing songs about, not you."

A THIEF IN THE NIGHT

With so many unexpected visitors, Princess Ned was kept busy that day airing cabins, baking bread, making cakes, and fetching preserves from the storerooms she'd established inside the old gatehouse. All the travelers felt a little embarrassed at imposing on the kind princess in this way, and they did their best to help. The Sable Conclave meekly presented her with a bottle of Mendervan wine they'd brought with them to celebrate the reconquest of Clovenstone. Even Skarper peeled some carrots. Twiglings, who seemed fond of Ned, came creaking and whispering out of the woods with woven baskets full of mushrooms. There was so much activity in the old ship that it was quite easy, toward the end of the afternoon, for Skarper and Henwyn to quietly slip away.

They felt the eyes of twiglings on them as they crossed the clapper bridge and went into the woods, but, as Skarper had hoped, they were known as friends of Fraddon and the princess now, and the people of the trees stayed high in the branches and let them pass. They climbed broad, grassy streets between the empty mansions, scrambled through thick stands of trees, which had once been parks or kitchen gardens or parade grounds, and Skarper took the chance to roll in piles of leaf mold and the pungent places where passing badgers had peed, until he no longer smelled of softlings, giants, or Princess Ned's ship.

As the sun dipped beneath the gray clouds and spread a bloody evening light over Clovenstone, they came again to the Inner Wall.

Skarper sighed with relief. No trolls, no goblins, no unknown monsters of the woods had tried to stop them. He hadn't needed Henwyn to protect him after all. For a moment he felt that he'd been foolish to tell the cheese-wright his plans and offer to share the treasure with him. But it had been good to have company on the journey through the woods, and besides, Henwyn's sword might still come in handy later, if any of Blackspike's sentries caught him on his way out with the map.

They slunk like shadows through the ruins below the wall, and soon came to the place where the goblins had attacked the day before. "Shhhhh!" warned Skarper, nose twitching as he sniffed for goblin scent. "We're going to keep creepy-quiet this time. No shouting about like that stupid Fentongoose."

Henwyn did as he was told. He hid himself in a bush and peered up nervously at Blackspike Tower. Lights burned in the mean little windows high above; distant snarls and drumbeats drifted down.

"What's happening up there?" he asked.

"They're gettin' ready to make this big raid," said Skarper. "We just need to watch, an' wait . . ."

They watched. They waited. Some of the lights went out. There were faint sounds of movement on the battlements. Skarper had never been out on a raid, but he'd seen some, and he knew that by now all the goblins of Slatetop and Redcap would have gathered in the Blackspike and they and the Blackspike Boys would be hurrying along the wall toward the eastside towers as quietly and quickly as ever goblins could. That wasn't *very* quietly, but it was pretty quick: He had not watched for long before he saw a tall gush of fire roar up from the roof of Sternbrow Tower, and the faint squeals and clangs of far-off battle came drifting over the ruins.

"Right," he said, turning to the bush that Henwyn was hiding in. "You wait here."

The bush gulped. "I should come with you."

"Not likely. The guards'll smell your man-stink as soon as you get near the entrance, but they won't notice my nice goblin scent."

The moon was rising, fat and full above the Bonehills. Skarper scampered to the secret entrance that the goblins had spilled out from the day before. He slipped his paws under the edge of the loose stone and heaved, but although it shifted just enough to prove it was the right one, he could not lift it. He hissed at Henwyn. "Don't just stand there! Come and help!"

"But you said . . ."

"Come on!"

Henwyn loped over to join him, and together they lifted the stone aside and laid it down. From the black hole beneath it came a stink of goblins. *Phew,* thought Skarper, flapping a paw in front of his nose. He'd only been out of the 'Spike for a day and a night, but he'd forgotten quite how badly it stank. He crouched down and swiveled an ear to pick up the sounds from inside the hole. As he'd hoped: faint snoring. King Knobbler always served out wine before a raid, and even the goblins who were being left behind made sure they got some. The sentries would have snuggled down to sleep as soon as Knobbler left.

Leaving Henwyn to sneak back to his bush, he dropped into the hole. It was about six feet deep, and from its bottom a long stone tunnel stretched under the wall. Skarper trotted along it, and soon saw the sentry, curled up at the bottom of a flight of stairs, which led up into the tower. As he crept past, he saw that it was his batch-brother Yabber, and he was tempted to kick him or set his tail on fire to pay him back for all the blows and kicks he'd landed on Skarper in the past . . . but the thought of Stenoryon's map kept him going, tiptoeing past the snoring goblin, up the stairs, and through the doorway at the top.

It felt strange to be back within the familiar walls of Blackspike. Strange and almost nice. He wanted to go back to his old hole and snuggle down and sleep. Maybe when he woke, his adventure would turn out to have been only a dream. But he made his way to the bumwipe chamber instead, along the weirdly empty passageways. The wind moaned in the tower's complicated guts. Somewhere high above a drunken goblin laughed, and Skarper froze until he was quite sure the sound was not getting closer, then went on.

The bumwipe heaps were just as he had left them. He groped inside and found the tight tube of the rolled-up map. In the dim glow from the bat droppings he drew it out and unfurled it, peering at it, searching for Stenoryon's secret markings as intently as he'd once sought for the meaning of all those scrawly letters. "Well, *I* can't see any invisible writing," he grumbled to himself.

That was when he realized the flaw in his plan. He'd been so excited by the thought that he knew where Stenoryon's map was that he'd forgotten its secret could only be revealed by the light of burning slowsilver. He smacked a paw against his face. "Where am I goin' to get slowsilver at this time of night?"

Then he remembered the ball that old Breslaw had squeezed together out of the scrapings and shavings of slowsilver from all the eggstones he'd helped to hatch. It lived in a secret hole in the wall of Breslaw's chamber, and although Breslaw didn't go out on raids, he liked a drop of wine as much as any other goblin.

And it wouldn't really even be stealin', Skarper thought, *'cause some of that slowsilver's off my eggstone, so he stole it from me in the first place!*

He rolled the map again, stuffed it down his trousers for safekeeping, and hurried upstairs toward the hatchery.

Outside, Henwyn was relieved to hear the sounds of the goblin battle growing fainter. The raiders had gone right through Sternbrow and were moving away along the wall toward Grimspike and the tall two-headed tower called Growler. As he watched, a flag of fire unfurled from Grimspike's roof, smudging black smoke across the moon. He heard a far-off scream as some unlucky goblin was pushed off the battlements, but the clash of weapons and the war cries were mostly too distant now to reach him.

He began to relax a little, listening to the soft whispers of the woods and the voices of the little streams that flowed among the ruins. He glanced behind him, checking the shadows for danger. A face stared at him through a gap in the weeds, white in a fall of moonbeams, making him start — but it was only a fallen statue. The Lych Lord himself, done in white marble. He had been handsome and noble-looking, as far as Henwyn could tell beneath the ivy and the owl droppings. He wondered why such a man had turned to evil, and the little whispery voice of his conscience said, "Perhaps he started out just the way you are: going behind his friends' backs; keeping secrets to serve himself . . ."

"You're right, conscience," Henwyn said aloud. All the way through the woods he had been uneasy; excited, but uneasy. He still knew that deceiving Princess Ned like this was wrong, whatever Skarper said. Skarper was a goblin; what could he be expected to know about right and wrong? Henwyn was a cheesewright of Adherak, and cheesewrights knew better.

Just then the pale moonlight that reflected from the statue showed him something else, something pale that lay among the brambles and dead leaves at the Lych Lord's feet. Henwyn stooped and picked it up. An ivory carving in the shape of a winged head, with the same face as the statue. It was the amulet that Fentongoose had dropped the day before, but of course Henwyn didn't know that; he had never seen it before. He almost threw it down again, but it looked so beautiful in the moonlight, and the shape of it felt so satisfying as it nestled in his palm that he decided to keep it. He knotted the frayed ends of the cord where it had snapped and looped it over his head, tucking the amulet down inside his shirt.

"I shall take it back as a present for Princess Ned," he said. "To make up for slipping off like this."

The statue stared down at him, and its marble mouth seemed twisted in a sneer.

At first, everything went brilliantly. The goblins Knobbler had left behind were all up in the top of the tower, busy rummaging through the possessions of those who'd gone on the raid. There was no one about at all in the middle section as Skarper hurried up the stairs from the bumwipe chamber to Breslaw's hatchery. When he paused outside the hatchery he could hear the old goblin's slow and heavy breathing, and when he stooped and peeked through one of the holes in the door (for it was very old and wormy) he saw Breslaw asleep on his nest of old tapestries in the far corner, an empty wineskin on the floor beside him.

Quietly, Skarper lifted the latch and slipped inside. He stood by Breslaw's nest and reached over the sleeping hatchling master to remove a small stone from the wall behind him. It made a little stony rasp as it came free, and Breslaw stirred and muttered, "Eh, what's that?" before mumbling off into his dreams again.

In the space behind the loose stone his secret treasures gleamed: an old gold ring; a couple of jewels prized out of sword hilts; and the misshapen orb of stolen slowsilver, faintly shining. Skarper lifted it out. It was as big as a duck's egg, surprisingly heavy, and faintly warm to the touch. *Hopefully I can just scrape off a little bit to burn and see the secret writing by,* he thought. *And the rest I'll keep for me.* It would be a good start to his new treasure hoard.

He put it in his pocket and carefully replaced the loose stone. Then he let out his pent-up breath and turned to go back to the door, but his tail whisked against one of the training cudgels that stood propped in a row against the hatchery wall. It fell and hit the cudgel next to it, and that one hit an old halberd, which toppled against a blunted battle-ax, and the whole row of weapons went crashing and clattering down. The last in the line was a three-pointed spear, and as it fell it hit Breslaw's food bowl, balanced on a high shelf. The bowl dropped, and Skarper leapt forward and caught it just before it hit the floor, but the shelf had been struck too; it came away from the wall at one end and a cascade of old eggstone shards came clattering down, pummeling Skarper like angry little stone fists and dancing on the wormy boards around him.

He stood there for a few seconds in the silence after the noise had finished. Slowly he started to hear the sounds of the tower again. The goblin voices still hooted and laughed way up above, and they did not seem to be coming any closer. Was it possible that they had not noticed the din? Perhaps it had not been as loud as he'd feared. . . .

He looked around.

Breslaw had lifted his head off the mound of tapestries, and was regarding Skarper with one bleary yellow eye.

Skarper waved the bowl at him. "I'm just a dream," he said. "It's all that wine that's done it. You're dreamin' me."

It was worth a try. Any other goblin would probably have taken Skarper's word for it and gone back to sleep, but Breslaw was wilier than most. "Skarper?" he said. For a moment he looked almost pleased to see his old star pupil standing there; then, as more bits of his brain stirred and yawned and came awake, he scowled suspiciously. "What you doin' sneakin' about . . . ?" He scrambled up and snatched the loose stone from its hole.

"Thief!" he bellowed.

Skarper was already running. Out of the hatchery and down the spiral stairs so fast it made him dizzy. Behind him he could hear other feet pattering down higher stairways as the goblins at the top of the tower came running down in answer to Breslaw's shrill shouts.

"Thieves! Burglars! Invaders!"

Down in the cellar, even Yabber had been woken by the noise. "Halt, who goes — *Skarper*?" he said, blocking the way as Skarper bounded down the final flight of stairs.

Luckily Skarper had forgotten to let go of Breslaw's bowl. He smashed it over Yabber's bony head and scrambled over the goblin as he subsided, burbling. A moment more and he was outside, breathing clean, cold air again and looking for Henwyn among the shadows and the moonlight. Behind him, though, he could hear the snarls of angry goblins, the stamp of their feet, and the clang of arms and armor as they came hurrying after him.

"Help!" he shouted, trying to drag the stone back over the hole, but it was too heavy for him to move. Then a hand grasped him by the back of his tunic and it was Henwyn, pulling him back toward the woods with one hand while with the other he waved his sword so that the blade flashed in the moonlight.

The cold reflections flicked across the angry faces of the Blackspike Boys emerging from the tunnel, and they hung back, remembering how fiercely the softlings had fought yesterday and ignoring Breslaw's angry voice that shouted orders at them from below. Henwyn let go of Skarper, and they fled together through the ruins and into the deep shadows of the woods until they reached a clearing where moonshine lay like a gray carpet on the stony ground.

"Did you get the map?" panted Henwyn.

"Course I did," said Skarper. He patted his trousers again. The slowsilver ball was still there, and Stenoryon's map gave a comforting papery rustle.

"Does it show the secret way?"

"I don't know, do I? I haven't had time to go burning up any slowsilver next to it, have I?" Skarper chuckled, remembering old Breslaw's face. "I got some, though. That's what they was all chasing me about."

"We will take it back to Ned's ship and show it to her," said Henwyn, smiling as he thought how pleased and impressed the princess would be with what they'd done.

"Oh, we don't want to bother her with it," Skarper protested. "Not with her so busy and all. Why don't we just keep it between ourselves, like . . ."

"Ned and the others must know of this," said Henwyn firmly. "Or shall I leave you here to find your own way home?"

He walked off through the woods, setting a brisk pace, and there was nothing that Skarper could do but follow.

"Henwyn!" called Princess Ned, going out across her garden in the moonlight. She had been looking forward to another night of talk and stories, but Henwyn was nowhere to be found, and it would not be the same without him.

"There is no sign of Skarper either," called Fenton-goose, from up on the stern cabin of her ship. "Perhaps they've gone off together somewhere?"

The princess felt a little chill settle on her. She remembered seeing Henwyn and the goblin talking that afternoon, wreathed in the steam that rose from the dung-filled barrow. She had wondered at the time what it was that they had been discussing. She wondered again now. Henwyn was lovely, and if he had only turned up thirty years earlier she would have rather liked to be rescued by him, but he was not very wise, and she was afraid he did not understand how treacherous goblins could be.

Not all goblins, she told herself. *They can't all be bad, any more than all men are good, and Skarper wasn't even hatched when the goblins attacked Porthstrewy.* But beneath all her good sense she could still hear the pleading voice of that deceitful goblin whose trick had led to the deaths of her mother and father. *Spare me! Spare me!* it said, and mingled with it in her memory there were other voices, the fierce voices of the raiders as they burst into her father's castle, bellowing, *Blackspike! Blackspike!* Wasn't Skarper a Blackspike goblin?

"Oh, Henwyn," she said softly, crossing the garden, finding her way to the clapper bridge by the sound of the water that gurgled beneath it. "I do hope you have not let him lead you into a trap . . ."

The moonlight that fell in patches through the branches showed her their footprints clearly, in the muddy hollow at the bridge's end. As she stopped to peer closer she noticed other footprints too, pressed in the mud and glistening wetly on the granite of the bridge itself; the prints of big, triangular, web-toed feet.

She had never seen marks like those before. The chill deepened. She straightened up, and there in the shadows all around her the moonlight reflected on watchful eyes.

She cried out and turned to run, but a net dropped over her, white and cold, tangling and tripping her, trapping her in strands of marsh mist as strong as any rope.

In Blackspike Tower, Breslaw was searching through the bumwipe heaps. "He came in here," he grumbled to himself. "His footprints is all over. He came in here and took something and then he came and stole my stuff. But why?"

Outside, he could hear the tower's guards shouting, "That's right, Libnog, you take that alleyway," and "Come on, let's check this building." He knew they weren't really looking for Skarper and the softlings, though; they were just standing in a scaredy bunch at the tunnel entrance, shouting those things to make him think that they were searching. He snorted. Why would Skarper have taken up with softlings? What could they have wanted from the bumwipe heaps? He looked at the books and papers scattered all around him, and thought, *That map. Maybe it's that map he wanted. But why steal my lovely slowsilver too? What are you playin' at, Skarper?*

Dimly, a faint memory came back to him, something he'd heard an old goblin tell him years and years before. "When slowsilver burns," he muttered, "it can show up secret writings sometimes; worms and lettuces what the old-times men wanted hidden . . ." Of course, he'd never tried it for himself: Slowsilver was shiny and precious; why waste it peering at a bunch of old secret scribbles?

"But if there was scribblings on that map, they must show the way to something. The way to something that the softlings want . . ."

There was only one thing worth going to that much trouble for. Breslaw's eye glowed with goblin greed.

"Treasure!"

KIDNAPPED

Long before they crossed the clapper bridge and came in sight of Westerly Gate, Skarper and Henwyn could tell that something was wrong. The woods smelled damp, and they were too quiet; no twiglings rustled in the treetops or scuttled along the branches. There was one sound, though. Drips were falling all around; drops were pattering onto wet earth.

"It's been raining," said Henwyn.

"I saw no clouds," said Skarper.

The path filled with puddles. The two companions squelched through mud that rose past Skarper's knees. They sloshed through fresh puddles, kicking the moon's reflection into dancing shards.

"A real storm, by the look of it," said Henwyn.

"I didn't hear no thunder," said Skarper.

They reached the clapper and barely recognized it; the swollen river had risen to brush its underside, and sprawled out in wide moonlit pools upon the bank. Eluned's garden had a wilted look; the shrubs were beaten flat as if by heavy rain. The old ship was gone from the gatehouse.

"A hurricane!" gasped Henwyn.

"I didn't hear any wind," said Skarper, and they both began to run, splashing through the streamlets that trickled down the path, slithering on patches of transparent slime. Everywhere there was the sound of water trickling.

The ship lay on its side at the tower's foot, its prow staved in by the fall. Some of the ropes that had been used to pull it down were still around it: thick white ropes with a strangely smoky look about them, as if they could not quite decide whether they were real or not. There were dozens of them. Henwyn seized the trailing end of one.

"Eugh! It's all wet!"

From the shadows inside the fallen ship there came a loud sneeze.

Henwyn stepped forward. "Who's that?"

"Henwyn?"

Three pale shapes emerged into the moonlight.

"Henwyn?" said Fentongoose, stifling another sneeze. "Skarper? Oh, thank badness! We thought those creatures had taken you too!"

"What creatures?" Henwyn asked. "Taken who? Taken where? Where is Princess Ned?"

"Gone!" said Carnglaze. "Those slimy goblins wrapped her up in nets of mist and carted her away!"

"Slimy goblins?" said Skarper. Goblins had been called many things in the long history of the world, but he'd never yet heard anyone call them "slimy." "This isn't goblin work. Goblins hate damp and wet."

"Well, whatever they were," said Prawl, "they came from the north, beneath a cloud of thick fog."

"North?" asked Skarper uneasily. "That would be Natterdon Mire. Goblins don't talk about Natterdon Mire, but there's supposed to be things living there . . ."

"What sort of things?" asked Prawl.

"I don't know. We don't talk about it."

Fentongoose said, "The first we knew of them was when they looped their white ropes around the ship.

We didn't think that they could pull it down, but there were many of them, and they must have been stronger than they looked, for down it came. After that they were everywhere, the slimy devils. They wrapped the princess up in more of their filthy mist ropes and dragged her away. There were so many of them; there was simply nothing we could do. They would have taken us too, except that our arcane wisdom gives us the ability to conceal ourselves from mortal eyes."

"He means we hid in a cupboard," explained Prawl.

"Didn't you try to stop them?"

"Stop them? When they had such powerful spells?" demanded Fentongoose.

"We were afraid," sniffed Carnglaze shamefacedly, and the sorcerers all hung their heads.

"Where did they take Princess Ned?" asked Henwyn.

"We don't know," replied Carnglaze.

"It was quite a dark cupboard," said Prawl.

"We heard them chuckling and chanting as they carried her off."

"They were singing something about 'Bospoldew.'"

"If you can call that racket *singing*."

"The noises faded away toward the north, into the woods."

"Back to Natterdon Mire," said Skarper.

"But what do they want with the princess? What are they going to do with her?"

"Nothing nice, that's for sure," said Carnglaze. "If they had just wanted Princess Ned to visit them for supper they would have asked, not tied her up and kidnapped her."

"Maybe Ned *is* supper," said Skarper. He had an uneasy, queasy feeling that he could not name. "It's my fault, isn't it? I'm to blame. If we'd not gone off to Blackspike tonight we'd have been here. We might have done something . . ."

Henwyn patted him encouragingly on the back. "Yes," he said, "we might have got ourselves wrapped up and stolen like Princess Ned. But thanks to you we're free, and we can go and rescue her."

"Rescue her?" croaked Skarper. The idea had not occurred to him, and now that it did it seemed like a bad one.

"It should be easy enough to track them," Henwyn went on, and he turned to look north. The rags of mist tangled in the trees there seemed to form a line, like a ghostly paper trail, leading away through the woods and over the high ridge that thrust out to the west of the Keep. "Fentongoose, you must come with us. We shall need your magic."

"But I don't have any magic!" cried Fentongoose, aghast. "I don't even have the Lych Lord's amulet anymore . . ."

"You should have more faith in yourself," said Henwyn. "Your spells worked well enough on my cheese. They may work again."

"But what if they don't?" said Fentongoose. "What if we confront these bog creatures only to find that the magic falls flat? Then we should feel like idiots."

"Don't you feel like that already?"

"Yes, but at least here we are *safe* idiots," said Prawl. "We are not warriors or adventurers. We are scholars. We shall stay here. Look at all poor Princess Ned's belongings, scattered around in the damp. How upset she would be, if she came home to find it all in such disorder. We shall stay here and tidy up and wait for your return."

"An excellent idea!" Fentongoose said firmly. "I'm sure such brave and noble souls as you will have no trouble tracking these moist bandits to their lair, and fetching back their fair captive. We would only slow you down, and get in your way."

"I could stay behind too," offered Skarper hopefully.

Henwyn shook his head. "I need you, Skarper; you are my guide to Clovenstone." Of the sorcerers he asked, "What did these creatures look like, by the by?"

Carnglaze led him across the garden. There in the shadow of the fallen ship lay four of the attackers, who had not jumped out of the way quickly enough when their ropes pulled it down. The ship had rolled over them before it settled into its present position. So far as it was possible to tell they'd been wet, gray-greenish things of goblin size, with the wide mouths and broad speckled faces of evil toads.

"They looked like that," said Carnglaze, "only not flat."

IN NATTERDON MIRE

The woods of Clovenstone seemed stunned and silent. Traces of the raiders' magic mist still lingered in the trees, but there was no sign of the twiglings; they were hiding in hollow trunks somewhere, in spaces between roots, waiting for the danger to be gone.

And Henwyn and Skarper were going toward the danger, following it as fast as they could along paths floored with puddles and covered with the wide, webbed prints of three-toed feet.

"What are these things, Skarper?" Henwyn asked, as the wet woods deepened around them. "I know you don't talk of them, but you must know something . . ."

"Boglin," said Skarper, dredging up a name he'd heard old goblins mutter sometimes. "That's what they're called, I think. Swamp things. Slime things. Bad things always. They've not left their marshes before; not in my time."

"That star's to blame, I expect," said Henwyn. "Princess Ned said herself; all manner of old things are waking."

Above the trees, the comet burned. The moon was low; the shadows long. The muddy path took them uphill to where an old road rose in zigzags past ivied temples with domes bashed in like breakfast eggs, mossy observatory towers where the Lych Lord's astrologers might have watched his star the last time it swooped over the Westlands. From the top of the ridge they looked north and east. Trees were fewer there, and instead of oak there were stands of alder lying like smoke in the hollows of the ground and birches standing ghostly in the moonlight. As their eyes moved away from the wall, out across the broad bowl of the marsh, there was nothing but mist, with here and there a gaunt tower or a tall tree's crown poking up above the billows.

"Natterdon Mire," said Skarper, and at the sound of its name all the hair on his ears prickled and stood up on end.

The boglins were returning to Bospoldew just as they had come: in a broad column of marching bog boys, the hatchlings on the edges holding tight to the misty strings that held a dense awning of fog above the army. The only difference was that on this homeward march they made more noise, their war horns booming like bitterns to let Poldew and the others who had waited behind in the mire know that their raid had been a success.

Actually, that was not *quite* the only difference. In the heart of the column, trussed in mist bonds and dragged along on a sled of woven rushes, was the Princess Eluned.

This is so embarrassing, she thought. *To be captured like a silly princess in a story. Why, only yesterday I was telling that nice young man that I did not need rescuing. Now I think I need it rather badly.*

When they seized her she had thought, uncharitably, that Skarper was to blame. As they manhandled her across the bridge in their wet net she had imagined that the goblin had gone sneaking back to Blackspike Tower with news that Fraddon was away, and brought all his friends to attack Westerly Gate. But as they carried her through the spills of moonlight on the wood paths, she soon saw that these were not goblins. During her years at Clovenstone she had talked with many of the old creatures of the place, and some had spoken of the horrors that lurked in the Natterdon Mire. Boglins: That was what these were. She felt the excitement of an Unnatural Historian encountering new creatures for the first time, mingled with a healthy dose of fear.

> To Bospoldew, to Bospoldew, (the horrid
> creatures chanted as they marched)
> *We'll boil your bones to make our stew,*
> *We'll bake your eyes to fill our pies,*
> *We'll take your ribs to roof our hall,*
> *We'll use your head for a bouncy ball,*
> *At Bospoldew, at Bospoldew . . .*

Most of them were as naked as frogs, but the bigger ones wore armor made from old slates and roof tiles lashed together with strands of tussock grass. Some had spears and knives made from old slates too, or from shards of glass they'd found in Clovenstone's countless shattered windows. *Of course,* thought Ned, *metal blades would dull and rust in no time in the dankness of their mires.* That was why most of the boglins were armed only with clubs of bog oak, blackened and stony hard after years in the mud, or with those long blowpipes made from hollowed reeds, and quivers of willow-splinter darts.

It was all most interesting, but Princess Ned found it hard to concentrate, for she kept wondering what the creatures planned to do with her when they reached this place that they called Bospoldew. They were moving steadily downhill now, the thickening fog concealing all but the vague outlines of the ruined buildings and stunted trees that lay about them. Ahead there were shifting lights behind the fog, and the hint of a great whale-backed shape like an upturned ship. She did hope the words of their marching song were not meant *literally. . . .*

> *At Bospoldew, at Bospoldew,*
> *We'll use each little bit of you,*
> *We'll take your guts to thatch our huts,*
> *We'll have your spine for a washing line,*
> *We'll use your appendix for um, er, what rhymes*
> *with appendix? Erm . . .*
> *At Bospoldew! At Bospoldew!*

The bittern horns boomed, and out of the fog ahead the upturned-ship-thing emerged clearly at last, and it was a hall, built badly out of tumbled stones and roofed with slabs of mildewed thatch. Long, colorless flags of flame wavered up from braziers on either side of the gate, and drifting balls of marsh gas dithered like fat phantom fireflies, reflecting in the black waters which stretched all around the hall.

By the light of these ghostly lamps the boglins hauled their captive across the causeway and in through the gate, and the tall doors of Bospoldew slammed shut behind them.

Meanwhile, the rescue party was starting to descend the northern side of the ridge, still following the broad trail left by the boglins. But as the first pools and reedbeds of the mire opened among the ruins on either side of them, they found their way barred by a net of mist. When Henwyn tried to plunge through it, the mist strands yielded like wet ropes but would not part.

"Hard mist," he said, plucking at one of the strands so that it twanged damply. "That's just unnatural. Like black snow, or dry rain . . ."

"Or hot water," agreed Skarper.

"Hot water's not unnatural. Don't you have baths in Blackspike Tower?"

"Er . . ."

Henwyn started hacking at the mist webs with his sword. The strands parted reluctantly, and immediately started to re-form. Through the gap he'd made, the two companions peered at the way ahead and saw that it lay down a long, narrow street between tall buildings, and that the mist webs were strung everywhere.

"It will take us hours to get through!" gasped Henwyn. "And the mist will form again behind us as we go. We shall be trapped."

"The boglins can prob'ly feel us twitching at it, like spiders feel flies in their webs," said Skarper.

They stood there for a moment, not sure what to do, both feeling hot and tired from their trek through the woods, both starting to fear that it had been in vain. Henwyn was the first to turn away. "I'm going back to the top of the hill," he said. "Perhaps from up there I can spy a better way."

He set off before Skarper could tell him that he was wasting his time and walked quickly uphill, trying to outpace his helpless anger. The heroes in stories never had this much trouble rescuing people. How was he supposed to slay monsters if the monsters wouldn't even let him get near them?

He felt better when he regained the ridgetop and left the mists behind. The setting moon had spread long carpets of silver light across the gaps between the buildings there, and the Lych Lord's star peeked at him over the Inner Wall. There was only one single cloud in the sky, and that was silvered by the moonshine too, so that it looked more like a puff of thistledown. Henwyn ran up the outside staircase of one of the old astrologers' towers and stood on the top, peering into the bowl of mist, which stretched away northward toward the Outer Wall.

Beneath the fog, a mile or two from where he stood, lights seemed to be moving. A far-off hooting rang among the ruins. As the fog eddied, Henwyn thought he could make out a shape: the roofline of a massive, whale-backed hall. Was that where the captive had been taken? But how to reach it when the mist lay over everything?

He looked eastward to the towering darkness of the Keep. It was so immense that you tended to forget about it, as you might forget about the sky or a mountain or anything else that seems a permanent part of the backdrop of the world. But this was the closest that Henwyn had yet come to it, and he looked at it afresh, at the moonlight shimmering on its strange walls. The sight filled him with feelings that he could not name. Without thinking, he raised a hand to finger the amulet that hung beneath his tunic, and suddenly into his mind there came a snatch of poetry he had once heard:

> *The white owl calls,*
> *As twilight falls,*
> *Behind the lofty towers and walls*
> *Where roofs decay*
> *And weeds hold sway*
> *From dawn to dying of the day;*
> *The wind in gusts*
> *Disturbs the dusts*
> *Where old bones bleach and armor rusts*
> *In Clovenstone.*
> *But in the Keep*
> *In darkness deep*
> *Where dead things creep*

Behind barred gates
And lychglass plates
The Stone Throne waits,
The Stone Throne waits . . .

"How I should love to see the Lych Lord's Stone Throne," Henwyn said to himself. "*Then* I could say I had had adventures, all right . . ."

"Oh, prince!"

The voice, coming suddenly out of the darkness, startled him, and made him remember that he was having an adventure already. Princess Ned still needed rescuing and these ruins were filled with unknown dangers.

"Cooee! Prince!"

He looked this way and that, but saw no one.

"Prince!"

A well-aimed hailstone bounced off his head, and more voices called, "Up here!"

They were peeking down at him over the edge of that thistledown cloud, which had come down to hover just above his head like a fluffy oversized halo. Cloud faces, with eyes of shadow and hair like wind-combed cirrus. Cloud hands reaching down to him.

"Come aboard, young prince!"

"Come, forsake your lonely quest and tarry in the air with us!"

"We'll show you the sky's sky!"

"We'll show you the Ice Crystal Mountains on the edge of the world!"

"That's very kind of you," Henwyn told them politely. "But I'm a bit busy at the moment . . ."

"Oh!" they said, dejected, pouting (who'd have thought a cloud could pout?). They seemed like nice girls to Henwyn, and he was sorry he had upset them. "Anyway," he told them, hoping to console them, "I am not really a prince. I am just a cheesewright. Though I *am* on a quest, as it happens; I have to rescue . . ."

An idea came to him. He did not get very many, so they were always welcome, and he smiled as this one arrived. The cloud maidens thought he looked gorgeous when he smiled, and they all forgave him at once for being only a cheesewright.

"Perhaps you could help?" he asked. "I need to reach the lair of these boglin fellows, down under the mists yonder. I don't suppose you could fly me there, could you?"

"Bospoldew?" The cloud maidens quailed, and their manner grew distinctly cooler, so much so that a little flurry of snow settled on Henwyn's upturned face.

"Bospoldew is a fearful place!" said one.

"Poldew of the Mire lives there."

"He is weaving his mist magic again!"

"He has power over clouds too. In olden times the boglins used to set snares for us, and use us and our clouds to stuff their mattresses."

"We dare not carry you to Bospoldew."

"Oh, but sisters," said one of the maidens, "he's the first prince we've seen for *years* and *years*."

"He's not a prince; he said himself that he is just a cheese-writer or something."

"Well, it is very nearly the same thing, and he's so beautiful."

"Ladies, please!" said Henwyn, who was a bit embarrassed at being called beautiful. "I can see no other way into the mire, and I have to reach this Bospoldew place and rescue Princess Ned."

"Princess? Princess?" whispered the cloud maidens. "Eugh! Princesses are lame! We don't like princesses at all."

"I suppose you are in love with her?"

"Oh no!" cried Henwyn, blushing. "It's nothing like that. She's quite a middle-aged princess. Though very nice."

The cloud maidens withdrew inside their cloud, and it bobbed and rustled there for a moment while a hasty, whispered debate took place within. Then, to Henwyn's delight, a kind of smoky ladder came dangling down, and the cloud maidens reappeared, gesturing for him to climb aboard. Before that night he would have been afraid to trust his weight to such a flimsy-looking thing, but he had felt the strength of the boglins' woven mists and he felt sure that this ladder would be just as tough. He set his foot on the bottom rung and started climbing, calling loudly over his shoulder as he went, "Skarper! Over here!"

"Who?" said the cloud maidens, startled out of gazing at him.

"A friend of mine," said Henwyn, looking up into their pretty, cloudy faces. "I'm sorry, I should have said. I can't go without him. Look, here he comes . . ."

The cloud maidens had already seen the little figure hurrying uphill toward the tower. The cloud lifted a little, and angry lightning fluttered in its belly.

"You did not say anything about *friends* . . ."

"Oh! It's that horrible *goblin*!"

Skarper looked up and recognized the cloud maidens at the same instant that the cloud maidens recognized him. He flattened himself against the tower wall as a lightning bolt fizzed past, exploding the flagstones below.

"Do be careful!" cried Henwyn anxiously. "That is my friend Skarper."

"No, no!" the cloud maidens said.

"We will not take him!"

"Not an earth-sprout . . ."

"A stone-born . . ."

"Not a goblin!"

"Oh, he may *look* like a goblin," protested Henwyn, "but he . . . Well, he *is*. Yet he is stout-hearted for all that. He saved my life."

"No goblins," said the cloud maidens firmly.

"Nasty creatures."

"'Specially that one. Throwing himself about in the sky where only birds should be, making horrible great holes in other people's clouds . . ."

Henwyn, who had almost reached the top of the cloud ladder by then, sighed loudly and started to descend again. "I am sorry, kind cloud ladies, but I cannot leave my friend behind. I'm a hero, you see — well, I'm hoping to be — and that wouldn't be heroic at all. It seems that we must find our own way to Bospoldew. . . ."

The cloud maidens all looked at one another. For a moment it seemed they were about to go back inside their cloud for another conference, but they came to some agreement without speaking, and one said, "All right. Just this once. You and your goblin may both come into our cloud."

DAMPDRAKE

Skarper didn't trust them. He thought they might be planning to frazzle him with a thunderbolt as soon as he stepped out into the open, or drop him off the cloud as soon as it rose high enough for the drop to do him harm. But no lightning seared him as he went up the tower steps and then climbed that cloudy ladder. He sat down, sinking only slightly into the cloud's soft billows as it lifted and began to waft northward. Apart from a few hard stares (and a smile from Rill) the cloud maidens ignored him and clustered around Henwyn, asking him how he liked it up here in the sky, and which of them he thought was prettiest.

Henwyn wasn't sure quite what to say. They were all as pretty as one another in their cloudy way, and having grown up with three sisters, he had a good idea of the sort of quarrel that would break out if he told one that she looked better than the others. So he said, "Oh look, a bird," pointing at a passing owl, and then noticed how high he was, how far above the towers and walls of Clovenstone, and came over a little faint. "Coo!" he said, turning roughly the color of a well-squashed boglin.

"What is it, sweet prince?"

"What ails you?"

"It's just — we're *flying*. It feels unnatural, some-how . . ."

The cloud maidens fussed around him, inviting him to lie back on plump cushions of cloud and bringing him cool drinks of rainwater in a cup of ice.

"It is not really high at all," they said.

"Not when you are used to it . . ."

"The sky is a lovely place."

"You should see it at sunset, when the long light fades all rose and gold on the long rim of the world, and the stars come out . . ."

And so on. If Skarper had been a bitter sort of goblin he might have thought, *That great dim-witted lump. I fall out of the sky through no fault of my own and ask them for help and they just scold and scoff and try to strike me with lightning. He only has to smile at them and they all start twittering about his lovely curly hair and telling him to make himself at home.* (And actually he *did* think that, because he *was* a bitter sort of goblin: There isn't really any other sort.)

"What on earth do they see in him?" he asked aloud. It was an unfair world, it seemed to him, and just as bad outside of Blackspike Tower as in.

The cloud maidens were now asking Henwyn what it was that a cheesewright did, exactly, and if he could remind them what cheese was, because they *did* know but they'd temporarily forgotten. When he explained that it was a food made from coagulated milk curds they giggled as if he had just made the most wonderful joke. Eat rancid cow's juice? All they ate up in the sky's sky were drifting flakes of water-ice, flavored sometimes with a speck of wind-borne pollen. They were certain he'd just made up this *cheese* to tease them.

Then the cloud maiden called Rill slipped down into the soft chambers at the cloud's heart and returned cradling something gently in her hands. "You should have this, cheese-prince," she said, bringing it shyly to where

Henwyn waited. "It is an earth-born thing, and you will be able to care for it much better than I can. It won't eat water-ice, or pollen. The wind brought it to me, poor creature. It must have been blown out of its nest up in the Bonehills, and flapped about until its poor little wings could flap no more, and landed on our cloud to rest."

Henwyn took the creature in his cupped hands and it was warm and light and throbbing with its own swift little heartbeat. He thought at first it was a bird; then a bat. Then, as it stretched its snaky neck and he saw its big-eyed reptile head clear in the moonlight, he realized that it was a tiny dragon. It made a mewling sound, and sank its teeth into his finger.

"Ow!"

"That means he likes you," the cloud maidens all assured him.

"Oh, does it? Ow! It's a snappish little thing, isn't it?"

By that time the cloud had drifted far out over the mire, and when they looked down the passengers could see again, in its coming-and-going way, the bulk of that great shapeless building in the mist. Lights were moving all around it, and the cloud maidens let their cloud waft over it before they made it settle toward the ground.

"We must be quiet now," the maidens hissed in stage whispers. "If Poldew of the Mire hears us he will send up snares of mist magic . . ."

"He will turn us into pillows . . ."

"Hush!"

The cloud descended, and the mist rose up and swallowed it so that you could not tell any longer where the cloud ended and the mist began. It was like sinking into a cold sea. There was nothing but pale gray darkness, and the figures of Henwyn and Skarper crouched in it (the cloud maidens were all quite invisible). The little dragon cooed, and nibbled at Henwyn's fingers as he stuffed it carefully inside one of the pouches on his belt. Then, below them, they saw the gleam of water; a dead tree growing on a grassy knoll between two black lagoons. The tops of crumbled walls poked from the waters, forming a path of sorts.

"This is as close as we dare to go," said a cloud maiden. "Farewell, sweet Henwyn. But we wish you would fly farther with us, and tell us more about your fascinating cheese. Are you sure you would not rather come and watch the sun rise behind the Ice Crystal Mountains?"

Henwyn looked down at the dark and threatening marsh and thought that he was not sure at all, but Skarper nudged him and he remembered his farewells and scrambled quickly down the cloud's side, down the ladder that showed dimly, a denser gray than the mist around it.

Skarper went after him, and the ladder dissolved when he was halfway down it, dropping him with a squelch on the moist earth. "Sorry!" giggled the cloud maidens, not sounding a bit sorry. He looked up angrily, but their laughter was already fading, the cloud already rising back into moonlight far above the fog.

Henwyn looked carefully around. "This way," he decided, pointing into the grayness.

From directly behind him came that booming, hooting noise again; the pale glare of light behind the drifting vapor.

"Or perhaps that way . . ." said Henwyn.

They set off, balancing like tightrope walkers along the tops of those slimy walls that rose out of the meres, whole sections of which sometimes slithered down into the water with sad sloughing noises. Reeds whispered, water gurgled, the branches of the mire's sparse trees rattled dismally together, and through the fog ahead came ugly voices. Through stands of rushes they saw the hall, and beyond the hall, beside the pool that opened there, the jerky hopping movement of many boglins and the dim, fitful flickering of scores of marshlights.

"What are they doing?" whispered Henwyn.

They crept nearer, parting the reeds and peering through. The boglins were coming out of Bospoldew in great numbers. Some held stone bowls in which marsh-gas flames stood wavering like snakes; others were dragging Princess Ned, still bound to the sled on which they had brought her there. They propped her up in the angle of an old wall on the brink of the black mere which lay before the hall. A boglin pricked her finger with a sharp glass knife. Then they all crowded backward, leaving their captive there alone.

Out from the hall came waddling a huge boglin. *"Poldew! Poldew! Poldew!"* chanted the rest, bowing down as he passed, pressing their flat faces into the slime. He waved a webbed hand and they fell quiet. The wind moved in the feathery tops of the reeds; the water lapped at the mere's edge and echoed from the green walls of Bospoldew.

"What're they doing?" wondered Skarper.

"Waiting for something," said Henwyn. He drew his sword, thinking that if he were to slay that fat bog king the rest might panic, and in the confusion there might just be a chance . . . But the boglins crowded so thick about Poldew that it was hard to see how Henwyn could reach him, and now the waters of the mere had started to ripple in a strange, greasy swell.

From the cut that the glass knife had made, the blood of Princess Ned dripped onto the earth, black in the glow from the bobbing marshlights and steaming faintly. It seeped into the waters of the mere. The water, thick with mud and moss and the dust of drowned buildings, was suddenly flavored with the faintest trace of hot and frightened human. Down in the roots of the mire a thing that had not tasted man-blood for a long, long time stirred in its sleep, and into its long, cold dreams came creeping the idea of breakfast.

"The dampdrake!" cried Poldew, and all his boglins echoed him, some in whispers, some in shouts. "Dampdrake! Dampdrake rises! Dampdrake wakes!"

"What's a dampdrake?" asked Henwyn, hidden in the reeds.

Skarper knew. The books he had read in the bumwipe heaps hadn't had much to say on the subject of boglins, but one or two of them had mentioned the dampdrake.

"It's another creature from the olden days," he said uneasily. "Also known as the *Mergh Dowr* or Water Horse."

"Oh, that's all right then! I quite like horses. . . ."

The waters bubbled. The waters boiled. The waters split, and up out of them there rose a huge, flat, pale, and faintly glowing head.

Serpentlike it was, yet not a serpent; dragonlike, yet not a dragon; the head of some ancient thing that had been sleeping through centuries down among the drowned oaks in the deepest oozes of the mire, but that had begun to stir and surface as the star of Slowsilver drew near, and that Poldew's blood offering had now brought wide awake.

"But that's nothing like a horse at all!" Henwyn hissed.

Poor Princess Ned just hung helpless in her web of mist, looking up and up at that dreadful head. It snorted, letting out two plumes of steam, which mingled with the drifting mist.

"Dampdrake!" the boglins kept calling.

"*Mergh Dowr!*" yelled a few of the better-educated ones.

"Quickly!" said Henwyn, turning to Skarper, his eyes shining. Here at last was a monster he could fight: a true monster, awoken out of ancient tales, and it wasn't made of cheese, and he had a sword in his hand. "Attract its attention!"

"What? Me?" asked Skarper, trying to burrow deeper among the roots of the reeds. "You mean, *don't* attract its attention. . . ."

"I have a plan," said Henwyn.

"Oh no!"

"I'll cause a diversion," he explained. "You free Princess Ned." And he gave Skarper a shove that sent him somersaulting out of the reeds into the full view of the boglins and the dampdrake and landing with a white splash in a puddle.

The dampdrake's pale, shortsighted eyes had not seen the two companions hidden in the reeds. Their scent had been masked from it by the scents of Ned and the boglins. Now a hot waft of frightened goblin tickled its nostrils. The great head swung toward Skarper. The barbels that trailed from its lower jaw quivered, and its feathery gills batted at the air like the feelers of enormous moths. Its mouth gaped wide. It roared, and its fetid breath engulfed Skarper like the wettest and smelliest wind there had ever been.

The dampdrakes were of dragon-kind; relatives to the great fire-breathers that had laired in the Bonehills long ago. But the breath of dampdrakes was not fiery; it was as chill and stinking as the wind off a marsh. As it huffed over Skarper, water droplets swelled and trickled on his skin, while white mold furred his clothes. His belt snapped and his trousers fell down; his tunic rotted and dropped from him in wet rags; he shivered and sneezed and tried to cover his private bits with Stenoryon's map, cowering naked in the blast of the dampdrake's breath.

"Eugh!" he said, and, "At-*choo!*"

The dampdrake reared above him, ready to reach down and gobble him up, but while it was busy with Skarper, Henwyn had been running along the mere's edge, getting around behind it. His idea had been to lure it away from Ned, and as he reached the far side of the mere he shouted loudly, trying to draw the attention of the boglins so that Skarper could run forward and cut her free.

"Don't be afraid, princess!" he yelled. "I am here to save you!" — and he slipped in a puddle and went down with a *splat*, face-first in black mud. From the far side of the mere Princess Ned saw him, and felt a deep, warm glow of thanks and happiness that he had come to rescue her. She also felt pretty sure he couldn't manage it on his own, and she began to struggle against her mist bonds with fresh vigor.

The dampdrake had sensed Henwyn too. It turned away from Skarper, and Skarper dived back into the reeds, whimpering with the cold and frantically checking the map. It was soaked through and crinkled, and thin white mushrooms sprouted from it, but miraculously it was still in one piece, and still readable. Or maybe it wasn't miraculous: Maybe Stenoryon had woven spells into the parchment to protect it. Anyway, he gave a sigh of relief . . . and then remembered that the map was useless without the slowsilver, which would show him its secrets.

He went to check in his pockets for the slowsilver, but his pockets were gone, fallen away with the rest of his rotted clothes. He peered out of the reeds and saw a whirl of confusion. Princess Ned had fought one hand out of the misty ropes that held her and was struggling to free the other. On the far shore of the mere, Henwyn was swinging his sword at the dampdrake's tail, which had burst from the water, lashing about like a whip. Boglins were hopping and scrambling everywhere, all trying to obey the marsh king's ever-changing orders. "Kill me that softling! No, not *that* one, *that* one!" Poldew roared. "Stop the prisoner! She's escaping!"

Down between their feet rolled Skarper's slowsilver, unnoticed as yet, booted this way and that like some priceless soccer ball.

Bunching the wet map in one hand, Skarper dived after it. Boglins ran over him as he scrabbled between them; boglins kicked him in the face with their stinky frog feet as he slithered on the wet earth under them, but he didn't care; nothing comes between a Blackspike Boy and treasure. He lost sight of the slowsilver for a moment, confused by the mad shadows cast by the marshlights, which were skittering about overhead as if in panic. A few had even fallen to the ground, and pale flames were leaping in the grass along the mere's edge.

And there was the slowsilver, trundling down the slope to the water.

Henwyn finally landed a blow on the damp-drake's tail.

Ned ran toward the safety of the reeds, shaking off the last knots of mist as she went.

Skarper's outstretched paw grasped the rolling slowsilver, but it was wet and it popped out from between his fingers and landed on one of the fallen marsh fires. They looked cold, those fires, but perhaps there was a magic in them that spoke somehow to the magic of the metal, for as Skarper snatched it up again the slowsilver ball burst into dazzling silver flames.

"Warggh!" he screeched, dropping it again. It lay on the wet ground and blazed, too bright to look at, giving off no heat, only a distant roaring sound and a tre-mendous light. The boglins hid their eyes and flung themselves facedown on the ground or dived into the mere, screeching and screeling. Black shadows wavered across the marshes. Poldew of the Mire howled and ran blindly back into his hall. The dampdrake howled too, its tail bitten through by Henwyn's blow, its eyes smart-ing in the weird glare of the slowsilver. In its rage it let out a great bellowing gush of wet breath that whiffled over Skarper's head and engulfed Bospoldew. Hundreds of toadstools sprouted instantly from the hall's mossy thatch and from the bog-oak timbers of its doors. Livid growths of fresh green moss enslimed its stones. It shifted and shuddered, and the voices of the boglins went up in a great wail as the weight of the sodden thatch pressing downward pushed the walls apart, and the roof settled slowly to the ground.

Henwyn came around the mire, thrusting his way through the panicky boglins to Skarper. The little dragon had escaped from his pouch and fluttered madly around his head. "Come!" he said heroically. "We must away!"

"Must *away*?" asked Skarper, angry at the loss of all that lovely slowsilver. "That's not even a proper sentence. You mean, 'We must *run* away.'"

"I suppose I do. It's funny, it doesn't sound half so heroic when you put it like that. Still, we really *must* run away."

Skarper knew he was right. In a few more moments the slowsilver would all be burned away, and when they could see again, the boglins and their great wet pet would all be looking for revenge. He could not bear the thought that all his cleverness in stealing the map and Breslaw's orb had been in vain. Frantically, he spread the map out on the moss at the mere's edge.

The light of the blazing slowsilver fluttered and stuttered, beginning to fail. Just for a moment, as it fell across the ancient parchment, a tracery of wire-thin lines shone there, drawn centuries ago with a pen dipped in slowsilver ink. Just for a moment, as the wild blaze faded, as the boglins howled, as Henwyn shouted at him to hurry, Skarper saw the secret way into the Keep, as plain as any of the other roads Stenoryon had drawn.

The light died suddenly, and left the darkness darker than before. The burned-out slowsilver had no luster left; it was just a little black lump of clinker, like something you might rake out of a stove. Henwyn grabbed Skarper by his tail and started hauling him bodily away. The dampdrake lunged toward them, missed, and scooped up a shrieking mouthful of boglins instead. Skarper had just time to snatch Stenoryon's map as Henwyn dragged him into the reeds toward Ned. On the backs of his eyelids the afterimage of the secret path still glowed: He, alone in all of Clovenstone, knew the way into the Lych Lord's Keep.

If only he dared to take it.

High on the Inner Wall, just west of Growler Tower, King Knobbler heard the boglin bull-roarers booming; heard the faint, far-off wailings, and the dampdrake's roar. He went to the battlements to peer down at the moonlit mist that swirled above Natterdon Mire.

His raid on the eastside towers had gone pretty well. Just as old Breslaw had promised, the Sternbrow, Grimspike and Growler goblins had been taken completely by surprise. Now the Blackspike Boys and their allies from Slatetop and Redcap were busy ransacking the towers for loot and food, and finishing off any eastside warriors who objected. It had been a good night, Knobbler thought, but now this new noise, booming up from the bogs, made him uneasy.

"What's that?" he asked his fellow goblin king, Tanbren of Redcap, Boss of the Chili Hats.

Tanbren scowled. Redcap was closer to the mires than any of the other towers, but his goblins had long since sealed up the old passageways that had once linked it to Natterdon Tower, and like all the goblins of the Inner Wall, they didn't talk about the things that lived in the marshes. The Redcap goblins were smaller than most, but their territory included an area of old glasshouses where they grew small, fiery redcap peppers, which they ate to drive themselves into a battle frenzy. They wore red leather hats shaped like these peppers, and so as well as Redcaps they were also known as the Chili Hats.

Tanbren pushed his own hat back now, and a frown creased his shallow forehead. "That's the bog boys blowin' their bull-roarers down in their squelchy places," he said. "We ain't heard anythin' outta them for a goodly while."

Knobbler nodded wisely. "The times they are a-changin'," he said. "You remember the old stories, how there's going to come a time when us goblins grow strong again? I reckon it's here. I mean, who's left? Manaccan got hisself splatted by that giant yesterday, and we've done for the kings of the eastside towers tonight."

"It's just you an' me then, Knobbler," said Tanbren. "You reckon we could rule over all the towers between us? Me the westside, you the east?"

"Yeah," said Knobbler.

"Yeah," said Tanbren. They studied each other thoughtfully for a moment, and then Tanbren pulled out a knife and drove it at Knobbler's belly and Knobbler jumped sideways so that the blade glanced off his leather fighting trousers and used Mr. Chop-U-Up to chop off Tanbren's head.

Flat feet flapped along the battlement. Knobbler spun around, raising his sword again. To his surprise, he saw Breslaw standing there.

"What are you doin' out of the Blackspike?" growled Knobbler, furtively checking his fighting trousers in case Tanbren's knife had gashed them and let his pink frilly underpants show through. "You never come on raids."

"I came to find you," said the hatchling master, coming closer. He was panting, winded by his long, hasty journey around the wall's eastern rim.

"Look," chuckled Knobbler, while Breslaw was catching his breath, "I chopped Tanbren's body off."

"Don't you mean you chopped his head off?"

"No, his head's still here; look. I chopped off everything *below* his head. That's strategy, see. I reckon with

Tanbren and Manaccan and the other kings out the way, I can rule over all the towers. King of the whole Inner Wall! I don't know why I never thunk of it before."

Of course, it wasn't Knobbler who had thunk of it at all; getting rid of Tanbren had been Breslaw's idea, and he had suggested it to Knobbler, in a roundabout sort of way, before the raid began, but he was happy to let Knobbler *think* it had been all his own. "Very wise," he said. "And you can be king of more than just the towers, maybe . . ." He glanced behind him to make sure no other goblins were in earshot. "Skarper's been back. To the Blackspike, tonight."

"Who? Oh, him. That traitorous, softling-loving . . ."

"He pinched an old map from me. That's like a picture of Clovenstone, with worms on it to tell you what's what. And he took a lump of slowsilver I happened to have lying about too, which makes me think there must be secret writin's on that map, and him and his softling friends are planning to read them."

"Writin's?" This was all getting a bit complex for Knobbler.

"I think they knows of a way inside there," said Breslaw, and he pointed a bony paw at the Keep.

"But there ain't no way in there. There hasn't been since . . ."

"Maybe there is. Maybe they've found one. What was it that that old beardy softling was shouting about yesterday?"

"I dunno, I didn't listen. Magic or something."

"Magic," said Breslaw greedily. "It's comin' back, Knobbler."

"You mean there's going to be a Lych Lord again? A big boss sitting on the Stone Throne, thinking up nasty stuff for us to do?"

"Maybe," said the hatchling master. "Or maybe not . . ."

"You speak in riddles, Breslaw. Normally when people starts speaking in riddles I bashes them. I hates riddles."

"It's not a riddle," Breslaw explained. "Why do we goblins always have to have a wizard or a sorcerer or some dark lord or other to tell us what to do?"

Knobbler pondered this. "It's 'cause we're thick and we like hitting things."

"No! Well, yes . . . Perhaps it was. But things have changed. Maybe us modern-days goblins are wiser than we were in the old Lych Lord's time. Maybe it's time we started lookin' out for ourselves. If you could sit yourself on that Stone Throne, you'd be more than just king of the Inner Wall, Knobbler."

"King of all Clovenstone, you mean?"

"King of the world, maybe."

Knobbler's eyes glowed like embers, dull and greedy and confused. "But it's Skarper and the softlings who knows the way inside, not us."

"So we'll watch them. I reckon the way in must be from down below. We'll set a watch there, and we'll wait . . ."

THE DARK WAY DOWN

The dampdrake slobbered and slithered back into the depths of its mere, bubbling in rage and misery. With it went all Poldew's hopes, for the marsh king had planned to keep and train the monster, and use its great strength and dismal breath to spread his swampy domain across the whole of Clovenstone. Now his dreams were all in ruins. Now he did not even have a hall anymore! Like a man fighting his way out of an enormous, soggy paper bag, he punched and clawed and struggled his way out from beneath the dank heap that had been Bospoldew, and roared at his battered boglins.

"Fetch me those softlings! Find them all! Find them and bring them back! If the 'drake don't want them, I'll eat them myself!" screamed the demented bog boss, and he snacked on a hatchling for starters.

And so the hunting parties formed, and set out this way and that, crisscrossing the water mazes of the mire. The boglins hated this work, for they'd seen the silver fire the softlings had conjured, and the dampdrake's severed tail-tip still twitching on the margins of the mere, and they were sure that their quarry were great warriors and mighty sorcerers too. But they were more scared of Poldew, so they did his bidding and looked high and low, near and far. Some harnessed the great gray raft-spiders that lived in the mire and went scudding across the lagoons to search the remotest reedbeds and islets. Some gathered marshlights and crept sniffing into the damp green shells of the old buildings where the water slopped and echoed eerily and their own huge shadows veered up the slimy walls to terrify them. They looked everywhere; they looked and looked and looked; but when the gray dawn came they had still found no trace of the companions.

Poldew did not seem *too* furious when they came creeping home at sunup, empty-handed. He bit the heads off a couple of the captains, just for form's sake, but he already had another plan. Ever since the dampdrake sank, his fat webbed fingers had been busy weaving. Nets and skeins and snoods of mist were draped in all the trees around the ruined hall like laundry. "We'll fence 'em in!" he burbled, passing out mist traps to his weary underlings. "We'll string such strands around our lovely mire they won't ever leave. If they won't show themselves, the creeping cowards, so be it: We'll sniff 'em out when they starve and start to molder . . ."

Skarper and his companions had been holed up on the third story of an old temple, waiting for the light. Halfheartedly they'd hoped the sun might show them some path that led back to drier places. But the sun barely rose in Natterdon; there was just a lightening in the grayness, and sometimes a glimpse of a pale disc behind the scudding vapors; a glitter of reflections on the puddles as Henwyn set out to scout for a way home.

As Henwyn left, the little dragon, which had been sleeping peacefully curled up on his haversack, woke and started whining. Princess Ned scratched its nose, and it lifted its head and closed its eyes, but it would not settle. "It is fond of Henwyn," said the princess. "It misses him."

"It misses the *taste* of him," said Skarper. With all his clothes rotted away, he had made a slit in the middle of

Stenoryon's map and put his head through it. Wrapped in this parchment poncho he sat miserably in a corner, his bony knees drawn up and his arms wrapped around them.

"It is not a true dragon," said Ned, tickling the creature's red tummy. "The great fire-breathers of old all perished at Dor Koth, and I doubt we shall see their like again, comet or no comet. This little one is a dragonet. The Lych Lord and his captains used them for hunting in the olden times, like hawks. I wonder where this one came from? Has Henwyn given him a name?"

"He calls it 'Ow, you little nuisance!' mostly. It keeps nipping his fingers, you see."

"You did well last night," Ned told him. "I was wrong to mistrust you, Skarper; you are brave and true. Thank you."

Skarper felt the blood rush to his ears. "S'all right," he mumbled.

Ned said, "The fight with the boglins would have ended badly for us if you had not thought to throw that ball of fire-stuff into the flames. That was quick thinking on your part."

Skarper did his best to look as if it had been deliberate. He narrowed his eyes and tilted his chin like the sort of person who scared off bog monsters with magic fire most nights. "It was nothing," he said.

"It was slowsilver," said Ned, looking questioningly at him. "It was a ball of slowsilver so big that it would have made you a very wealthy goblin indeed if you had taken it to the markets of Clovelly or Coriander instead of staying here to help us."

"Would it?" asked Skarper. "Bumcakes! I mean . . ."

"While it was burning, did you chance to see the secret way marked on the map?" the princess asked, and her gaze dropped to the parchment draped over his knobbly knees.

"Map?" he asked innocently.

"I presume that is *Stenoryon's Mappe of All Clovenstone* that you have been using as a nightshirt?" she asked, and he could tell that she knew full well it was, and that she was laughing at him in some secret, inward way. "I saw your ears prick up when I mentioned it yesterday, and then when you went sneaking off with Henwyn . . ."

Skarper held up the parchment, and tried to look surprised at all the words and markings on it. "Oh! This old thing . . ."

"What did you see," she asked, "when the light of the slowsilver fell upon it?"

Skarper couldn't meet her eyes: so bright, so humorous, so wise; she seemed to be able to see what he was thinking. And what he was thinking, of course, was, *The way into the Keep's my secret! Mine! I found it, not them!* He folded the map and said, "I didn't see nothing. There was boglins tromplin' all over me at the time, and I was more interested in rescuing you lot."

"Most heroic," said Princess Ned, and she smiled that private smile of hers, watching the dragonet scrabble about on her lap.

A little while after, they heard movements below. Ned reached for Henwyn's knife, which he had left with her when he went out. But the newcomer was Henwyn himself, returning with bad news.

"There are boglins patrolling all along the borders of the mire," he said. "They have strengthened their mist traps. There is no way out."

"If only those nice cloud girls would come back," said Ned. They all looked hopefully at the sky, but they knew that the cloud maidens would not see them beneath the mist, and even if they did, they were probably too scared of Poldew to descend. The dragonet flew eagerly to

Henwyn and fluttered around him, and he tried telling it, "Go find the cloud maidens, boy! Go fetch!"

"Nuisance is too little to understand you," said Skarper.

"Nuisance?" asked Henwyn, looking surprised.

"Well, you keep calling it Nuisance so I thought that might as well be its name. It will save time."

"Ow! Did you see that? He bit my ear!"

"What if we got it to fly up above the mist and breathe flame?" asked Skarper. "These cloud maidens might see it and guess we were in trouble."

Ned shook her head. "Dragonets cannot breathe flame," she said. "Anyway, cloud maidens are flighty creatures; they have probably forgotten all about you by now, and flown off to throw lightning bolts at mountain trolls up in the Bonehills."

Nobody could think of anything else to suggest. The dragonet settled happily on Henwyn's shoulder and did a wee down his cloak.

"Then are we to just wait here," asked Henwyn, "until the boglins find us?"

Skarper clutched Stenoryon's map close to himself. He could feel some dreadful words forming deep inside him. He could feel them scrambling up his throat. Now they were in his mouth. He didn't want to let them out, but he could not stop them. They were most un-gobliny words, and they were brewed by that same un-gobliny feeling that he'd first noticed when he met Henwyn in the woods. He *liked* these people. He knew he could easily sneak away and leave them to the boglins while he went and explored the Great Keep and its treasures for himself, but he didn't want to.

"I know a way out," he said.

The others turned to look at him. Even Nuisance.

He unfolded the map. There was no sign now of the hidden words and dotted pathway that he had seen glow so brightly last night while the slowsilver blazed, but that didn't matter; Stenoryon's secret was branded on his memory. He drew a claw across the parchment. "It's not far from here," he said. "Into the stump of old Natterdon Tower and then down. Down to the lava lake. There the map will show us something called the Firefrost Stair, which leads up inside the Keep."

"Inside the Keep?" Ned came and took the map from Skarper's paws. "It *is* the map," she said, frowning at the old brown words upon the parchment. "It is Stenoryon's map. Thank you for sharing it with us, Skarper." She made a little curtsy. Skarper blushed. "But dare we take this secret way?" Ned went on. "Wouldn't going inside the Keep be rather like jumping out of the frying pan into . . . well, into a different frying pan?"

"I don't see that we got any other choice," said Skarper.

Henwyn said, "We must do it! Even if there was some other way to escape from the boglins, it would be cowardly to have Stenoryon's map and not to use it!" He was gazing at the map, and there was a light in his eyes that reminded Skarper, just for a moment, of goblins he had known. "Inside the Keep!" he said. "Just think of it!"

Boglin bull-roarers were booming in the fog as the companions left their place of shelter and turned away from the borders of the mire, moving south in the direction of the Inner Wall. Twice they had to stop, crouched silent among reeds or mossy trees, while a patrol of grumpy boglins went splashing past only a few paces away. "Shhh," said Henwyn, calming the dragonet, which had gone back inside the pouch on his belt. Luckily the swamp creatures didn't have the same keen sense of smell as their cousins in the goblin towers; in fact, living in the damps of Natterdon had given most of them terrible colds, so that not only could they not sniff out their prey, their prey could hear them coming from a hundred yards off by their constant snufflings and snifflings and sneezes.

At last the Inner Wall emerged out of the coiling fog ahead, and the travelers cast along it till they reached the stump of Natterdon Tower, which still rose forty or fifty feet high, its shattered top lost in the grayness. Deep, dark pools had formed between the heaps of tumbled masonry at its foot, but the travelers waded across them, with Skarper riding on Henwyn's shoulders, and came to a low doorway half blocked with stones.

"Lead on, Skarper," said Princess Ned.

Skarper paused with one paw on the threshold. It was all very well saying, "We go into old Natterdon Tower," but now, looking into that black opening, he was starting to think of all the horrible things that might live in there.

"Let me!" said Henwyn bravely, and pushed past him, squeezing in through the old doorway. "It stinks," he said from inside, his voice all echoey. "And half the roof's come down. But it's empty . . ."

After a few moments had passed and nothing had eaten Henwyn, Skarper went in after him. The inside of the tower was not altogether dark. Cave-bat droppings had drizzled down the wall and gathered in heaps among the piles of fallen stones which covered the floor. Their soft blue glow made Skarper almost homesick.

"It's all right, boy!" Henwyn was saying, trying to calm Nuisance, who clung to his shoulder, flapping nervously at the stench of the bats. Beyond him, in the far wall, Skarper could see a little pointed doorway. Its iron door was still in place and locked, but the fittings had been so eaten away with rust that Skarper and Henwyn were soon able to pull it clean off its hinges. Nuisance cooed, soothed by the hot air that came out of the dark behind the door. Stone stairs, shallowed with long use, descended into gloom.

"Is this it?" asked Henwyn.

Skarper nodded. "Must be the path the Natterdon goblins' hatchling masters used to reach the lake. The map just called it 'The Dark Way Down.'"

Henwyn peered into the passage. "Well, it's dark all right. And it definitely goes down. But is it a way? I can't see how far it goes. It might be blocked by more of these stones. What if the roof has caved in?"

"We'll need light," said Skarper. "Bat poo will do. We just smear some on our noses and . . ."

"Eugh!" cried Henwyn, who had been thinking that the one good thing about setting off down that dark tunnel would be that he wouldn't have to smell the stench of bat droppings any more.

Outside the tower a boglin bull-roarer blarted in the fog. Others answered it from all around, the deep notes echoing flatly off the Inner Wall. Henwyn ran to the entrance and looked out. There were shouts behind the mist, and running shadows.

"They have found us!" cried Ned, scrambling inside. "There are boglins everywhere. Henwyn, help me bar the way. . . ."

Boglin darts were clattering and ticking against the stones around the door. Henwyn heaved at a huge fallen slab that lay slantwise on a pile of lesser rubble just inside. It shifted, slithered sideways, and set off a sudden avalanche. He jumped backward out of the path of the tumbling rocks, and for a moment there was noise and dust and danger, the floor quaking, Skarper coughing, Ned shouting, "The whole tower is coming down!"

It wasn't, but when the dust thinned enough for them to see again it revealed that the rockslide had sealed the entrance entirely. Faint boglin voices came through chinks between the rocks, saying, "They're sealed in good and proper they are now," and, "At-choo!" and, "*Now* what'll Poldew eat for his breakfasts? *Us*, I reckons!"

Henwyn brushed dust from his hair in a thick cloud and said, "Does anyone happen to have a tinderbox about them? I seem to have lost mine somewhere. . . ."

The princess shook her head.

"Because there is a way down from here," Henwyn explained, "just as Skarper said, except it's rather dark . . ."

"That does not matter," said Princess Ned. "Dark or not, it is the only way left to us now."

THE BRIGHT WAY UP

The way was dark indeed, but it did not go always down; the passage rose and fell, looped and wound, burrowing deep into the summit of Meneth Eskern. They soon reached the stone-lined chamber where the hatchling master of the Natterdon goblins had kept his egg wagon (its iron wheel-rims still lay there, the wood long since rotted by the water that trickled through the chamber from the mires above). Beyond that, the way had been bored and hewn through the living rock. Water still dripped into it in places, and sometimes too, the roots of trees reached down from the world above and caught at the companions' hair like bony fingers.

They walked for a half a mile or so, lit only by the blue glow from the bat poo smeared on Skarper's nose and on the hunks of wood and shards of stone the others carried. No bats lived in the tunnel. Nothing seemed to live there at all, although it was warm and mostly dry, and as they walked on, the companions began to see that a faint silvery light was coming from ahead. It grew brighter and brighter until soon they were able to abandon their smelly bat-poo glow-sticks. A long stair took them winding down and down, the light gathering all the time, and they emerged at last upon a black beach beneath a vaulted roof, lit by the unearthly glow of the lava lake.

"So this is where the Lych Lord's goblins were made!" said Ned, in awe. "But it is not really lava, is it? It is not hot enough or red enough . . ."

Henwyn ran a hand over the gleaming black walls of the cavern. The lake gave him a strange feeling, a little like that longing for adventure he had felt when he was younger, back in Adherak; a desperate yearning for something that he could not quite name. "It's molten slowsilver," he said. "Molten magic! This black stone is slowsilver too, but in another form. The whole Keep . . ." He looked up. "The tales are wrong. The sorcerers did not make the Keep; the Keep just *grew* here . . ."

Ned laughed. "Henwyn, that's very poetic!"

Henwyn shook himself. "I'm sorry. It gives me a funny feeling, that's all."

Skarper had a funny feeling too as he went down to the shore, blinking into the fumes that hung above the lava, looking for a sign of the Firefrost Stair the map had told him of. He could not see anything that looked like stairs at all. There was only the lake, covered in a char-black crust, which kept heaving and splitting, swelling into blisters that burst with lazy belching sounds to let white-hot slowsilver lava splurt up from the depths. Through the smoke and gases he could dimly make out other beaches where the dark ways down from other towers let out. On one of those strands his own egg had been thrown up, and been collected by old Breslaw . . .

From the beach where the companions stood, a long black promontory reached out almost to the center of the lake. Skarper picked his way along it while the others hung back and watched him.

"Is that the way?" called Henwyn. "Can you see the Firefrost Stair?"

"Oh, not *more* stairs!" said Princess Ned. "My knees aren't as young as they once were."

"I see no stair," said Henwyn. "What did the map say, Skarper?"

"It just said, '*Here the map will show you the Firefrost Stair,*'" Skarper replied irritably. He was irritable because he had come all that way on the promise of a Firefrost Stair and there was simply no stair there; only the black shores, the glowing lake, the fumes, and, high above, a cluster of big, round openings in the domed roof of the cavern, as if he were standing inside an enormous pepper shaker and looking up at the holes that let the pepper out. He could feel the others all watching him. He had a feeling that he had let them down, and this made him angry and inclined to snap.

"Perhaps if you had another look at it?" urged Henwyn.

"All right!" snapped Skarper. "I know! What do you think I'm doing?" He pulled the map off over his head and held it out in front of him, hoping desperately that he'd see something there that would jog his fading memories of the slowsilver writing. He could see the very place where Stenoryon's spidery words had shone; he could see them in his mind: *"Here the map will show you . . ."*

"Have you got it the right way up?" asked Henwyn helpfully.

"Of course I have!" shouted Skarper, rounding on him and flapping the map angrily. Which turned out to be a big mistake, because he lost his grip on it and the hot updrafts from the lava lake plucked it out of his paws.

"Bumcakes!" he shouted.

It seemed impossible that such a large and weighty sheet of parchment should just take to the air, but it did. It fluttered up and over Skarper's head like a gigantic, playful moth. He jumped up and snatched at it, but missed. He threw himself after it, but too late. It settled gently on the lava just off the end of the promontory, an inch from his outstretched paws. A white flame sprang up in its very center. Around the flame the parchment blackened, crisped and curled, folding in on itself in crinkling charred scales and scollops. Then, with a *woof,* the flame engulfed it and it was gone, with only a drifting ghost of silver smoke to show that it had ever been.

"My map!" shouted Skarper, stretched out on his tummy on the hot black stone with the heat of the lava singeing all his nose hairs off. He scrambled up and turned to Henwyn. "See what you made me do, you great lumbering cheese-herder!"

Henwyn didn't seem interested in what he had to say. Nor did Ned. They were both staring straight past him, and Henwyn was pointing. "Look!" he said, and then changed his mind and said, "I mean, *behold!*" for what was happening behind Skarper's back was definitely the sort of thing you needed to behold rather than just look at.

The patch of lava where the map had lain grew calm. Up out of it there arose a curl of something that looked like white smoke and then hardened into — no, how could it be *ice?* Up and up it rose, spiraling, reaching toward the high roof like the tendril of some climbing plant. It twined around a stalactite to steady itself, and its tip kept questing upward, circling like the head of a caterpillar, high over the lake, until it found one of those circular holes and slipped inside it. Then, all down its shining length, like leaves, it sprouted steps.

"The Firefrost Stair!" cried Henwyn.

"Yes," said Skarper, trying to look as if he had been expecting this all along. "I was wondering when it would do that."

"Is it real?' asked Princess Ned. "Will it take our weight?"

Henwyn lobbed a stone at it. It rebounded from the stairs with a pretty chiming noise, leaving no mark. He reached out, took hold of the crystal stem, and stepped off the promontory to stand upon the lowest stair. It was firm and solid, the crystal cool to the touch.

"Stenoryon wove powerful magics into that map," said Ned.

"I wish he had thought to give his stairs a handrail while he was at it," said Henwyn. He did not want the others to see that he was nervous, though, so he started to climb. It was just as he'd feared; creeping up from one diamond stair to the next with nothing to hold on to but the stalk from which they'd sprouted was unnervingly like walking on nothing at all.

Skarper, climbing behind him, felt no fear at all. It was different for goblins. He'd been scrambling about on Blackspike's roof since he was new-hatched, and besides, he could always use his tail to save himself if he fell. All he was thinking as he climbed was, *I wonder if this stuff is valuable?*

▼   ▼   ▼

On the beach under Blackspike Tower two things that looked like wet rocks moved slightly, unseen by the companions toiling up the stair. Breslaw the hatchling master had wrapped himself in his old leather apron, and beside him crouched King Knobbler, hidden under a thick black cloak. Only their eyes showed, glowing watchfully in the light from the lava lake, with the frail-looking stair and the climbers reflected in their pupils.

"So that's how you gets inside!" muttered Knobbler, and under his cloak he rubbed his paws together hungrily. "You wait here, Breslaw. I'll fetch the lads and we'll scamper around and get up there before those softling filth can nick all the treasure."

"Wait!" said Breslaw. "Look!"

What was this? Unseen by the climbers on the crystal stairs, more figures were emerging from the black passage that led up into Natterdon Tower. Breslaw growled in alarm, and the apron that covered him fell aside as he straightened, pricking his ear up and staring through the lake's smoke. Across the lava he heard ugly voices: "There they goes!"

"They're on that shiny thingy!"

"Get 'em, boys!"

Poldew of the Mire had not been pleased when his boglins came home to his fallen-down hall to report that the
softlings had escaped. He'd been so displeased that he
had led them back to Natterdon Tower himself, and
stood watching while they scrabbled a pathway through
the fall of stones that blocked its door. Now, heaving his
great gray-green bulk along the narrow passageway, he
had followed his prey all the way down to the lava lake,
with his boglins hopping and gibbering behind him.
The heat dried out their slimy skin and the silvery light
hurt their eyes, but Poldew kept pressing onward, and
none of the others dared defy him and turn back. Now
they urged one another on as their king went waddling
out along the promontory, squinting through the haze
at the distant figures on the stair.

"What are *they*?" asked King Knobbler, squinting at the
boglins from the far shore of the lake.

"Bog boys," growled Breslaw. "Frog hoppers." He'd
always thought boglins were just a nasty rumor. Now it
looked as if they were going to get inside the Keep while
he just sat and watched, because he could see no way of

crossing the lava lake and reaching the stair. He quivered with a furious envy.

Far above, Henwyn was nearing the stair's top. "Don't look down," he kept telling himself, and he looked up instead, at the domed roof that was now so close, and the circular openings, which he could now see were huge, copper-lined flues, carrying the heat of the lava lake up inside the Keep. Even so, he could sense that dreadful drop below him as the stair rose up into the largest of those flues, curved around upon itself in a narrowing spiral, and ended at last against a circular metal door.

He needed all his courage to take his hands off the stairs and reach out to try the handle. *What if it's locked?* he thought. *We'll have to go all the way down again!*

But there had never been any need to lock that door, for the only way to it was by the Firefrost Stair. The handle was stiff, but it opened at last, and Henwyn shoved the door wide open and scrambled through it into a sort of antechamber, very glad to have solid stone beneath him again. Skarper followed, then Ned. None of them, not even Skarper, had dared look down during the final few hundred feet of the climb; none of them had seen the pale little figures of Poldew and his boglin huntsmen below them, clustering at the end of the promontory, jumping across one by one onto the stairs.

The companions lay catching their breath for a while on the floor of the antechamber, watching the light from the lava below play on its high, stony ceiling. Strange noises came to their ears, like deep voices singing an unearthly song. "It is only the wind," said Ned. "It is the air stirring in all those flues and chimneys."

"Nothing could be alive in here," said Henwyn. "It is centuries since the Keep was sealed. Nothing could have lasted all that time."

The others all agreed, and hoped that he was right, but even he didn't sound very sure about it. Skarper was recalling those strange lights he'd seen behind the Keep's lychglass-scabbed windows on the night when he lay in the bratapult. The others were all thinking of legends they'd heard about the place: how the very stones of its walls were said to breathe out evil. Those old stories hadn't seemed important when they were fleeing from the boglins or struggling up the Firefrost Stair, but now they were impossible to forget.

At last Princess Ned clambered to her feet and went to explore. The antechamber was perhaps twenty feet deep, and quite empty. At the end farthest from the door they'd entered by there was another door, a normal rectangular one, made not of metal but of some dark wood. This too was unlocked. She opened it cautiously, and stepped through it, and the others heard her voice echo in a much larger space.

"Oh!"

They followed her through, all except Skarper. He could not quite bear to leave behind the lovely diamond stairs he'd conjured. *That firefrosty stuff,* he thought, *that must be valuable. That would make a good start for a hoard, that would.* As his companions vanished through the door he scurried back to the entrance and leaned out. He gripped the topmost stair firmly between his paws and heaved, but of course he could not break it off — *it must be strong,* he thought, *to have took the weight of those great lumbering humans.* He tried the tip of the stalk instead, which was as slender as a twig. As he closed his paws around it and started to strain he felt it trembling, as if with the footfalls of people coming up. He looked down, but the hot fumes from the lava got into his eyes and he could see nothing. *Sort of echoes from when we climbed up, maybe?* he wondered.

Then he blinked away his tears and saw the boglins, about thirty feet below him, ungainly as frogs as they scrambled from stair to stair. And Poldew of the Mire looked up and saw him looking down, and reached behind him to take a blowpipe from one of his hunters . . .

At that same instant the tip of the firefrost stem broke off in Skarper's paw with a lovely glassy chime. With tinkling, chinking sounds a web of tiny cracks spread down the stem and rushed out to fill each stair, the clear crystal structure whitening as if with a sudden frost. Then, with a tuneful crash, it burst into tiny fragments, which hung in the hot air for a moment like a smoke, still in the shape of the twining stairs, before falling back into the lava, taking the surprised boglins with it. *Glop, glop, glop,* they went, dropping one by one into the hot lake, and then one last, particularly large *GLOP*, which was Poldew.

Skarper scrambled back into the antechamber and opened his paw to look at the treasure he had stolen, but that had shattered too, and when he breathed on it, it lifted from his palm and blew away like a little spreading cloud of ice crystals.

"Bumcakes!" he said, and went after the others, wondering what they were going "Ooh!" and "Oh!" and "Ah!" about on the other side of that big door, and hoping it was treasure.

Knobbler and Breslaw watched the straggles of smoke, which had been boglins, fade like disappointed sighs above the lava lake. "Well, that's that then," said Knobbler grumpily. "The bog boys can't get up there now. But nor can we."

"Maybe we can . . ." said Breslaw, thinking hard. "Maybe there is another way . . ."

"What?"

"You remember that softling yesterday; that beardy one? Said he could do magic? Maybe he wasn't lying. Maybe *he* could get us into the Keep!"

THE SILENT ROOMS

They had climbed so far that it seemed they must be very high, halfway up the tall Keep already. But, of course, the lava lake lay deep beneath the Keep, and the antechamber they had climbed into was actually part of the Keep's cellars. They stepped out of it into a huge space, its roof held up by black pillars. The broad copper flues, as wide as massive trees, emerged from the floor and rose up through the ceiling, carrying the heat and magic of the lava lake up into the rest of the Keep. The light which slanted down through high windows far above had a rusty color, because the windows, like all the openings of the Lych Lord's Keep, were webbed with lychglass.

It was what the light revealed that had made Henwyn and Princess Ned go "Ooh!" and "Ah!" This massive cellar was where the Lych Lord had kept his larger treasures. There were ships there: great warships and caravels; dragon-prowed longships won in battles against the pirates of the Nibbled Coast in olden times. There were coaches decorated in gold and silver and narwhal ivory; there were golden towers such as the Leopard Kings from the lands beyond the Musk Desert used when they rode to war upon the backs of elephants.

There was a carriage carved from one huge semiprecious stone, with gold ornaments on its roof in dragon-shape, and Henwyn's dragonet escaped from his pouch and went whirring up to squeak at them.

There were chariots, and palanquins, and slender little sailing boats. There were kites big enough to carry a man, hanging from the roof on long wires. There was a sort of carriage that looked like a little room made of silver metal sitting on four small wheels, with a long prow poking out at the front, and a little statue of a lady with silver wings standing on the very tip of it. Skarper peered in through the windows at all the lovely red leather seats and a walnut shelf with little clocks set in it.

"I've read of this," said Princess Ned, running her fingers through the dust on the curving mudguards. "It is the 'Rolls-Royce Silver Shadow'; a chariot that the Lych Lord fetched here by magic from another world."

"Where do the horses go?" asked Henwyn.

"It needed none," the princess said. "It was powered by sorcery. Here is your treasure trove, Henwyn. These things must be worth kings' ransoms."

"Even if we could slip these longships in our pockets," said Henwyn, "there is no way out of here, is there?"

"Back down the Firefrost Stair into the mire," said Ned. "I expect the boglins will forget us in a day or so."

"Ah," said Skarper.

They turned to look at him.

"About the Firefrost Stair," he said. "It sort of cracked. Went all to pieces. Nothing to do with me. It just smashed. It was a once-only kind of thing. Cheap and nasty."

"Accursed magic!" said Ned. "So we are trapped here in the Keep? I suppose at the top we might find a way out, and be able to signal to Fraddon; he should be coming down from the Bonehills later today."

"Or perhaps Henwyn's cloudy girlfriends will see us . . ." suggested Skarper.

"They're not my *girlfriends* . . ." said Henwyn.

On the far side of the strange museum they found a staircase, and started up it. ("I never realized that adventures involved quite so many stairs!" said Ned.) The stairs led through a doorway, curled around inside the Keep's thick walls, and emerged into a wide dining hall with long wooden tables down the center, silent as a tomb, empty except for the dust, and the red light that strained in through the lychglass on the high, thin windows. Not as cold as a tomb, though, for the flues rose from floor to ceiling and sent out broad branches, which vanished through the walls, so that it was like standing in a spinney of great copper oaks. The flues gave off a faint heat, filling the quiet room with the smell of warm metal. There were little doors and hatches set into their sides. Skarper opened one and peered in, and the light of the lava lake spilled out into the room, reflecting off the burnished inner curves of the flue. It reminded him suddenly of the lights he'd seen, or thought he'd seen, inside the Keep.

"Maybe somebody opens these sometimes," he said nervously, "and the light shines out."

"Who?" asked Henwyn. "There's no one here. There aren't even bones. Everyone must have fled before the place was sealed up. Look at the dust on the floor. The only footprints are ours. Not even a spider lives here."

"Pity," said Skarper, who was feeling peckish and could have done with a nice plump spider. "What are we going to eat in this place?"

It was a good question. None of them had eaten since the night before, and, although they were all too polite to mention it, the main sound in the Keep was the rumbling of their empty bellies.

"I have some flour in my pack," said Henwyn. "And some water . . ."

"Wonderful," grumbled Skarper. "We can make *glue* . . ."

"There must be kitchens here somewhere," said Henwyn. "Larders. Perhaps there will be something there."

"After all these years?" snorted Skarper. "If the Lych Lord left any loaves in his bread bin they will be stale as stones by now."

"There might be something," said Ned. "This is a strange place, and perhaps time does not pass here as it does outside. These chairs and tables have not rotted or grown wormy . . ." She settled herself gratefully in one of them and kicked her shoes off. "I'll sit and wait, and let you young people search the rooms around and see if you can find the Lych Lord's larder."

On Henwyn's shoulder little Nuisance flapped and squeaked.

"Look!" said Henwyn. "I think he's got the scent of something! Is it food, boy? Can you lead us to the larders?"

The dragonet took flight, whirred once around Henwyn's head, and shot across the hall and through a low, open doorway in the far wall. A moment later he reappeared, hovering just inside the door and squeaking at the companions as if to say, "Follow me," before darting out again.

"I'm sure he understands every word we say!" cried Henwyn. "He'll lead us to food and water."

"Take care!" called Ned, as Henwyn hastened after the little dragon with Skarper at his heels. "Don't get lost!"

"We'll be all right," said Henwyn. "You said yourself — nothing lives here."

His words went whispering away up staircases and chimneys into the highest parts of Clovenstone; into the ears of the ones who waited there.

▼   ▼   ▼

Evening was already falling in the world outside the Keep. The three sorcerers, who did not fancy spending another night alone at Westerly Tower, were making plans to leave.

"We have to assume," said Fentongoose sadly, "that our friends were all eaten by those bog creatures."

"Poor Princess Ned," said Prawl sorrowfully.

"Poor Henwyn," sighed Carnglaze.

"Poor what's-his-name," said Fentongoose. "You know, the little one with the tail . . ."

"Poor *us*," said Carnglaze, "left alone and defenseless in this fearful place."

"I don't think we are cut out to be evil sorcerers, brothers," said Fentongoose. "If we were truly evil, we would not feel such sorrow at the deaths of our friends. We would just go, 'Ha! Ha! Ha!' or something. I think we should leave this place and take our chances on the moors. With luck we shall find a southerly-bound barge at Sticklebridge and be back in Coriander by the turning of the month."

And so they crammed what provisions they had rescued from the wreck of Princess Eluned's ship hastily into their packs and went hurrying out through Westerly Gate with the low sun in their eyes, bidding a glad good-bye to Clovenstone.

Clovenstone, however, had other ideas. As they passed beneath the shadow of the gate-arch, something landed heavily on the road in front of them, straight-ened up, fixed the startled sorcerers with a beady yellow eye and growled, "'Allo!"

More goblins landed all around, swinging down on greasy ropes or just jumping out of windows and down from nearby roofs. A red-capped Chili Hat jabbed Fentongoose in the bottom with his three-pronged spear; a Blackspike Boy knocked Carnglaze's pointy hat off.

"That's enough of that, lads," growled a gruff voice, and King Knobbler himself swaggered out in front of the sorcerers, picking his teeth with the point of Mr. Chop-U-Up. Six of his biggest goblins stood close behind him, idly swinging flails and brandishing complicated axes with homemade eye-gouging attachments.

"We come in peace," said Knobbler. "And you lot will come in *pieces*," he added wittily, "unless you does what we asks. You're coming with us."

"But *where*?" they all wailed, as grimy goblin paws seized hold of them. "But *why*?"

"Grab 'em and gag 'em, lads," called old Breslaw, from a safe place at the back of the goblin mob. "Quick, before they can do spells and stuff on us."

Fentongoose opened his mouth to protest that he couldn't really work magic, but instantly a grimy goblin sock was shoved into it, and one of Knobbler's lads hoisted him onto his shoulders. The other sorcerers, kicking and struggling, were treated likewise. "Your magic's going to get us into the Keep," Knobbler explained, and the goblins set off toward the Inner Wall.

"But we don't have any magic, it's all a mistake!" Prawl tried to say, but all that came out through his gag was a muffled murmuring.

"I know what you're doing," said Knobbler, waving his fearsome sword at the sorcerers. "You're trying to work spells, ain't you, and turn us into frogs or logs or something? Well, save your magic for when we get to the Keep. If I hear another peep out of you before then, Mr. Chop-U-Up here will be getting acquainted with your squelchy bits."

THE DRAGONBONE MEN

In their chamber near the top of the Keep, the Dragonbone Men had been waiting for a long, long time. For most of it they had not even been aware that they *were* waiting. They had slumped in those narrow niches in the walls like forgotten dolls, not sleeping, for they did not sleep; not dead, for they had never been alive. But there were windows in that high place of theirs, and even through the scales of lychglass that had grown across them the pale light of the new star had crept. It lit reflections in the flakes of slowsilver that served the Dragonbone Men for eyes, and they awoke. When they heard the voices of Henwyn and Skarper and Princess Ned come drifting up the Keep's stairways they had roused themselves and paced with solemn, birdlike steps to the flue that rose through their floor, and opened the door in the side of it, and climbed in, one by one.

The glow of the lava lake so far below shone through the thin sheets of stuff that they were made of, and showed the shadows of their dragonbone skeletons beneath. They were so light that the heat coming up the flue was almost enough to buoy them up — almost, but not quite. They spread their capes of dry skin like paper wings and descended slowly, following the scent of men down this branch and that of the immense system of flues, which spread through the Keep like a copper tree.

Skarper and Henwyn made their way meanwhile down dusty corridors, up little stairs, through armories and guardrooms. Racks of armor stood in rows. Helmets watched with empty eyes as the intruders passed. Skarper helped himself to an old leather tunic, made for some human warrior; it was scratchy and musty and it came down past his knees, but it felt good not to be wandering about nude anymore. Henwyn found a pair of leather gauntlets and put them on. The dragonet was flying excitedly ahead of the companions through the lofty rooms, but every few minutes it would loop back to land on Henwyn's wrist and nip his fingers, urging him onward.

At last Nuisance screeched and came to a stop, flapping in midair outside a low, half-open door. Henwyn and Skarper hurried toward it.

"Is this the larder, boy?"

"Maybe there'll be honey! Honey keeps!"

But it was not a larder. It was a mews where hawks and hunting birds had been kept back in the Lych Lord's time. Jesses and lures hung from hooks on the ceiling, lit by the evening sunlight filtering through the scabs of lychglass on the window. Empty perches lined the walls, and plumed hoods stood in a row on a shelf above. One of the great copper flues passed through this room from floor to ceiling, and the air tasted warm and dry.

"There is no food here," said Henwyn. "Come on, little Nuisance. Larder. Where's the larder?"

He turned to leave, but Nuisance would not let him. With a mewling cry the dragonet darted in front of him and flapped its wings in his face, driving him back into the room, then whisking away to hover and mewl above a long wooden tray that rested on a stone shelf beneath the window.

Skarper and Henwyn went closer. "Eggs . . ." said Skarper.

"A dozen. Do you think they're fresh? We could scramble them . . ."

"Don't be soft!" said Skarper. "They're dragon's eggs. Well, dragonets'. Probably poisonous or magic or something. Look: That one's bust. Maybe it's the one little Nuisance hatched out of . . ." He looked up, and the Lych Lord's star winked in at him through a crack on the lychglass that sealed the window. "Look! That must be where Nuisance squeezed out . . ."

"Could we get out that way?" asked Henwyn.

"Never. We must be halfway up the Keep by now, and we can't fly like a dragonet can. There's nothing outside but a long drop to a sticky end."

Henwyn, who had been working at the edges of the crack with his swordpoint, stopped. "I can't widen it anyway," he said. He felt an odd sort of relief. It was thrilling to be exploring the Keep at last; he was almost glad that there was no way out.

Nuisance mewed again, fluttering to and fro over the tray of eggs. Henwyn looked closer, and saw several of the eggs give small movements. He thought he could hear the dragonets squeaking and struggling inside. "Well, I hope they don't hatch," he said. "It's bad enough having Nuisance nibbling and pecking at me all the time; I don't want his eleven brothers and sisters having a go too."

Skarper picked up the shards of Nuisance's eggshell. Thick, it was; not eggstone-thick, but nearly. "Maybe he wants you to help them," he said. "I 'spect in olden days there was mother dragonets or men or goblins or something to look after this place and help the dragonets to hatch. Look; that hammer hanging on the wall . . ."

Henwyn looked. Sure enough, a little hammer dangled there, but before he could reach for it strange sounds filled the room; a rushing and a rustling; a slither and a scrape.

Skarper and Henwyn looked at each other. By the time they realized that the sounds were coming from the flue it was too late. They turned in time to see a copper hatch swinging open, and the Dragonbone Men stepping out.

There were four of them. Their hollow bodies had been folded out of sheets of dragon-skin parchment; their arms and legs were brittle arrangements of dragonbone.

Inside their chests, stiff leather cogs revolved. Their heads splayed into wayward points, like tall crowns. Behind the eyeholes of those parchment masks there was a glint of slowsilver. They made little ticking noises, like clinker cooling in a grate. Their tiny feet, which were made from dragons' claws, went *scritch* and *snick* as they stepped from the flue, and their dry capes settled around them like corn husks.

Henwyn raised his sword. Nuisance squeaked with alarm and fluttered up to hide in the folds of his cloak. Skarper just stood and stared as the creatures surrounded them.

"What *are* they?" he hissed at Henwyn.

Said Henwyn, "I'm not sure. But I think . . . In the old, old tales, the seven sorcerers who raised this place made seven servants for themselves. Dragonbone Men, brought to life by magic. They were the most dreadful of the Lych Lord's warriors. But toward the end the magic left them, and they became just mannequins again. That's why they were not there to help him at the Battle of Dor Koth."

"Well, they look as if they're brimful of magic again now," said Skarper.

"Adherak!" roared Henwyn, suddenly and at the top of his voice. The noise scared Skarper and Nuisance, but it did not seem to trouble the Dragonbone Men, who just stood and watched as the cheesewright swung his sword at them. One caught the blade as it descended; another lashed out at Henwyn with a hand like a bundle of ivory hooks. Henwyn let go of the sword and leapt backward just in time to avoid being ripped open, and the slashing claws ripped his clothes instead.

Back to the egg-tray, breathing hard, he waited for the next blow, but it did not come. The Dragonbone Men stood still again, and watched him. Their eyes glimmered with something more than the reflection of the star outside. They stared at Henwyn; at the bare white skin that showed where his torn tunic hung open. They stared at the grim, winged face of the amulet staring out at them. The mouths of the Dragonbone Men were slots; their tongues were dried-up knots of dragon tendon, which they rattled inside their hollow heads to make rustling, clattering noises like rattlesnake tails.

The rattling sounds formed words.

"Welcome," whispered the Dragonbone Men.

"We have waited . . ."

"So long . . ."

"What are they talking about?" asked Henwyn in a whisper.

"That's Fentongoose's amulet you're wearing!" Skarper hissed back. "They think you're him! The leader of the Sable Conclave! The Lych Lord's heir!"

"I didn't know!" whispered Henwyn. "I found it in the ruins! I'd forgotten I even had it!"

"Well don't tell them that," Skarper warned. It seemed to him that amulet had saved their skins. If these Dragonbone weirdies wanted to treat Henwyn like the Lych Lord come again, that was fine by him.

"Come with us," clattered the Dragonbone Men. "Come with us. Let us lead you to your throne of stone."

The sun had set, and the Lych Lord's star was blazing in the top of the sky like a squib that never went out as the goblins carried their captives through the gateways of the Inner Wall, past the shabby glasshouses where the Chili Hats' peppers grew, and up the last steep streets to stand at the foot of the Keep. It was the first time since the Fall of Clovenstone that so many goblins had been seen all together in one place and not fighting one another. Grimspikes and Growlers, Slatetops and Chili Hats, Blackspikes and Browbeaters. As the host tramped up the final weed-choked ramp to the black gate they sang the old goblin marching song:

Goblins come!
Goblins come!
From Clovenstone with horn and drum!
To the Lands of Man with fire we come!
Over the mountains,
Over the moor,
Goblins are marching,
To war! To war!

. . . which wasn't entirely true, because this was a raid on the Keep, not the lands of men, but they hadn't had time to think of a song about the Keep, and it was certainly true that they had fire, in the form of scores of flaming torches, and horns and drums, which they used to accompany their singing, making a horrendous din. Anyway, if Knobbler really could open the Keep, maybe the man-lands *would* be next. Even goblins knew that there were meant to be powerful magics in there along with all the treasure. Maybe King Knobbler's goblin armies would be able to conquer the whole world . . .

At the front of the army, old Breslaw stepped up to the gates and thumped thoughtfully on them with his teaching mallet. They let out a low bonging sound, muffled by the sheath of lychglass that covered them like cataracts on an old goblin's eye.

King Knobbler watched him. The king had put on his new fighting hat, a huge dark helm, which he had captured from the king of Growler. It covered his head like an upturned bucket. In fact, it *was* an upturned bucket, but it was a very fancy one, with a spike on the top, a bull's horn stuck to each side, and a long slot cut across the front like a mailbox, through which the king's mad yellow eyes blinked out. He motioned to the goblins who stood behind, and they dragged the battered, frightened members of the Sable Conclave out of their ranks and dumped them among the nettles at the king's feet.

"Go on then," Knobbler growled. "Open it."

The three sorcerers clung together, trembling and making little *eep* noises.

"OPEN IT!" bellowed Knobbler, so loudly that the echoes slamming off the gates blew the sorcerers' hair and beards out behind them like a gale while the goblins standing nearby all leveled spears, swords, pikes and spiky egg-whisk things at them.

"Very well," said Fentongoose, although he had never felt less capable of doing magic in his whole life. He raised his hands, shut his eyes, and said in as loud and commanding a voice as he could manage:

"OPEN!"

A THRONE OF STONE

The Keep narrowed as it rose, and a stairway spiraled through the heart of it, up and up again, winding about the warm branchings of the copper flues. Doorways opened off the stairs, some leading out onto lofty battlements where catapults and war machines stood beneath bubbles of lychglass like museum exhibits in dusty cabinets. Others led into rooms in whose shadows, dimly shining, Skarper saw chests of coins and precious stones, golden idols from far Zandegar, the skins of leopards, bears and hippogriffs. He saw curtained anterooms where harps and viols stood waiting for the ladies of the Lych Lord's court to return and stir them into life with long, pale fingers.

Skarper's goblin senses prickled; his paws itched

with the desire to gather up these precious things and stuff them in his pockets. But the Dragonbone Men allowed no tarrying, and whenever Skarper slowed or tried to turn aside into one of the rooms they would come rustling around him, plucking at their clothes with dragon-claw hands, their dry voices rattling and buzzing in their wasps' nest heads, urging him on and up.

Once Henwyn tried to stop too. "Princess Ned will be afraid for us," he said.

"That does not matter," whispered the Dragonbone Men.

"Where are you taking us?"

"The time has come," rustled the Dragonbone Men. "The star is risen and the Stone Throne waits."

Skarper didn't much like the sound of that, but there was nothing he could do, only let the Dragonbone Men hustle him on up the stairs. Nuisance was still cowering under Henwyn's cloak, and Henwyn wondered if it might be possible for the little dragonet to slip away and go winging back down to where Princess Ned waited, carrying a warning. Ned needed to know that dreadful things were loose inside the Keep . . . but he could not think how he could make Nuisance understand that, and before he could come up with an idea another staircase joined the one that he and Skarper were climbing, and up came another group of Dragonbone Men, three this time, leading Princess Ned.

"I am so sorry," she said, when she saw Henwyn and Skarper. Her hair had come down in a tumble of gray; she blinked at them between its strands. "They came out of the chimneys and there was nothing I could do. I am forever being captured these days. It isn't like me at all. You must think me such a silly princess."

Still they climbed, and still the Keep narrowed, and the doors they passed were mostly shut tight now, and made of bronze or iron, not of wood. Then, quite suddenly, there was the brightness of moonlight above, and they came up into a huge chamber: the very top of the Keep. The roof was one great misshapen dome of lychglass. Through it Skarper and Henwyn could see the weird towers and horns of the Keep's top jutting toward the moon, the black stone of them all glittery with veins of slowsilver. Moonlight spilled in through the lychglass and lit the floor of the room, which was made of many different sorts of metal, arranged in curious, intricate patterns. There were patches of platinum; swirls of gold; broad fields of copper, green with verdigris. But the moon was not the only light they had to see all this by, for in the middle of the floor there was a round opening, fifty feet across. It was the mouth of a great copper flue, into which all the other flues that carried the warmth of the lava lake up through the Keep must feed. A faint silver light came out of it, and a haze of magic rippled the air above. A thin stone bridge arched out over it to meet a slender pinnacle, which rose from its very center, the top of a craggy stone claw that jutted through the flue's side, farther down.

Upon that pinnacle, at the top of a last flight of seven steps, there stood a stone chair. Black it was, and burnished; shining; its facets veined with slowsilver and other magic metals. Hard and high and dangerous it looked, and Princess Ned went to the bridge's end and gazed up at it, and said in an awed and shuddery voice, "Oh! It is the Stone Throne!"

The Dragonbone Men rustled like dry leaves in a wind. "The magic has returned," said one.

"The Lych Lord must take his seat again, and rule."

"But don't you understand?" shouted Henwyn. "He's dead! He's been dead for centuries, and the world is free of him! There is no one to sit on your horrible hard old throne. . . ."

The Dragonbone Men swung their dry heads toward him. They fixed him with silverfish eyes. Folding at the waist, they bowed low before the bewildered young cheesewright and their voices buzzed like seven swarms of bees trapped in seven paper bags.

"The star has risen . . ."

"A new Lych Lord has come to wield its power."

"Lord of Clovenstone," they whispered.

"Lord of Ash and Shadows."

"Come. Sit upon your Stone Throne."

"Me?" Henwyn touched his own chest. He looked for help to Ned and Skarper. "I'm just a cheesewright!" he protested. "I'm not a sorcerer! Just because I found this silly amulet? It isn't even mine! Perhaps it's Fentongoose you're waiting for . . ."

"Come."

Henwyn took a step toward the bridge and drew back nervously, appalled by the great drop beneath it.

"And again, no handrail," he complained. "I mean, is it just me? I like to think I'm pretty steady on my feet, but when I'm crossing stairs and bridges above gulfs of magic lava I like something to hold on to. . . ."

"Come," whispered the Dragonbone Men.

And suddenly Henwyn found that he wasn't afraid of the drop after all — or, if he was, that his need to reach that black throne was greater than his fear. He crossed the bridge and climbed the steps, and as he climbed he saw that there was something lying on the throne, and as he reached the top he realized that it was a man.

How had none of them noticed him there before? Perhaps it was because the throne was so big and the man was so small; because the throne was so richly carved and the man so plainly dressed in shabby old black robes; because the throne was magnificent, and the man was a shriveled up, little, wizened, wrinkled thing, more like an old gnarled heather root than a human being. But he was alive, and watching his visitor with pale yellow eyes.

"So you've come at last," he whispered. "You took your time!"

From beneath the cobweb hair at the old man's temples black wings jutted, attached to a circlet of silver that ringed his brow.

"You are Him! You are the Lych Lord!" said Henwyn in astonishment.

"I was," the old man said.

"But all the songs and stories say you're dead!"

"Of course I'm not! I'd hardly be sitting here talking to you if I were, would I?" snapped the old man. He frowned — one more wrinkle in a face made of wrinkles — and just for a moment Henwyn caught a glimpse of the proud and frightening person he had been. Then his voice faded to a whisper again. "Songs are mistaken sometimes, and you can never trust storytellers. They got it wrong, as usual. That last day, when the magic was fading and my people had fled and King Kennack's armies were battering down my gates, I gathered what little power remained and cast one last spell. I sealed the Keep. I slowed time to a trickle. And here I have waited ever since. Keeping the Stone Throne warm for you, as it were."

"For me?" said Henwyn. "That's what they said, those leathery chaps, but . . ."

"You have my token about you, I suppose?" the Lych Lord said.

Henwyn fumbled the ivory carving out on the end of its string. He pulled the loop of string over his head and held the amulet out. "This old thing?"

The old man nodded. "He who carries my token home to Clovenstone, shall take my place upon the Stone Throne. That's the way it works, you see."

"But I didn't bring it here!"

"Yet there it is, around your neck."

"It was Fentongoose who has guarded it! Fentongoose who brought it here! Fentongoose, master of the Sable Conclave! *He* should be the new Lych Lord if anyone should! Although . . ."

"Ah!" said the old man. "But does the blood of the Lych Lord run in this Fentongoose's veins?"

"I, er . . ." said Henwyn. "Well, it certainly doesn't run in mine!"

"Are you certain of that, Henwyn of Adherak?" The old man heaved himself upright like a shock of dry sticks. "When I guessed that all was lost, I sent my household away. I sent Stenoryon to Coriander, to keep the knowledge of me alive till the magic grew strong again. But my daughter? My own small daughter, who was heir to all my empires, yet too little then to even know it? I could not entrust her to a lot of silly would-be wizards. I sent her where she would be safest, into the household of King Kennack himself, where, I believe, she became a dairy maid. You are of the royal line of Clovenstone, Henwyn of Adherak."

"I'm not!" said Henwyn. "I don't feel royal or evil or any of the things a Lych Lord ought to feel . . ."

"Have you not felt Clovenstone calling to you, all your life?" asked the old man. "Did not the Sable Conclave seek you out — led to you by the power in the amulet, although they knew it not. Did your cheese not come to life?"

"*I* did that?" said Henwyn, amazed.

"Well, sort of. I did it. I saw you through the eyes of the amulet, and I set in motion the events that would lead you here. If I could have only controlled it a little longer, the cheese demon would have snatched you up and run here with you; you would have arrived weeks ago. But the magic is weak nowadays. It is hard for even I to work a spell on anything beyond the borders of Clovenstone. Only the presence of the amulet allowed me to influence the cheese at all, and when that fool of a Fentongoose panicked and ran away I lost the link; the spell was broken."

"The cheese-creature exploded . . ." remembered Henwyn.

"What sort of an evil sorcerer is it who panics at the sight of a cheese-demon?" scoffed the old man. "Sable Conclave indeed. Standards have slipped. But you'll put that to rights once you sit upon the Stone Throne." He reached out one thin, trembling claw of a hand and took the amulet from Henwyn. He set it on the arm of the throne, and it quivered a moment like a blob of mercury, then sank into the stone.

"From the throne it was made, and to the throne it returns," said the Lych Lord. "The throne is the source of it all, you see. Raw magic from the deep places of the earth is stirred into life by the coming of the star. When the star draws close, the power waxes; when the star soars away, it wanes. The star is coming close again now; the power is gathering. It flows up through the Keep, through the throne, out into the world.

"But it needs a *mind*. It needs a person sitting on the throne to give it shape and meaning and direction.

Without that it would just flail about, creating random giants and useless woodlings and the like for want of any better way to express itself. Someone must control it or there would be chaos."

He patted one arm of the throne. "Take your seat, Henwyn of Clovenstone. You'll understand."

He slid himself forward, reaching down his withered legs, his bony toes. He gave a sharp sigh as he raised himself from his stony seat. Regret? Or relief? It was hard to tell. He stood in front of the throne, and reached up to pluck the winged crown from his head. "Here," he said, holding it out toward Henwyn. "Take it!"

"But I don't want it," said Henwyn, and then realized that perhaps he did. All his life he'd known that he was special; that he had a destiny. Perhaps he'd just been wrong about its nature. Perhaps that was why he'd been no use as a hero — because he'd been a villain all along! "Me?" he wondered. "The new Lych Lord? The king of all the world?"

"Take it," said the Lych Lord, in a voice as faint as a breeze in a tomb, and he tottered and fell forward. Henwyn reached out to catch him, but it was like catching a toppling pile of sand; the dry grains and cinders that had been the old man poured between his fingers, spilling in a gray drift down the steps, settling as dust upon the dust of Clovenstone. All that remained was the winged crown, solid and cool in Henwyn's hands.

"Henwyn!" called Princess Ned, from the far side of the bridge.

He looked back; saw her and Skarper watching him.

"Throw it away!" called Ned. "Please, Henwyn! There is dreadful magic here!"

"No, it's all right!" said Henwyn. He wished he could explain to her that this was what he had been waiting for, all through his dull and cheesy life. He sat down upon the Lych Lord's throne.

He felt it change. He felt it shift and stir, shaping itself to him. He set the winged crown upon his head.

There was a huge groaning sound, a cracking and a shattering, and across the lychglass dome above there reached a spider's web of thread-thin cracks. Skarper and Princess Ned clapped their hands over their ears and cowered at the enormous noise, but Henwyn only laughed, because he knew it was not just that dome that was breaking but all the lychglass upon all the doors and windows of the Keep, as if Clovenstone was shaking off a thick frost that had settled on it while it slept.

From every window, every balcony, every battlement and arrow-slit of the Keep, the plugs of lychglass cracked and fell. A great fissure opened in the lens that covered the main gate. The noise it made startled King Knobbler, who had been about to bring down Mr. Chop-U-Up on Fentongoose's scrawny neck. He stumbled backward, gaping, and behind him his horde of goblins cowered, throwing up their shields to shelter from the shower of shards. But no jagged blades of lychglass came plummeting to spear them: It had splintered into such tiny crumbs that most of it just blew away on the breeze, surrounding the Keep with a glittering mist. The few pieces that did hit the ground came down as a gentle snowfall of crystals, shining in the moonlight and the light of the goblins' torches, settling on their heads and shoulders like mystic dandruff.

Knobbler looked at the three sorcerers, cowering among drifts of lychglass dust on the cobbles in front of him. "Did you do that?"

"Of course!" fibbed Fentongoose. "Open it, you said, and we, ah . . ."

A long, discordant creak drowned out the rest. The Keep's gate, freed of its lychglass seal, was swinging open, letting out a smell of dust and dry air; letting in the moonlight. The goblins stared in silence for a moment, then surged forward, big ones trampling small ones underfoot, small ones scrambling over the big ones' heads, swirling into the halls of the Lych Lord like a smelly sea.

THE LYCH LORD

The new Lych Lord sat upon his throne and felt the ancient power of Clovenstone course through him. It was not all it might be yet, and wouldn't be until the star came closer, but it thrilled him all the same as he began to realize what he would soon be able to do. He looked out over his throne room and saw how the squirls and splodges of different-colored metals on the floor made a map: hammered silver for seas and rivers, green copper for the forests, bronze for the moors, and burnished brass for deserts, gold and platinum and lapis lazuli for cities. He looked out across the world that he would rule: the cities that he would conquer, and the kingdoms that would pay him tribute . . .

And he saw his friends standing there, looking up at him with worry in their faces, and remembered he was

Henwyn of Adherak as well as the Lych Lord. It touched him to see how concerned they were. "It's all right," he said, forgetting for a moment about his destiny, his vast new power. "I'm still Henwyn. I'm not going to be, you know, *evil* . . . Magic can be used for good, as well, can't it? Skarper, my friend, I won't desert you. Look!"

He let the powers of Clovenstone lift his hand and flex his fingers. He felt it raise the hairs on the nape of his neck. He whispered words he'd never heard before, and something like a smoke enveloped Skarper. When it cleared, the goblin's shabby clothes had changed. The old tunic he had found himself had turned into a fish-bright hauberk of silver scales, and there were golden rings upon his paws and a circlet of gold about his head. Even his shoes were made of gold, etched with threads of slowsilver and studded with rubies. Skarper looked down at himself and flinched in surprise. Coins cascaded from his sleeves.

"You wanted treasure?" asked Henwyn. "You will have more treasure than a goblin ever dreamed of!" And he saw Skarper's eyes shine, and felt glad that the first deed he had done as Lych Lord was something generous. To give your friends what they had always wanted; wasn't that the best use of power?

Next he turned to Princess Ned. She took a step away and held up one hand, palm toward him. "I do not want riches, Henwyn," she said.

Again the magic prickled; he felt all the branchings of his nerves tingle as it surged through him. Smoke wrapped the princess. When it blew away, she was not dressed in finery; she still wore the same patched frock and bog-soggy boots, and the necklace around her throat was still just string and stones. But the lines of laughter on her face had smoothed themselves away; her long hair had turned from gray to gold. She looked at the hand that she still held out, upraised in front of her, and she saw that all the creases and crinkles of age were fallen from it, and it had become soft and white again. She was a girl, as young and beautiful as she had been on the long-ago Tuesday when Fraddon hoisted her ship from the choppy seas off Choon Head. She touched her fingers to her lineless face, and Henwyn, looking on, saw wonder there, then a little fear, then dawning joy. He had found the thing she wanted too. Who wouldn't want a chance to live again?

"See?" he said. "I have rescued you after all. I have rescued you from time."

Skarper looked up at his words. He had been so busy admiring the fine new rings and silver wristlets that Henwyn had magicked for him that he had not even seen the transformation being wrought on Princess Ned. Now he stared at her, and despite his new riches, a little creeping feeling of unease came into his mind. He was remembering what the princess had said about power, and what power did to people. He remembered her saying it, sitting on the sofa in her cozy old ship, with her knees drawn up under her chin and her nice gray hair spilled over them. He had liked her that way; she looked prettier now, more like a storybook princess, but less like herself. He wanted the old Ned back. And he missed the old Henwyn too. He'd wanted a friend, not some all-powerful Lych Lord who dished out magic presents to his companions, and did who knows what to his enemies . . .

Skarper shook his paws, and the new rings flew off and landed clattering on the floor. He took a step backward, and the ruby-encrusted shoes Henwyn had made him felt heavy and uncomfortable. They clumped across the metal map as he turned and fled between the silent Dragonbone Men to the stairs.

"Skarper?" he heard Henwyn call behind him. "Skarper! Come back!"

The Dragonbone Men skittered into life, sprinting after Skarper with their strange, stiff-legged run, but Henwyn halted them with a gesture. "No, let him go."

Skarper glanced back over his shoulder as he reached the top of the stairs, and saw the Dragonbone Men freeze in mid-stride. Then he tripped over his strange new shoes and pitched forward. "Bumcakes!" he cried, curling into a ball like a scared hedgehog, putting his paws up to protect his head, and his mail coat rang upon the stones as he went tumbling head over heels down the long spiral of the stairs.

Princess Ned looked up at Henwyn. No, not Princess Ned any more; Eluned. *Ned* was far too ordinary and mannish a name for someone so young and beautiful. She said, "He is afraid of you, my lord."

Henwyn laughed. It seemed such a strange idea, that anyone should be afraid of him. Little Nuisance crept out from beneath his cloak, and Henwyn worked another spell — it was easy, once you got the knack — and turned him from a dull brown dragonet into a perfect miniature dragon, his scales blazing with rich colors. *Isn't that what a dragonet must dream of?* thought Henwyn. *To be a proper dragon?* He almost made him dragon-sized as well, but decided he had better wait until his powers were stronger and he was quite certain of his dragon-taming abilities.

Nuisance hiccupped and let out a little flare of orange flame, which startled him so much he took flight and went whirring away to hide among the ornate carvings that ringed the chamber. Henwyn felt irritated, and a little sad. Did no one appreciate his kindness?

"Are you afraid of me?" he asked Eluned.

"A little," said Eluned, and she looked so beautiful that Henwyn could not resist changing her clothes for her; her homespun kirtle kindled into bright silk, and splashes of bog mud on her skirt's hem became lush knots of gold embroidery.

"Don't be afraid," he said. "I'm not like *him* . . ." He pointed to the ash of the old Lych Lord, sprinkled down the steps of the throne. "I'm going to do good things. All this magic is waiting to be used, you see. It needs harnessing, power like that. Like a wild horse or something. That's what Clovenstone is for. I'll use the magic to bring rivers to the deserts of Zandegar! I'll use it to build fine palaces for my sisters, and a new cheesery beyond compare for my father. I'll use it to throw down bad kings and tyrants everywhere. That lout the king of Choon, for instance; I'll show *him* a thing or two!"

If Ned had been herself she might have told him that that's how it starts; you set out to punish bad people and end up punishing anyone who does not think exactly as you do. But she was not herself; an unusual meekness had come over her. The magic that Henwyn had called upon had not just made her young again, it had turned her into everything Henwyn thought a princess should be: beautiful and ladylike and a bit wet. Deep inside her somewhere, muffled, the old Ned struggled to break free, but the new one just stood there, drooping picturesquely and gazing up adoringly at Henwyn while he told her of his plans.

"Of course, I shall need an army," he said. "Goblins would be best. Oh, why did Skarper have to run off like that? I would have made him captain over all the goblins of Clovenstone. Still, there are plenty more to do my bidding, I suppose. I expect they will all be knocking on the door when they know that the Lych Lord has returned . . ."

The goblins were not just knocking at doors; they were kicking them, head-butting them and smashing them down with axes as they milled through the lower levels of the Keep in search of treasure. At the sight of all those riches the alliance between the different towers had unraveled in an eyeblink; Mad Manaccan's Lads fell upon Chili Hats, while Growlers fought with Blackspikes, none wanting to let another tribe grab the best of the loot. After that, the members of each tribe started fighting among themselves. The floors of the treasure chambers grew slithery with spilled blood and dropped coins; fallen torches sparked small fires in piles of torn-down tapestries and smashed-up furniture, until the walls were flickering with the spiny shadows of the goblins, all thumping and throttling and hacking and impaling one another.

Through the din strode Knobbler, with old Breslaw hurrying at his heels, and all the biggest and fiercest of his goblin mob about him. With him too went Skarper's batch-brothers, Yabber, Gutgust, Bootle, Wrench, and Libnog. They had seen other hatchlings like them being bludgeoned by greedy Chili Hats or kebabed on the long spears of Growlers, and they had decided that the safest place to be was next to Knobbler.

"Leave that!" the king bellowed at two small Mad Manaccan's Lads carrying a golden shield. "That's mine!" he roared, thumping another looter. But each time he was tempted to turn aside and stuff his own pockets with the shiny stuff he saw, Breslaw would lean close to him and whisper, "There's a greater prize here, Knobbler. The Stone Throne, remember? Rest your fat goblin bum on that and all these treasures will seem only toys and trinkets."

Knobbler grunted and looked around, squinting through the eye-slit of his bucket. "Where is it then? This throne?"

Breslaw jabbed a claw toward the ceiling. "Up."

With another grunt, King Knobbler stomped toward the nearest stairway and started hurrying upward. But he had only climbed a few floors when one of the other goblins, sharper eared, said, "Listen! What's that?"

It was a rattling and a crashing and thudding, faint at first but growing louder, and coming from some-where above them. Soon even Knobbler could hear it inside his bucket. Mixed with the steady thumps and crashes there were yelps, and an occasional woeful cry of "Bumcakes!"

Around the bend of the stairway there came bounding what looked like a small wheel made of hair and metal. It bounced off a landing three stairs above the one where Knobbler stood and struck him square in the belly, knocking him backward. He cannoned into Breslaw, who cannoned in turn into the goblins behind him, and they all went sprawling down to the landing below in a dropped-pot clatter of dinged armor and lost weapons.

Knobbler was the first to recover (it was reflexes like that that had made him king in the first place). He snatched up his sword and looked around angrily for the thing that had struck him down.

The thing uncurled and peered up at him.

"It's that little runt!" he growled. "That Whot-sisname . . ."

Skarper whimpered and hid his head in his paws again, as if that could protect it from the king's wrath. Still dazed from his long tumble down the Keep's stairs, he couldn't imagine how Knobbler and the rest had come there.

Breslaw sadly shook his head. "Skarper," he said. "What's got into you, turning against your own kind and taking up with nasty softlings?"

Skarper peeked up at him. "They're not nasty. They're my friends."

"Friends?" roared Knobbler, swinging Mr. Chop-U-Up. "Goblins don't have *friends!*"

Skarper yowled and threw himself sideways as the massive sword swished down. It missed him by a whisker and bit deep into the stone of the stairs.

"Get him!" roared Knobbler, trying to tug the blade free, but the goblins behind him were still untangling themselves, bruised and groaning. None of them had the chance to grab Skarper as he sprang up and scampered frantically over them and through a doorway at the far end of the landing.

Knobbler finally prized Mr. Chop-U-Up out of the stair and made to go after him, but Breslaw grabbed him by the ankle. "Up!" he said. "The Stone Throne, remember?"

Knobbler nodded. "Get him, Dungnutt!" he bellowed again, and his second-in-command set off on Skarper's trail. Knobbler straightened his helmet and started on up the stairs, running now, because he had worked out that Skarper's softling friends must be somewhere inside the Keep as well, and he didn't want them getting to the Stone Throne ahead of him. Up, up, up he went, past landings and doorways. Some of those rooms they passed were stuffed with treasure, and one by one the goblins who had followed him slunk off, bored with the long climb and eager to stuff their pockets. Soon only Breslaw was left, and Yabber, Gutgust, Bootle, Wrench, and Libnog, who were too wary of the old hatchling master's watchful eye and massive mallet to desert.

And then there were suddenly no more stairs to climb, and they all emerged behind Knobbler onto the metal map that floored the throne room.

Eluned keened with fright. Her memories of recent days had blurred when Henwyn made her young, but the memories of her girlhood were suddenly fresh and clear again, and the sight of Knobbler reminded her horribly of the night the Blackspike Boys had raided Porthstrewy and killed her mother and her father.

The goblins stood in a bunch at the head of the stairs. They saw the waiting Dragonbone Men, and the Stone Throne. Breslaw and the others drew back in fear, leaving Knobbler to stand alone before the gaze of the dark figure who sat waiting there.

"Hello!" said Henwyn. "What is your name, goblin?"

Knobbler mumbled something. He felt shy, which was a strange new feeling for him. He couldn't help it, though. The goblins of Clovenstone had been servants for so long to the power of the Stone Throne that he could not help but bow before this new Lych Lord. "Knobbler," he said. "*King* Knobbler. King of all the seven towers."

"Excellent!" said Henwyn. "Then you shall be their captain when I get a proper goblin army sorted out. Things have been allowed to get pretty slack around here, Knobbler, but that's all going to change now. I'm the new Lych Lord, it turns out. So kneel, and swear your loyalty to me."

King Knobbler did not kneel, but he looked as if he half wanted to, and behind him Yabber, Gutgust, Bootle, Wrench, and Libnog all sank to their knees.

Henwyn jumped up from the throne and came striding down the steps, and vague dark robes swirled around him like smoke and shadows. "My lord!" said Eluned in a warning voice as he went past her and strode across the bridge, but he paid her no heed. The Dragonbone Men stood aside to let him pass, and as he walked toward Knobbler the goblin king bowed lower and lower, until at last he was down on his knees, while Yabber, Gutgust, Bootle, Wrench, and Libnog pressed their ugly faces against the floor and stuck their ugly bottoms in the air.

There was a clink of metal on metal as Knobbler set Mr. Chop-U-Up on the floor before him. He was laying his weapon at the Lych Lord's feet just as the goblin kings of long ago had done. But at his shoulder Breslaw gave a scathing hiss. "Lych Lord? That's no Lych Lord, Knobbler! Shams and trickeries is what he's working! He's naught but a softling! A stupid sniveling softling such as you've slaughtered by the score! Ignore him! Look at the throne, Knobbler! The throne! Ain't it time it felt a goblin's behind upon it?"

And to Knobbler it seemed that the smoky robes of the tall man who stood before him thinned and melted, and instead of the Lych Lord, grim-faced, terrible, he was looking at some shabby boy out of the softlands, with travel-stained clothes and a secondhand sword at his side. Indeed, it was the same shabby boy who had faced him two days before in the woods by the Oeth; the same secondhand sword that had left such a dent in his old helmet.

"You're going to let yourself be owned and ordered by the likes of him?" asked Breslaw.

"Never!" grunted Knobbler. "NEVER!" he roared, and he snatched up the great blade that he had laid before the Lych Lord's feet and, rising, swung it at his head instead.

THE TROUBLE
WITH MAGIC

Skarper was fast, but Dungnutt was faster. Skarper hared through the dim, vaulted passageways of the Keep, running he knew not where, and Dungnutt's angry cries grew louder behind him, and the clatter of Dungnutt's iron-shod paws came closer and closer.

Then, suddenly, from the shadows at the entrance to another stairway, a figure leapt out. Skarper, thinking it was more goblins come to head him off, squealed in terror and threw himself flat on the floor. Lucky for him that he did, for something big and dimly shiny swung above him and smashed into Dungnutt's face. There was a loud, hollow dong like the note of a cracked bell: Dungnutt reeled backward, and friendly hands heaved Skarper up and thrust him onward, around a corner, up yet another stair.

It was a few seconds before he understood that he'd been rescued, and not until they paused for breath on a deserted landing that he saw who by.

The Sable Conclave had been forgotten by the goblins as soon as the lychglass broke. Ignored and half-trampled, they had followed Knobbler's boys into the Lych Lord's halls and slunk up a narrow side stair to avoid the looting going on in the main part of the Keep. They had been looking for the Stone Throne, of course, but they soon got lost, and wandered vaguely among old bedchambers and wardrobes, doing a little genteel looting of their own.

It was pure luck that they had found themselves in the path of Skarper and his pursuer.

It was pure luck that Prawl had recognized him.

It was pure luck that Carnglaze happened to be carrying an enormous copper frying pan, which he had taken from a pantry they'd explored. That was the thing he had used to wallop Dungnutt. It was still ringing faintly with the impact of the blow, and bore a deep dent in the shape of Dungnutt's face.

"Did you see that?" Carnglaze chuckled, patting the pan. "*Whang!* That will teach those louts to tangle with the Sable Conclave!"

"And Fentongoose can work proper magic!" said Prawl excitedly. "'Open,' he said, and the lychglass shattered!"

Skarper shook his head. "That wasn't Fentongoose," he said. "That was the Lych Lord's doing."

Carnglaze shook his head. "Poor goblin! His adventures have sent him funny in the head. There is no Lych Lord, Skarper; he has been dead for years. . . ."

"There is a new one!" explained Skarper. "And it's Henwyn! He sat down on the Stone Throne. He's descended from the old Lych Lord, it turns out, and now he's flinging spells about. Look!" He showed them the glorious coat of mail he wore; his one remaining shoe (he'd lost the other tumbling down the stairs). "He made this stuff! He turned Princess Ned young again!"

"Henwyn? Descended from the Lych Lord?" Fentongoose said. "Then that explains why the cheese spell worked; why we picked on him in the first place! The old powers were not working through *us*, but through *him*." He sounded both disappointed and a bit relieved. "All the prophecies — the Lych Lord's return — it was young Henwyn all along."

"Then the power of Clovenstone is in good hands," said Prawl.

"Idiot!" said Skarper. "There aren't no good hands for power like that! You remember what Princess Ned said? Power poisons people. You wait, he'll be just like the old Lych Lord; conquering this and trampling that."

"Then we must stop him!" said Fentongoose. "We must save him from himself!"

"How? Haven't you been listening? He's gone all magic!"

"Not yet," said Fentongoose.

"Not wholly," agreed Prawl.

"The power of Clovenstone will not wax full until the Lych Lord's star hangs directly overhead," explained Carnglaze. "Whatever spells Henwyn is weaving now, they are weak things, and will not have much power outside the chamber of the throne. Look . . ." And he reached out and pulled one of the scales from Skarper's golden armor. It crumbled in his hand, dry and brown like a dead leaf, and Skarper looked down and saw that all the rest had withered too. He touched them with a paw and they dissolved into a drift of dust, and he was standing in his own clothes again.

"We may still persuade him to give up his power," said Fentongoose.

"And hand it over to somebody who knows how to use it, you mean?" asked Skarper.

The old sorcerer blushed, and mumbled something about having spent a lifetime preparing to sit upon the Stone Throne and what a pity it would be if all that training went to waste, but his companions looked angrily at him.

"If we've learned one thing from our adventures here," said Carnglaze, "it is not to tangle with goblins and magic and the old powers of the earth. Let us save Henwyn if we can, and then go home and take up a safer hobby."

"Let's save Henwyn," said Skarper, "and then smash that Stone Throne up so there can never be another Lych Lord at all."

Henwyn leaned backward just in time, and Knobbler's sword whisked past a half inch from the tip of his nose. He tried to work a spell, but although he could feel magic flaring and weaving all around him, it no longer seemed to flow through him; he couldn't shape it or command it. It was the throne, he realized; he had to sit upon the throne. He turned to flee back across the bridge, but

Knobbler blocked his way, breathing hard inside his bucket and readying his sword again. Magic lightning flamed and flared between the horns of Clovenstone, kindling a wicked gleam on Mr. Chop-U-Up's cutting edge.

"Dragonbone Men!" Henwyn shouted desperately.

With a leathery rustle the Lych Lord's servants sprang forward to defend him. The other goblins cowered against the chamber walls, but Knobbler was braver than your average goblin, and Mr. Chop-U-Up was not just any old goblin sword. Gods knew where Knobbler had come by it, in what deep armory or warrior's tomb, but it had been forged in the great furnaces of Clovenstone in days of old, and spells were layered in the folds of its steel. (It had probably had a better name than Mr. Chop-U-Up in those days, but that was long forgotten.)

Swish! Flicker! Snick! The heads of three Dragonbone Men went bowling on the floor like wasps' nests knocked down from the rafters.

"Hooray!" cheered the watching goblins.

"Nice one, King Knobbler!"

"Anchovies!"

Flicker! Swish! Spiff! Three more Dragonbone Men were felled. Arms and heads and spindly, kicking legs tumbled over the flue's brink and away down the long drop into the lava lake.

The last of them landed one blow, drawing black blood from Knobbler's shoulder and opening a long gash in his armor, but then Mr. Chop-U-Up went through him too and with a wrench and a kick Knobbler sent him after his comrades down the flue.

"The softling!" shouted Breslaw. "He's getting away! Don't let him reach the throne!"

Knobbler looked around. Sure enough, while he had been distracted, Henwyn had made it past him and out onto the bridge. Knobbler roared and leapt after him, and Henwyn, knowing that he could not reach the throne without a fight, turned to face him, drawing his own sword and trying to remember the moves he'd practiced in his bedroom at the cheesery.

That was when Skarper arrived, scrambling up the stairs with the Sable Conclave panting and complaining behind him. He felt his eyes turn wide as saucers as he took in the scene. He saw the strewn wreckage of the Dragonbone warriors. He saw Eluned pale and beautiful beside the throne. He saw Henwyn and King Knobbler facing each other on that narrow bridge.

He did not see Breslaw and the other goblins, who had drawn back into the shadows around the edges of the room to watch the fun. He didn't see them until it was too late. "Stop him!" hissed Breslaw, and he found himself wrestled to the floor by Yabber and Libnog while the rest of his batch-brothers lay in wait to grab the sorcerers, one by one, as they came to the top of the stairs.

Out on the bridge, Henwyn swung his sword, but it rebounded from Knobbler's gnarly armor. He raised it again to parry the blow that Knobbler swung at him, and Mr. Chop-U-Up bit through the secondhand blade in a shower of sparks. Henwyn was left nursing a jarred arm and clutching the useless stub of his sword while the broken-off shard went ringing and dinging away down the shaft beneath him, down, down, down toward the lava far below. Knobbler started to laugh, but Henwyn, in desperation, jabbed the broken blade at him, and luck guided his hand. The sharp stub grated across the goblin's breastplate and slid through the gash the Dragonbone Man had opened there, biting deep into Knobbler's vitals.

The watching goblins gasped and growled.

"Henwyn!" shouted Skarper.

"Oh, well done!" called the sorcerers.

"Arrghle!" said Knobbler, swaying backward. Mr. Chop-U-Up fell from his paw and clattered on the bridge. He collapsed slowly, like a goblin-shaped tent with all its guylines cut, till he was kneeling in front of Henwyn again. Black goblin blood twined down his thighs and puddled around his knees like oil.

"Ow!" he said. "Help! Spare me!"

Henwyn had been just about to discard his broken sword and snatch up Mr. Chop-U-Up. It was a far more fitting blade for the Lord of Clovenstone, he thought, and it would easily split Knobbler's head in half, war-bucket and all. But although he was the Lych Lord now, he was still Henwyn as well, and Henwyn wasn't the sort of person who cut down unarmed and wounded enemies, even if they were goblins. *Wouldn't it make a change,* he thought, *to begin my reign with an act of mercy?*

Don't! warned the Lych Lord part of him, the cold, greedy voice of the Stone Throne in his mind. *Goblins respect strength, not mercy.*

"Don't!" yelled Skarper, fighting his way free of Yabber and Libnog and running toward the bridge, with some idea of tackling Knobbler from behind. "You can't believe anything goblins say! Except this, obviously . . ."

"Don't!" warned Eluned, waiting behind Henwyn at the bridge's end. "I know that goblin! I'm sure I do! Not his size or strength, but that whining voice! *'Spare me!'* Oh, slay him, Henwyn, for he is the very one that betrayed my father with that cowardly trick at Porthstrewy all those years ago!"

Henwyn reached out and lifted the bucket off Knobbler's head, revealing his sweaty, pain-strained face.

Those jutting fangs . . . Those yellow eyes . . . That nose patch . . .

"Oh," said Eluned, quite surprised. "Oh, no, it isn't him at all. My mistake."

"I think *I* am the goblin you is thinking of, actually, my dear," said a voice out of the shadows behind Knobbler. Old Breslaw, whom everybody had forgotten, hobbled toward the bridge, batting Skarper aside with a shrewd blow from his teaching mallet. "It was *me* that tricked your daddy and let the Blackspike Boys inside his castle, Princess," he said, as he stepped onto the bridge. "Last fight I was ever in. Cowardly, did you call it? Well, I takes that as a compliment. I'm clever, see, and clever folk are always cowards. Just ask young Skarper here. Why should we risk these bulging brains of ours when there are big, brainless lunks like Knobbler here to do the fighting for us?"

"Who are you calling brainless?" asked Knobbler, confused.

Breslaw's teaching mallet fetched the king a vicious clout on the back of the head. Knobbler's eyes crossed, and he toppled sideways off the edge of the bridge.

"All right, lads," called Breslaw, to the confused goblins clustering behind him. "Let's send these soft-lings to the lava too, and then the Stone Throne will be mine, and won't we have some fun, terrorizin' and rampagin' and stuff?"

"You shall not pass!" said Henwyn, trying to retrieve that Lych Lord tone of voice, which had come so easily to him before. He took a step backward toward the Stone Throne, hoping he could sit down on it again before this latest goblin worked out that he couldn't do magic without it. But it was an uneasy feeling, walking backward on that spindly bridge, above that deadly drop. He turned, and as he did so Breslaw snatched Mr. Chop-U-Up and drove it into Henwyn's back.

Eluned shrieked. Skarper and the sorcerers howled, struggling against the strong goblin paws which held them back. Henwyn went down on his knees, down on his face on the narrow bridge.

As a boy in Adherak he had always imagined that he would be wounded once or twice when he was a hero; it was only to be expected with all those battles and things, and a scar or two was part of the look. He had just never imagined that it would *hurt* quite so much, or that quite so much red blood would come gushing out of him. Dizzily, he raised his head and saw Eluned at the bridge's end, white hands outstretched toward him. He saw the Stone Throne waiting. If he could just climb onto it all would be well; the powers of Clovenstone would heal his hurt and give him the strength to defeat this traitorous goblin. But the throne looked so far away; the steps that led to it seemed so steep and high; and now Breslaw was stepping over him, stopping to look down at him, lifting the bloody sword.

"Oh, won't I have some fun when I'm the Lych Lord?" the goblin chuckled. "But I'd better finish you off first, my lovely. I may be only a poor old goblin, but I know better than to turn my back upon a foe."

But he had done exactly that, for he was forgetting Eluned. Henwyn's magic was definitely wavering now, and the princess felt more like her old self again. She ran at Breslaw from behind. She drew her knife, but it had been transformed along with her clothes and was now just a diamond-studded toy; a piece of royal jewelry. She tossed it aside and leapt at the hatchling master, wrapping an arm across his throat, biting his ear, clawing at the paw that held the sword.

Breslaw grunted, swore, writhed. He stumbled; he jabbed a bony elbow backward into Ned's chest and she lost her grip on him; he ducked and flung her forward over his head, and she shrieked as she followed Knobbler off the bridge's brink. Her shining hair swirled upward as she fell.

"No!" cried Henwyn — but there was nothing he could do about it, and Breslaw, chuckling some more, turned back to him.

Then, out of his hiding place among the pillars, like a mewling scarlet arrow, little Nuisance came shooting. He whirred twice around Breslaw's head, while Breslaw slashed wildly at him with Mr. Chop-U-Up. All the new jewels of the dragonet's skin shone. He seemed to glow from inside like a tiny paper lantern. Suddenly he backed in midair and hung in front of the old goblin to breathe a hot, bright belch of flame into his face.

"My nose!" screeched Breslaw, letting go of Mr. Chop-U-Up and clapping his hands to his face. "My toes!" he added, as the sword landed on them. Hair on fire and hopping blindly backward, he veered off course over the bridge's edge, hung horrified in the hot air for an instant and was gone. For a long time the sounds of his fall could be heard as he went tumbling and sliding away down the branching flues, until at last there was silence, and then a faint brief brightening of the light that came up the shaft to show that the old hatchling master had plunged at last into the lava lake.

Henwyn watched it fade. Then he noticed, beyond the fallen sword and Breslaw's scattered toes, eight dark claws clutching the edge of the bridge.

"Help!" said Knobbler, dangling there.

"Help!" called Eluned, clinging to his ankles, which she had managed to grab hold of as she fell.

"Get off!" growled Knobbler, kicking his feet. Eluned shrieked and clutched at his trousers, which came down, revealing huge, pink, frilly flannel underpants that made her shriek again.

With a great effort Henwyn forced himself closer. He did not really want to help Knobbler, but there was no way to save Ned without saving the goblin too, so he took hold of Knobbler's hairy wrists and heaved.

Skarper struggled against his batch-brothers. "Let me go!" he grunted. "I've got to help!"

They fought for a bit, but they were not sure what they were fighting for now that neither Knobbler nor Breslaw was around to tell them what to do, and Skarper managed to drag himself toward the bridge. There they all caught sight of Knobbler, the princess dangling from Knobbler's trousers and Knobbler's startling underpants. In amazement they let go of Skarper, and he broke free of them and ran across the bridge to help Henwyn. After another moment, Fentongoose, Prawl and Carnglaze were there too. Between them, puffing and gasping and panting, they heaved first Knobbler and then Ned to safety. While the goblin king struggled to pull his trousers up, the three sorcerers stared at the princess in wonder. They were used to seeing friends who had grown old, but they'd never seen one who had grown *young* before.

Skarper, meanwhile, went scrambling over them all. He grabbed Mr. Chop-U-Up and scampered with it up the steps of the Stone Throne. Nuisance was perched on one of them, looking almost as startled as Breslaw by the fire he'd breathed. Two curls of smoke still leaked from his nostrils, but he was fast returning to his ordinary colors and when he tried to breathe more fire only a few damp sparks came out. Skarper stepped carefully over him and stood before the throne itself. Even without sitting on it, he could feel its power. It looked comfy, despite being made of stone. "Sit down on me," it seemed to say. "Sit, and you shall be King Skarper; Skarper the Great; Skarper the lord of a thousand ravaged lands." *I could be the new Lych Lord*, he thought, and he saw for a moment all the ruined miles of Clovenstone restored and rebuilt, and all the men and goblins of the wide world doing as he told them.

But in the end, he just wasn't that greedy. He didn't want to tell people what to do. He didn't want castles and kingdoms. He couldn't be bothered with all that. "I like a quiet life," he said, as he swung Mr. Chop-U-Up at the throne. "Peace and quiet, and a little hoard of my own. Is that too much to ask?"

A shard the size of his head sheared off the top of the throne. Cracks like the shadows of winter branches spread across the rest. A thin, high scream rang through the Keep, and the floor shivered and the goblins who had been gawping at Knobbler's underpants all turned and started scrambling over one another to get down the stairs.

"Skarper, no!" cried Henwyn, looking up and seeing what he was about. "My throne!"

"Silly," said Princess Ned, looking fondly at him. "Let him smash it. You are much nicer when you're not being the Lych Lord."

"But all that power!" said Henwyn, and despite his wound he rose and stumbled toward the throne, making ready to run up the steps and stop Skarper. "All my magic!" he groaned. "The gifts I gave you . . ."

"They were not really yours to give," said Ned. Already her golden hair was graying and the lines were returning to her face, and she could feel her joints growing stiffer and the weight of her years settling on her again as the little magics that Henwyn had worked on her unraveled. It was like a door into summer closing, and tears ran down her face and caught in the little laughter lines, but she said, "Let him smash it, Henwyn."

"Let him do it, lad," said Fentongoose, who was busy ripping strips off his robes to help Prawl bandage Henwyn's wound. "The world's best off without it."

A great wave of anger rushed through Henwyn. *If I'm not a hero and I'm not the Lych Lord, what am I?* he thought. *Perhaps I'm just a cheesewright after all.* Then he looked down at all the blood that was puddling around his feet and he thought, *Perhaps I shall soon be nobody at all. . . .*

And he sank to his knees on the bridge, and watched while Skarper smashed the Stone Throne to pieces, and the pieces scattered down the dais steps and went tumbling and echoing back down the shafts into the lava lake.

The screaming sound grew louder as the throne shrank. The shaking in the floor was worse. Cracks were spreading up the chamber walls. Skarper struck the stump of the throne a last great blow, which shattered it into shards and broke the blade of Mr. Chop-U-Up into seven pieces. A big section of the chamber wall collapsed, and there was the moon looking in at them, and the Lych Lord's comet arched above it like a wry eyebrow.

"I think we should probably get off this bridge," said Prawl uneasily.

"I think the whole Keep is falling down!" shouted Carnglaze.

Skarper had been hoping the shaking and cracking would stop when the throne was gone. Instead, it seemed to be getting worse. One of the spines that rose from the Keep's top cracked, and the topmost half came crashing down and smashed to pieces on the metal floor.

They helped Henwyn up and made their way off the bridge. As Skarper hurried across to join them, the bridge cracked and dropped in pieces down the flue, and the pinnacle where the throne had stood began to crumble as well. Nuisance, startled from his perch on the steps, circled among the falling splinters for a moment before fluttering down to settle on Henwyn's shoulder and tug at his cloak.

"The eggs!" said Skarper, suddenly remembering.

"What eggs?" asked Fentongoose.

"Nuisance's brothers and sisters," said Henwyn. He struggled free of his helpers' hands and tried to stand, but he sagged, and Ned had to catch him to save him from falling. "We *promised!*" he said. "We can't just leave them here to be crushed!"

"Yes we can," said Skarper, but he knew Henwyn was right. He was an egg-born thing himself, and he could not help but imagine those poor mewling hatchlings trapped inside their too-thick shells, liable at any moment to be smashed flat by falling debris. He shoved the three sorcerers toward the stairs. "Halfway down you'll find an open door into a sort of mews. There's a hammer on the wall to smash the eggshells open with. Nuisance will show you the way. . . ."

They hurried off, with the dragonet swooping and squeaking above their heads. Skarper ran back to Henwyn, and together he and Princess Ned helped the wounded would-be hero down the stairs. Behind them they heard more of the Keep's horns fall, and shards of glass and fragments of stone came bounding down past them.

THINGS FALL APART

On the lower levels, greedy goblins were still running from room to room, weighed down with necklaces and plush curtains and ivory statuettes. They were too busy filling their pockets and squabbling among themselves to pay any heed when first the sorcerers and then Skarper, Ned, and Henwyn came rushing by, but Skarper shouted at them, "Get out! Run! The Keep is falling!" The floors heaved, and the dark jagged shapes of falling masonry flashed past the windows. For a while Skarper kept catching glimpses of the three sorcerers hurrying down the stairways in front of him, but Henwyn could only move slowly, and soon the Sable Conclave was far ahead. Then there came a terrible lurch — a wrenching feeling, as if the whole Keep were twisting — and when the awful noise subsided and the swirling dust had thinned they saw that the stairs below them had collapsed. They looked down the dark shaft of the stairway, filled with dust and the long moans of warping flues.

"It's not really a *stair*way any more," said Henwyn.

"It's not really *any* sort of way," agreed Skarper.

"Unless we want to *jump* . . ." said Ned.

They looked at one another, and decided that on the whole they didn't.

"What do we do?" asked Henwyn.

"I don't know!" said Skarper.

And then he did.

They turned and started up again, and went off the main stair along side ways choked with rubble and the bodies of goblins who'd killed one another fighting over trinkets. Coins and bits of jewelry and strings of pearls lay strewn there too, but there was no time to stop and pick them up. The floor was listing like a ship in steep seas. With all the dust in the air it was hard to see much, but at last Skarper found what he'd been looking for: an arched doorway leading outside. They emerged onto a high rampart that had not yet fallen, although half the parapet had gone and the rest was crumbling. A massive catapult squatted there, with a pile of great rocks still heaped beside it. Skarper scrambled past it and peered out between the collapsing crenellations.

With all this commotion going on, he thought, those cloud maidens were sure to be around.

"Hello!" he shouted, looking up into the sky, and jumping up and down to attract the attention of anybody looking down. "Cloud maidens! Cloud girlies! Here we are!"

"Help!" cried Ned, catching on.

"Help!" agreed Henwyn weakly. "Help! Over here, good ladies!"

"Come on, you vapor-faced puffs of wind!" hollered Skarper. But over the tremendous racket of the disintegrating Keep he doubted anyone could hear him, and the only clouds he could see in the sky above were clouds of dust.

A crack as black as midnight and as spiky as a winter thorn came creeping across the stonework between his feet. The rampart sagged. The great war machine behind him groaned as the stones beneath it tipped and shifted. Pieces of battlement fell away, revealing a giddy view down toward the Inner Wall and the roofs of the towers far below. *I've got even farther to fall this time than I had when they shot me out of the bratapult,* he thought. *It's going to take ages . . .*

"Skarper!" shouted Ned behind him. He looked around, hoping to see the cloud maidens' cloud descending. What he saw instead was the princess struggling to wind the capstan of the war machine.

"Skarper! Help her!" Henwyn yelled, struggling to help her himself, but hampered by his wound.

"Oh no!" said Skarper firmly, guessing their stupid plan.

Just then a sizeable chunk of what he was standing on decided not to be there anymore. He leapt onto what remained of the rampart and ran to help his friends. The catapult seemed not to have suffered much during the Keep's long slumber. The hide hawsers that powered it were as stiff and strong as if they'd just been fitted. Grunting and sweating, the three companions wound the capstan until the great throwing arm was pulled right back, then climbed into the cup.

The edges of the rampart were crumbling quickly now, like a giant cake being nibbled by hungry invisible mice. The catapult stood upon an island, a wobbling pillar of stone. As the pillar cracked at the bottom and started to topple, Skarper leaned out of the catapult cup and hit the release handle.

The throwing arm sprang upright, crashing against the frame. The catapult slid off the toppling pillar and fell down, down, while Skarper, Ned, and Henwyn went hurtling in the opposite direction: up and out into the howling spaces of the sky.

"Aaaaaaaaaaaaaaaa . . . !" they said.

Far below them, Prawl, Fentongoose, and Carnglaze had reached the main gate; any goblins who might have thought of stopping them or making trouble were scared off by Nuisance and the little swarm of screeching, new-hatched dragonets which flapped and whirred around the sorcerers' heads, wings still wet from the egg. But most of the goblins were fleeing anyway, and did not so much as notice the members of the Sable Conclave. Outside the gate a storm of shattered stonework was coming down like a bombardment, with goblins darting and dodging through it as they fled the Keep. A huge stone sculpture of the winged head squashed a running

Growler and burst into splinters, which rattled at the cracking walls.

Shielding their faces as best they could from the rain of dust and shards, the sorcerers stopped, and turned, and looked up at the Keep. It was not falling as a felled tree would: It was just crumpling in on itself, collapsing down into the cloven mountaintop from which it had emerged so long ago. The bits that were dropping off it were just the extra towers and ramparts with which the Lych Lord had encrusted it: gutterings and gargoyles.

"What about the other buildings?" Prawl shouted through the din. "Will they fall too?"

Fentongoose shook his head. "The Keep is different. Men made those other buildings. They ought to stand. Unless the Keep actually falls *on* them . . ."

A whole tower came slamming down. A fleeing Chili Hat was flattened by a huge siege catapult which had come tumbling down the Keep's flank from some disintegrating rampart high above. The sorcerers with their escort of newborn dragonets went hurrying into the shelter of an alcove near the gate, a useful alcove that was not part of the Keep but carved into one of the crags of Meneth Eskern itself. Goblins were still running past, dragging large pieces of loot they'd liberated, some forming bickering gangs to try and haul away whole ships and carriages. Even they were growing wary now, and quite a few came to lurk in the lee of the buttress too, not seeming to care that they were sharing it with softlings.

"There goes the Keep, then," said Fentongoose sadly, as they watched the great tower grow shorter and shorter, folding into itself like a telescope.

"We are well rid of it," said Prawl. "It was nothing but trouble."

Then nobody said anything for a while, because no one could be heard above the enormous bellowing of rock and stone as the remnants of the Keep collapsed into the caverns beneath. Upflung lava glopped and spurted, angry orange in the dark. A few last fragments fell like hammer blows. Dust swirled and settled. Where the Keep had stood there was now emptiness, and the Lych Lord's star pinned to the high sky.

Nuisance took flight, and the newer dragonets went with him, rising higher and higher as they searched for some sign of Henwyn and the others, and their thin, sad cries faded into the rattle and slither of the settling stones.

"Poor Princess Ned," the sorcerers whispered, as the silence slowly gathered around them. "Poor Henwyn. ...rper . . ."

". . . rrrrrrrrrrrgh!" said Henwyn and Skarper and the princess, plummeting. They had started off clinging to one another, but somehow they had been parted, and now they fell separately, three plunging specks screaming the same long scream.

Then Skarper saw it, bright in the last of the moonlight: the cloud of the cloud maidens, gusting around the corner of the collapsing tower and rushing into place below them. The cloud maidens stood on its top, faces raised to the fallers and arms outstretched.

"Let us catch you, O Prince!" called Rill.

"Quickly!" said another. "We must not tarry long; this horrid dust will make our cloud all dirty . . ."

"They are falling as fast as they can, Bree. They cannot fall faster. It's to do with gravity."

"Oh, look; he has that horrid goblin with him again . . ."

"They're here!" Skarper shouted to the others, who were falling with their eyes tight shut, and he flailed his limbs and tail, flapping himself closer to Ned and Henwyn so that they would all land in the center of the cloud. At the last moment he shut his eyes too, bracing himself for the soft impact, while cloud maidens scattered nervously to make a landing space . . .

There was a ripping sound, and a feeling, familiar to Skarper, of sinking fast through sparse, wet wool. He felt himself slow, grabbed fistfuls of cloud-stuff, and climbed up out of the pit he'd made. Princess Ned was emerging shakily from her own hole just next to his. She took his paw and they scrambled up together onto the cloud's top, where the cloud maidens were waiting. They'd all gathered around Henwyn's hole, of course.

"Well, *we're* all right," Skarper announced cheerfully, annoyed that they were only interested in his friend.

None of the cloud maidens so much as glanced at him.

"Oh no!" breathed Ned.

Skarper pushed his way between the sorrowing cloud maidens and looked down the hole that Henwyn had made.

It went clean through the cloud, like a hole in a shape sorter designed for giant babies to fit bricks in the

shape of spread-eagled cheesewrights through. Skarper
could see right through it to dark trees and ruined roofs.

"...as heavier than you," said Rill.

"The cloud is thinner here . . ." said one of her
sisters.

"He went straight through!"

"He is still falling!"

"Oh, poor Henwyn!" cried the other cloud maidens.

The dust of the fallen Keep had stained their faces,
and they leaned over the hole and let their big, gray tear-
drops fall upon the Inner Wall, a thousand feet below.

Henwyn plunged the rest of the way in silence, too
surprised to start screaming again. Rags of torn cloud
unraveled, caught between his clutching fingers. He fell
face-upward, watching the cloud shrink above him, and
he thought that was a good thing, because he couldn't
see the hard stones rushing up toward him from below,
the sharp stone spikes and broken tiles and rusty railings
waiting like teeth to tear at him, the broad expanses of
stone pavement on which he would soon smash like
an egg.

His landing was like a great blow.

It was not nearly as bad as he'd thought it would b
Whatever he had landed on, it was surprisingly soft and
yielding. After a few seconds he found that he badly
needed to breathe, which he supposed must mean he
wasn't dead. He opened one eye, and a face the size of a
ceiling returned his curious gaze.

"Are you well, little softling?" rumbled Fraddon.

Henwyn lay in the hat the giant had held out to catch
him. He breathed deeply in and out, and couldn't think
of anything to say.

"I came down from the mountains when I heard all
the commotion," said Fraddon. "I feared you small ones
might be in trouble. Then I saw you tumbling. The old
Keep's gone, I see. And now on top of everything, it's
raining. . . ."

Henwyn felt the raindrops on his face. Above him, a
dirty cloud was lowering, the hole he'd made in it already
half-healed. Cloud maidens and a scruffy goblin and a
princess of a certain age were looking down at him over
its edges, and around it in the moonlight flew eleven
tiny newborn dragonets.

EVER AFTER

The comet called the Lych Lord's star (though it had other names as well, on other worlds) rushed on through space, minding its own business, never guessing the trouble it caused, or the magic that stirred on the worlds that it passed as its train of slowsilver dust sifted down through their skies. It soared over the moon, and forests of white trees sprouted there and raised pale crowns to its silver light like daisies turning to the sun. It swung twice around the world, and magic woke there; there were trolls in the rivers again, and giants in the hills; sea serpents and mermaids sported off the beaches of Coriander, and Quesney Prong's latest lecture on *Why Magick Doth Not Exist* was interrupted when an angry fairy flew in through the window and punched him on his learned nose.

There was no one to direct the old things this time; no one to form them into armies; no dark tower tempting men to turn the magic to their own ends. Yet many of the creatures who woke as the star went by still found their way to Clovenstone. There, instead of a new Lych Lord, Princess Eluned and her friends were waiting for them.

The Great Keep was gone, of course, and in the quakings and shakings that had accompanied its fall, large sections of the Inner Wall had fallen too, but the towers still stood, ringing the cloven summit of Meneth Eskern. Fraddon had carried Princess Ned's ship there as soon as it was repaired. He had set it on the top of Blackspike Tower, from where she could keep an eye on the new fields and gardens that the goblins were laying out on the south-facing slopes of the summit.

At first they had been a little bewildered by the idea of gardening, and they'd tended to use their hoes and rakes and spades to hit one another instead of hoeing or raking or digging with. They had soon come to understand, however. Most of the really big, greedy, dangerous goblins had been slain during that last battle in the Keep, or been squashed afterward as they tried to haul their loot away. The lesser ones seemed glad of a bit of peace for a change, and they had turned for leadership to Princess Ned, the Lady of Clovenstone. In the lands of men there were already stories being told about the Goblin Queen. ("But you're better off without kings *or* queens," Ned told the goblins. "People who like telling other people what to do are usually trouble. As long as you don't interfere with anyone else, you should do as you like. Though it might be a nice idea, don't you think, to plant some apple trees upon the old parade grounds down behind Southerly Gate?")

The apple-tree saplings had been delivered quite recently by a trading caravan that had ventured over the Oeth Moors on the orders of Carnglaze. Carnglaze had retired from the Sable Conclave and gone home to Coriander, and since he had taken a few small but valuable items from the Keep with him, he was now one of the richest merchants in that city of rich merchants. He was keen to trade with Clovenstone, giving useful things in exchange for any trinkets and gewgaws which had escaped the collapse of the Keep — and it was surprising how many had, and were still being found by sharp-eyed goblins, scattered around among the ruins.

Carnglaze had even bought the Lych Lord's Rolls-Royce Silver Shadow, which some enterprising Growlers had dragged clear of the Keep before it came down. He rode around Coriander in it now, the envy of the other merchants: A good cartwright had put new wheels on it, and it was pulled by a team of gray horses.

Carnglaze's personal bodyguard stood on the running boards, causing almost as much amazement as the Silver Shadow itself, for he was none other than Knobbler. The goblin king had slunk away from Clovenstone in shame after the Keep fell. He knew that he could be king no more. What goblin would obey him, now that news of his knickers had got out? He could rage and roar and beat them, but they would only giggle and make jokes about his underpants. So, wishing he had fallen down that flue after all, he went off alone across the moor, and somewhere on the road Carnglaze overtook him, and felt sorry for him, and offered him the job of bodyguard.

It had worked out very well. As the only goblin in Coriander, the former king was something of a celebrity, and beneath his elegant new armor he wore not just underpants but socks and undershirts of exquisite warmth and softness, tailored to fit his squat and scaly body by the finest seamstresses in the undergarment district.

His master was content too, for one glance at Knobbler's massive fists and ugly face was enough to scare off any burglar or cutpurse who might have hoped to separate Carnglaze from his newfound riches.

The other members of the Sable Conclave had stayed at Clovenstone. Princess Ned had said that it would be nice to have some wise gentlemen to talk to, and they were so flattered and surprised at being called wise that they completely forgot the vows they'd made to go back to their homes and have no more to do with magic. They were busy ransacking the bumwipe heaps of all the goblin towers for scrolls and books that could be salvaged. (There was no need at all now for the bumwipe heaps, since Carnglaze's caravan had brought to Clovenstone great reams of soft, absorbent paper; Princess Ned was forever reminding the goblins to make use of it.)

The caravan had also brought cows: good red cows from the softlands, who grazed the grass outside the Outer Wall, and whom Henwyn taught the goblins how to milk. Henwyn sent word to Adherak, and his family came hurrying over the moor roads, bringing some old cheese vats and all their knowledge of the cheesemaking process. They were nervous of the goblins at first, but Ned calmed their fears, and Henmor soon declared that goblins were natural cheesemakers, and that Clovenstone cheese would one day be among the finest in all the Westlands. (He had quite forgiven his son for destroying his cheesery. A nice new one had been built with Henwyn's share of the treasure salvaged from the Keep. He had decided, against all the customs, to hand it on to Herda, Gerda, and Lynt.)

For a month or so after the Keep fell everyone had thought the lava lake was choked with rubble, and that no more eggstones would ever come from it. Then, from the crevices of the summit, a few bewildered hatchlings emerged, blinking in the daylight and looking about for rocks and planks to thump each other with. So investigations were made, and it was found that the lake was still there, a little smaller than before, but still throwing up eggstones. The tunnels that led to it had fallen in, but after a little work, the dark ways down from Blackspike and Growler Towers were opened again, and Fentongoose became the first softling hatchling master; he moved into Growler Tower, and there he patiently instructed new-hatched goblins in the goblin lore.

It took a long time for Henwyn's wound to fully heal, and longer still for him to get over the shame he felt for having given in to the power of the Stone Throne; for almost having become another Lych Lord.

"I always thought I was a hero," he confessed to Ned and Skarper one day at summer's end. The three of them were sitting eating apples on the top of the Inner Wall, watching Nuisance and the other dragonets play tag with young twiglings in the treetops below. The Lych Lord's star, visible even in daylight by then, hung above them in the dusty blue sky.

"You *are* a hero," said Ned. "All that rescuing people and fighting monsters."

Henwyn shook his head. "All those things I used to feel, that need I had for magic and adventures, it was just his blood in me, calling me to Clovenstone. All I really wanted was the Stone Throne. That's what led me here."

"Then that makes you even more of a hero," Ned said firmly. "To know you could have such power, and give it up. I think that's the most heroic thing I've ever heard of." And if she had still been young she would have kissed him, but she wasn't, so she gave him a good, friendly punch on the arm instead, and then went back into her ship; she had some scones in the oven, and wanted to see if they were ready.

"You're just feeling a bit down, that's all," said Skarper, when she had gone. "That's the trouble with adventures. When you're having them they're really, really scary and uncomfortable, and you've got bog water in your boots and your paws are wet and you ache all over and monsters keep trying to kill you, so you just wish the adventures would stop. And then when they *do* stop, you sort of miss them, and you wish they'd start again."

They thought about this for a time, while big white clouds trailed their shadows across the ruins and the woods.

"I think the trouble with *not* having adventures," said Henwyn, "is that it's sort of dull. Dull in a nice way, but still dull."

Skarper finished his apple and tossed the core out into the air, where one of the dragonets swooped by and caught it. He had been enjoying himself since the Keep fell: It had been interesting, watching all these changes taking place. He had a cabin of his own in Ned's ship, and he'd built up quite a little hoard for himself out of bits and pieces he'd found among the ruins. Yet somehow it was not quite enough, and in these warm, end-of-summer days he often found his mind turning to thoughts of the world beyond the Outer Wall: those vast lands he had seen mapped out in metal on the Lych Lord's throne-room floor.

"It seems to me," he said, "there must be all sorts of adventures waiting to be had. It seems to me there must be other places in the world like Clovenstone. Places where magic happens."

"They say there's a chasm in Barragan which leads right down into the Underworld," said Henwyn. "In Musk the sorcerers ride about on flying rugs."

"Flying *rugs*?" scoffed Skarper, waving to Rill as the cloud maidens' cloud went drifting overhead. (They'd sculpted it into an O, and the dragonets had left their games among the trees and were zipping through it like trained puppies jumping through a hoop.) "Your trouble is, you believe everything you hear in stories."

"There are whole mountains filled with treasure in

the country of the Leopard Kings," Henwyn said, ignoring him.

"Treasure, eh?" said Skarper thoughtfully. "And I suppose there might be different sorts of goblins in those other lands . . ."

"We should go and see!" declared Henwyn. "The two of us! Skarper and Henwyn: Gentlemen Adventurers! Companions together in the wild places of the world! With my swordsmanship and your cunning . . ."

"Well, I couldn't let you go off alone," said Skarper. "You'd prob'ly end up selling all you have for a handful of magic beans or something . . ."

"Ooh, magic beans?" said Henwyn, sounding interested.

"Course," Skarper went on, "we'll come back to Clovenstone sometimes. For rests, and tea and stuff, and to tell Princess Ned of our discoveries . . ."

"Clovenstone will always be here," said Henwyn, but his eyes were still on the horizon, and his mind was wandering among stories that had come from much farther and stranger places than Clovenstone. "The Autumn Isles," he murmured. "The Ice Crystal Mountains at the Edge of the World . . ."

"Tea!" called Ned, and the smell of the fresh-baked scones reached them at the same time as her voice.

They scrambled up, making ready to go back toward the ship, but just for a moment they lingered there, the two of them, looking beyond Westerly Gate to the long silvery line of the wet road shining in the heather. South and west it stretched away, across the moors and over the hills, into a blue distance filled with the promise of adventures.

ACKNOWLEDGMENTS

Hearty thanks to my editors, Marion Lloyd and Anna Solemani; to Sam, who started it all; to Jeremy Levett and Sarah McIntyre for help and advice and being Good Eggs; and to Eluned Gramich, who let me borrow her name.

ALSO BY PHILIP REEVE

No Such Thing as Dragons

Here Lies Arthur

Fever Crumb
A Web of Air
Scrivener's Moon

Mortal Engines
Predator's Gold
Infernal Devices
A Darkling Plain

ABOUT THE AUTHOR

Philip Reeve was born in Brighton and worked in a bookshop for many years before becoming a bestselling author. His debut novel, *Mortal Engines*, the first in an epic series, was published to great acclaim around the world. He has won the CILIP Carnegie Medal, the Smarties Gold Award, the Guardian Children's Fiction Prize, and the Blue Peter Book of the Year. He lives with his wife and son on Dartmoor, where the wildest places are probably full of boglins, dampdrakes, and other mysterious creatures.